Likely Stories

A Postmodern Sampler

Edited by

George Bowering

and Linda Hutcheon

Coach House Press

Toronto

Published with the assistance of the Canada Council, the Ontario Arts
Council and the Ontario Ministry of Culture and Communications.

Canadian Cataloguing in Publication Data
Main entry under title:

Likely stories : a postmodern sampler

ISBN 0-88910-446-8

1. Short stories, Canada (English).* 2. Canadian
fiction (English) – 20th century.* I. Bowering,
George, 1935-   II. Hutcheon, Linda, 1947-

PS8329.L55 1992   C813'.54   C92-094745-X
PR9197.32.L55 1992

Likely Stories

Contents

Acknowledgements

The following selections were originally published by Coach House Press and are reprinted in this anthology with the kind permission of the authors:

Atwood, Margaret, 'Women's Novels,' from *Murder in the Dark*, © 1983 by Margaret Atwood.
Cohen, Matt, 'A Literary History of Anton,' from *The Story So Four*, © 1976 by Matt Cohen.
Scott, Gail, 'Tall Cowboys and True,' from *Spare Parts*, © 1981 by Gail Scott.
Watson, Sheila, 'And the Four Animals,' from *Five Stories*, © 1984 by Sheila Watson.

Acknowledgement for the other stories in this volume is made as follows:

Arnason, David, 'A Girl's Story,' from *The Circus Performers' Bar*, © 1984 by David Arnason. Reprinted by permission of Talon Books Limited, Vancouver, Canada.
Brand, Dionne, 'Blossom,' from *Sans Souci and Other Stories*, © 1988 by Dionne Brand. Reprinted by permission of Williams-Wallace Publishers Inc.
Bromige, David, 'Ann and Dan Got Married,' from *Men, Women and Vehicles: Prose Works*, © 1990 by David Bromige. Reprinted by permission of Black Sparrow Press.
Fawcett, Brian, 'Malcolm Lowry and the Trojan Horse,' from *Cambodia, or, Stories for People Who Find Television Too Slow*, © 1986 by Brian Fawcett. Reprinted by permission of Talon Books Limited, Vancouver, Canada.
Findley, Timothy, 'Dreams,' from *Stones*, © 1988 by Pebble Productions Inc. Reprinted by permission of Penguin Books Canada Limited.

Glover, Douglas, 'Dog Attempts to Drown Man in Saskatoon,' from *Dog Attempts to Drown Man in Saskatoon*, © 1985 by Douglas Glover. Reprinted by permission of Talon Books Limited, Vancouver, Canada.

Harris, Claire, 'Butterfly on a Pin,' from *Drawing Down a Daughter* (Goose Lane Editions, 1992). First published in *Frictions: Stories by Women*, edited by Rhea Tregebov (Second Story Press, 1989). © 1989 by Claire Harris. Reprinted by permission of the author.

Joe, J.B., 'Cement Woman,' from *All My Relations: An Anthology of Contemporary Canadian Native Fiction* (McClelland & Stewart, 1990). © 1990 by J.B. Joe. Reprinted by permission of the author.

McCormack, Eric, 'Twins,' from *Inspecting the Vaults*, © 1987 by Eric McCormack. Reprinted by permission of Penguin Books Canada Limited.

McFadden, David, 'Hiroko Writes a Story,' from *Canadian Sunset* (Black Moss Press, 1986). © 1986 by David McFadden. Reprinted by permission of the author.

Munro, Alice, 'Bardon Bus,' from *The Moons of Jupiter*, © 1982 by Alice Munro. Reprinted by permission of Macmillan Canada.

Nichol, bp, 'Two Heroes,' from *Craft Dinner: Stories and Texts, 1966-1976* (Aya Press, 1978). © 1978 by bpNichol. Reprinted by permission of the estate of bpNichol.

Rooke, Leon, 'Art,' from *Who Do You Love?* © 1992 by Leon Rooke. Reprinted by permission of the author and The Canadian Publishers, McClelland & Stewart, Toronto.

Shields, Carol, 'Home,' from *Various Miracles*, © 1985 by Carol Shields. Reprinted by permission of Stoddart Publishing Co. Limited, Don Mills, Ontario, and Viking Penguin, a division of Penguin Books U.S.A. Inc.

Swan, Susan, 'The Man Doll,' from *Tesseracts*, edited by Judith Merril (Press Porcépic, 1985). © 1985 by Susan Swan. Reprinted by permission of the author.

Thomas, Audrey, 'The Man with Clam Eyes,' from *Goodbye Harold, Good Luck*, © 1986 by Audrey Thomas. Reprinted by permission of Penguin Books Canada Limited.

Tostevin, Lola Lemire, 'Le Baiser de Juan-Les-Pins,' excerpted from the forthcoming *Frog Moon*. © 1992 by Lola Lemire Tostevin. Used by permission of the author.

Tremblay, Mildred, 'Lily and the Salamander,' from *Dark Forms Gliding*, © 1988 by Mildred Tremblay. Reprinted by permission of Oolichan Books.

Urquhart, Jane, 'The Death of Robert Browning,' from *Storm Glass*, © 1987 by Jane Urquhart. Reprinted by permission of The Porcupine's Quill Inc.

Canada's 'Post': Sampling Today's Fiction

LINDA HUTCHEON

THEY SAY WE live in an age of electronic reproduction and information technology, an age that has been called 'postmodern.' That's one of the more polite things it has been called, of course, and the label has itself come to be the subject of much debate. So too have all the various mass culture and 'high art' forms to which anyone has dared to give that label. The postmodern seems to worry people ... even people who rather enjoy it. For instance, they worry about the digital sampling music computer, the most postmodern musical instrument yet invented, because it can manipulate and reproduce any sound it has encoded. In so doing—and here is where people really get worried—the 'sampler' erodes the tried and true (read: romantic, capitalist) distinction between original and copy, just as the modernist collage form in the visual arts had done before it.

You may have noticed that the cover of this book has 'sampled' Gail Geltner's *Closed System*, just as her collage itself 'samples' Ingres's famous *Grande Odalisque* and Magritte's bowler-hatted men, not to mention television's images of romance. Geltner's work does this in the name of challenging not only the standard definition of originality in art, but also the seemingly benign innocence of these and other representations of women in Western culture. *Her* Odalisque turns away from the conventional male gaze, addressing perhaps a different viewer than Ingres had in mind. This is a visual version of the kind of formal sampling or self-reflexive, parodic manipulation—with a political edge—that you'll find in much of the short fiction inside the cover of this book of *Likely Stories*.

This collection is a 'sampler' in other ways too, though. It does not—because it cannot—represent all the postmodern short stories written in Canada; it merely samples from them. Its very variety implicitly acts as a (postmodern) refusal to create a so-called 'master narrative' or general, neat explanation of what the postmodern might be. Instead, it offers a taste, a sampling of some of the many literary manifestations of this thing called 'postmodernism,' this thing that we can't ignore any more than we can ignore the air we breathe.

The reason we can't ignore it has nothing to do with its 'reality' and everything to do with the sheer amount of public attention given to the word in the last ten years. Many people—with very different opinions, beliefs, interests, and politics—still seem to think that there is something here worth talking about, something important enough even to argue about. They all appear to feel that the word 'postmodern' relates to a set of perspectives or cultural stances that have proliferated in a particular place (Western metropolitan centres) at a particular time (the late twentieth century). Though most would go along with the idea that the postmodern instigates a questioning of the claims of any particular set of cultural beliefs to being universal and value-free, that's pretty well where the agreement would end. Some associate the word with oppositional politics, with resistance and challenge; for others, however, it connotes only a contamination by (and complicity with) the benighted culture of 'late capitalism.' Still others see it as both: that is to say, as demystifying and contesting, because it is always part of the culture it nevertheless seeks to criticize.

Only you can decide which way you choose to read the postmodernism you live. (That in itself is a postmodern statement, I suppose.)

This doesn't mean that there aren't common denominators in the short stories collected in this sampler: it is, after all, a version of the postmodern that we have chosen to construct and present. For example, whether you see it as arch or honest, as irritating or entertaining, the self-reflexivity of postmodern literature—its concern for itself as text, as language—is hard to ignore in these particular fictions. However, it takes many different forms: Carol Shields's 'Home' illustrates in the very shape of its narrative the community constructed by the 'million invisible filaments of connection, trivial or profound' that is its subject; Alice Munro's 'Bardon Bus' makes the ironies and secrets of its love story into the ironies and secrets of storytelling. While David Bromige's 'Ann and Dan Got Married' and Douglas Glover's 'Dog Attempts to Drown Man in Saskatoon' both describe works of art that reflect the lives being lived in the stories, these allegories then also reflect back on the fiction in which they have been created.

Some stories are pretty overt about their interest in their own identity. Glover's narrator, for instance, presents his writerly worries ('Already this is not the story I wanted to tell') as well as his awareness of narrative conventions ('An apology for my style. I am not so much apologizing as invoking a tradition'). Brian Fawcett's 'Malcolm Lowry and the Trojan Horse' reminds us that it is a fiction even as it explores both the social and cultural climate that makes fiction possible and also the consequences and inadequacies of the novel form as it has developed over time.

David McFadden's 'Hiroko Writes a Story,' with its story within a story, opens with a self-reflexive statement: 'The problem with this story is its lack of motivation'—and continues to remind us of its status as fiction through remarks such as '"—" (as a character in Malcolm Lowry might say).' In Lola Lemire Tostevin's 'Le Baiser de Juan-Les-Pins,' creation and decay, 'beauty' and 'ugliness,' Picasso's painting and an uncanny cabby, art and life—all come together in the story of a kiss that is *not* just a kiss.

Perhaps no sampled story here is quite as self-conscious about itself as is David Arnason's 'A Girl's Story'—in part because it is politically difficult in some quarters these days to write a girl's story if your name is David. As his narrator says: 'I'm going to have trouble with the feminists about this story.' One of his ways to try to head off that trouble is to invite his female reader into the text: 'You've wondered what it would be like to be a character in a story ….' Playing openly with the conventions and clichés of romance, he explores the relation between freedom and control, between writing and reading. This is the exactly same relation you as readers get your own chance to explore as you make your way through the challenging experimental writing of Matt Cohen's 'A Literary History of Anton' or bpNichol's 'Two Heroes.'

The fictional Malcolm Lowry's advice to the narrator of Brian Fawcett's story is 'to live in the interzones between the worn-out Cartesian universe and the wilderness.' This space in between—the interzone—is the postmodern space *par excellence*, and it comes in many forms. In Leon Rooke's 'Art,' it is the space of paint and pain, of creation and destruction, of the generic ('the cow,' 'the wife') and the intensely personal. Postmodernism always exhibits this kind of 'both/and' (rather than 'either/or') thinking: Eric McCormack's 'Twins' brings this—what to some people is a 'disease of words'—to literary life in its double-tongued two-in-one protagonist. The interzone can also take the form of the surreal world of the memory 'interludes' in Gail Scott's 'Tall Cowboys and True,' of the psychotic and oneiric visions of Timothy Findley's 'Dreams,' of the verbally incantatory, textually-inspired escapist fantasy of Audrey Thomas's 'The Man with Clam Eyes,' or of the puzzling arithmetical eerieness of Sheila Watson's 'And the Four Animals.' All these are versions of what McFadden calls 'reality through different eyes.'

On a formal level, the interzone is the space between forms and genres: between poetry and prose, in Claire Harris's 'Butterfly on a Pin'; between critical essay and ironic story, in Margaret Atwood's 'Women's Novels'; between biography and fiction, in Jane Urquhart's 'The Death of Robert Browning'; between performance and writing, in J.B. Joe's 'Cement Woman.' In this last story, the interzone is also the space between the oral and the written. Here it has its source in the Native art of storytelling, an art rooted in a particular voice, eye, and (as this story demonstrates) body. In a related way, the interzone comes into being as well where the rhythm, syntax and diction of West Indian speech work to capture the vibrant particularity of 'voice' in Dionne Brand's 'Blossom.'

The postmodern is said by many to celebrate a plurality of voices instead of accepting the singular voice of 'neutral universality,' the kind of voice that implicitly denies social and cultural difference. In recognizing the partiality of all so-called 'universals,' postmodernism offers (as a corollary) an awareness of the multiplicity and particularity of the local, an awareness that has been made possible by decades of work by activists operating in the name of equality based on gender, race, ethnicity, class, religion, and sexual orientation. Nootka writer J.B. Joe's portrayal of her traditional community and its ties with nature contrasts with her vision of the grim and grey commercial world of urban 'cement people.' In 'Butterfly on a Pin,' the displacement of Trinidadian immigration is all the more strongly felt when situated in the cold of a Calgary winter. In both stories, there is little of the hope that the ideals of Canadian multiculturalism have aimed to instil, a hope that intercultural relations could be the source of a renewal of humane values based on tolerance and understanding.

The intersection of racism, classism, and sexism in stories like 'Blossom' and 'Cement Woman' illustrates clearly what some have referred to as the 'holy trinity' of political concerns in postmodern literature. Sometimes these issues are addressed with pointed irony—as in Atwood's 'Women's Novels' or the *Frankenstein* parody in Susan Swan's 'The Man Doll'; at other times, as in Gail Scott's story, it is a more tragic mode that is deemed appropriate for exploring a world of violence, prejudice, and evasion of responsibility. The same range of tone can be found in the postmodern, politicized treatment of that staple theme of so much narrative fiction, interpersonal relations— from the satiric edge of Swan's image of the cyborg lover (and politician) to the depiction of the pains of both commitment and loss in the selections by Findley or Thomas, or in Mildred Tremblay's moving and disturbing story of 'Lily and the Salamander.' Often there are more questions than answers. But that too may be postmodern, for in a world where the old stories about gender and about sexual relations have come under scrutiny, the old answers may not be very convincing anymore.

What the postmodernism constructed through this particular sampling of fiction suggests is that what many have come to see as important political issues of our day are unavoidably implicated in the stories we tell. In other words, the postmodern does not simply mean formal experiment or self-conscious play with language and conventions. It can mean that, of course, but in each case the point is not to stop there, but to look at what is at stake when narrative form is treated with irony, when a story becomes a 'likely story.'

But, once again, this is only *one* construction of the postmodern; it is only one sampler. You can make your own; you inevitably will. George Bowering will ... and so he gets the last word on Canada's 'post.'

A Girl's Story

DAVID ARNASON

You've wondered what it would be like to be a character in a story, to sort of slip out of your ordinary self and into some other character. Well, I'm offering you the opportunity. I've been trying to think of a heroine for this story, and frankly, it hasn't been going too well. A writer's life isn't easy, especially if, like me, he's got a tendency sometimes to drink a little bit too much. Yesterday, I went for a beer with Dennis and Ken (they're real-life friends of mine) and we stayed a little longer than we should have. Then I came home and quickly mixed a drink and started drinking it so my wife would think the liquor on my breath came from the drink I was drinking and not from the drinks I had had earlier. I wasn't going to tell her about those drinks. Anyway, Wayne dropped over in the evening and I had some more drinks, and this morning my head isn't working very well.

To be absolutely frank about it, I always have trouble getting characters, even when I'm stone cold sober. I can think of plots; plots are really easy. If you can't think of one, you just pick up a book, and sure enough, there's a plot. You just move a few things around and nobody knows you stole the idea. Characters are the problem. It doesn't matter how good the plot is if your characters are dull. You can steal characters too, and put them into different plots. I've done that. I stole Eustacia Vye from Hardy and gave her another name. The problem was that she turned out a lot sulkier than I remembered and the plot I put her in was a light comedy. Now nobody wants to publish the story. I'm still sending it out, though. If you send a story to enough publishers, no matter how bad it is, somebody will ultimately publish it.

For this story I need a beautiful girl. You probably don't think you're beautiful enough, but I can fix that. I can do all kinds of retouching once I've got the basic material, and if I miss anything, Karl (he's my editor) will find it. So I'm going to make you fairly tall, about five-foot eight and a quarter in your stocking feet. I'm going to give you long blonde hair because long blonde hair is sexy and virtuous. Black hair can be sexy too, but it doesn't go with virtue. I've got to deal with a whole literary tradition where black-haired women are basically evil. If I were feeling better I might be able to do it in an ironic way, then black hair would be okay, but I don't think I'm up to it this morning. If you're going to use irony, then you've got to be really careful about tone. I could make you a redhead, but redheads have a way of turning out pixie-ish, and that would wreck my plot.

So you've got long blonde hair and you're this tall slender girl with amazingly blue eyes. Your face is narrow and your nose is straight and thin. I could have turned up the nose a little, but that would have made you cute, and I really need a beautiful girl. I'm going to put a tiny black mole on your cheek. It's traditional. If you want your character to be really beautiful there has to be some minor defect.

Now, I'm going to sit you on the bank of a river. I'm not much for setting. I've read so many things where you get great long descriptions of the setting, and mostly it's just boring. When my last book came out, one of the reviewers suggested that the reason I don't do settings is that I'm not very good at them. That's just silly. I'm writing a different kind of story, not that old realist stuff. If you think I can't do setting, just watch.

There's a curl in the river just below the old dam where the water seems to make a broad sweep. That flatness is deceptive, though. Under the innocent sheen of the mirroring surface, the current is treacherous. The water swirls, stabs, takes sharp angles and dangerous vectors. The trees that lean from the bank shimmer with the multi-hued greenness of elm, oak, maple and aspen. The leaves turn in the gentle breeze, showing their paler green undersides. The undergrowth, too, is thick and green, hiding the poison ivy, the poison sumac and the thorns. On a patch of grass that slopes gently to the water, the only clear part of the bank on that side of the river, a girl sits, a girl with long blonde hair. She has slipped a ring from her finger and seems to be holding it towards the light.

You see? I could do a lot more of that, but you wouldn't like it. I slipped a lot of details in there and provided all those hints about strange and dangerous things under the surface. That's called foreshadowing. I put in the ring at the end there so that you'd wonder what was going to happen. That's to create suspense. You're supposed to ask yourself what the ring means. Obviously it has something to do with love, rings always do, and since she's taken it off, obviously something has gone wrong in the love relationship. Now I just have to hold off answering that question for as long as I can, and I've got my story. I've got a friend who's also a writer who says never tell the buggers anything until they absolutely have to know.

I'm going to have trouble with the feminists about this story. I can see that already. I've got that river that's calm on the surface and boiling underneath, and I've got those trees that are gentle

19

and beautiful with poisonous and dangerous undergrowth. Obviously, the girl is going to be like that, calm on the surface but passionate underneath. The feminists are going to say that I'm perpetuating stereotypes, that by giving the impression the girl is full of hidden passion I'm encouraging rapists. That's crazy. I'm just using a literary convention. Most of the world's great books are about the conflict between reason and passion. If you take that away, what's left to write about?

So I've got you sitting on the riverbank, twirling your ring. I forgot the birds. The trees are full of singing birds. There are meadowlarks and vireos and even Blackburnian warblers. I know a lot about birds but I'm not going to put in too many. You've got to be careful not to overdo things. In a minute I'm going to enter your mind and reveal what you're thinking. I'm going to do this in the third person. Using the first person is sometimes more effective, but I'm always afraid to do a female character in the first person. It seems wrong to me, like putting on a woman's dress.

Your name is Linda. I had to be careful not to give you a biblical name like Judith or Rachel. I don't want any symbolism in this story. Symbolism makes me sick, especially biblical symbolism. You always end up with some crazy moral argument that you don't believe and none of the readers believe. Then you lose control of your characters, because they've got to be like the biblical characters. You've got this terrific episode you'd like to use, but you can't because Rachel or Judith or whoever wouldn't do it. I think of stories with a lot of symbolism in them as sticky.

Here goes.

Linda held the ring up towards the light. The diamond flashed rainbow colours. It was a small diamond, and Linda reflected that it was probably a perfect symbol of her relationship with Gregg. Everything Gregg did was on a small scale. He was careful with his money and just as careful with his emotions. In one week they would have a small wedding and then move into a small apartment. She supposed that she ought to be happy. Gregg was very handsome, and she did love him. Why did it seem that she was walking into a trap?

That sounds kind of distant, but it's supposed to be distant. I'm using indirect quotation because the reader has just met Linda, and we don't want to get too intimate right away. Besides, I've got to get a lot of explaining done quickly, and if you can do it with the character's thoughts, then that's best.

Linda twirled the ring again, then with a suddenness that surprised her, she stood up and threw it into the river. She was immediately struck by a feeling of panic. For a moment she almost decided to dive into the river to try to recover it. Then, suddenly, she felt free. It was now impossible to marry Gregg. He would not forgive her for throwing the ring away. Gregg would say he'd had enough of her theatrics for one lifetime. He always accused her of being a romantic. She'd never had the courage to admit that he was correct, and that she intended to continue being a romantic. She was sitting alone by the river in a long blue dress because it was a romantic pose. Anyway, she thought a little wryly, you're only likely to find romance if you look for it in romantic places and dress for the occasion.

Suddenly, she heard a rustling in the bush, the sound of someone coming down the narrow path from the road above.

I had to do that, you see. I'd used up all the potential in the relationship with Gregg, and the plot would have started to flag if I hadn't introduced a new character. The man who is coming down the path is tall and athletic with wavy brown hair. He has dark brown eyes that crinkle when he smiles, and he looks kind. His skin is tanned, as if he spends a lot of time outdoors, and he moves gracefully. He is smoking a pipe. I don't want to give too many details. I'm not absolutely sure what features women find attractive in men these days, but what I've described seems safe enough. I got all of it from stories written by women, and I assume they must know. I could give him a chiselled jaw, but that's about as far as I'll go.

The man stepped into the clearing. He carried an old-fashioned wicker fishing creel and a telescoped fishing rod. Linda remained sitting on the grass, her blue dress spread out around her. The man noticed her and apologized.

'I'm sorry, I always come here to fish on Saturday afternoons and I've never encountered anyone here before.' His voice was low with something of an amused tone in it.

'Don't worry,' Linda replied. 'I'll only be here for a little while. Go ahead and fish. I won't make any noise.' In some way she couldn't understand, the man looked familiar to her. She felt she knew him. She thought she might have seen him on television or in a movie, but of course she knew that movie and television stars do not spend every Saturday afternoon fishing on the banks of small, muddy rivers.

'You can make all the noise you want,' he told her. 'The fish in this river are almost entirely deaf. Besides, I don't care if I catch any. I only like the act of fishing. If I catch them, then I have to take them home and clean them. Then I've got to cook them and eat them. I don't even like fish that much, and the fish you catch here all taste of mud.'

'Why do you bother fishing then?' Linda asked him. 'Why don't you just come and sit on the riverbank?'

'It's not that easy,' he told her. 'A beautiful girl in a blue dress may go and sit on a riverbank any time she wants. But a man can only sit on a riverbank if he has a very good reason. Because I fish, I am a man with a hobby. After a hard week of work, I deserve some relaxation. But if I just came and sat on the riverbank, I would be a romantic fool. People would make fun of me. They would think I was irresponsible, and before long I would be a failure.' As he spoke, he attached a lure to his line, untelescoped his fishing pole and cast his line into the water.

You may object that this would not have happened in real life, that the conversation would have been awkward, that Linda would have been a bit frightened by the man. Well, why don't you just run out to the grocery store and buy a bottle of milk and a loaf of bread? The grocer will give you your change without even looking at you. That's what happens in real life, and if that's what you're after, why are you reading a book?

I'm sorry. I shouldn't have got upset. But it's not easy you know. Dialogue is about the hardest stuff to write. You've got all those 'he saids' and 'she saids' and 'he replieds.' And you've got to remember the quotation marks and whether the comma is inside or outside the quotation marks. Sometimes you can leave out the 'he saids' and the 'she saids' but then the reader gets confused and can't figure out who's talking. Hemingway is bad for that. Sometimes you can read an entire chapter without figuring out who's on what side.

Anyway, something must have been in the air that afternoon. Linda felt free and open.

Did I mention that it was warm and the sun was shining?

She chattered away, telling the stranger all about her life, what she had done when she was a little girl, the time her dad had taken the whole family to Hawaii and she got such a bad sunburn that she was peeling in February, how she was a better water-skier than Gregg and how mad he got when she beat him at tennis. The man, whose name was Michael (you can use biblical names for men as long as you avoid Joshua or Isaac), told her he was a doctor, but had always wanted to be a cowboy. He told her about the time he skinned his knee when he fell off his bicycle and had to spend two weeks in the hospital because of infection. In short, they did what people who are falling in love always do. They unfolded their brightest and happiest memories and gave them to each other as gifts.

Then Michael took a bottle of wine and a Klik sandwich out of his wicker creel and invited Linda to join him in a picnic. He had forgotten his corkscrew and he had to push the cork down into the bottle with his filletting knife. They drank wine and laughed and spat out little pieces of cork. Michael reeled in his line, and to his amazement discovered a diamond ring on his hook. Linda didn't dare tell him where the ring had come from. Then Michael took Linda's hand, and slipped the ring onto her finger. In a comic-solemn voice, he asked her to marry him. With the same kind of comic solemnity, she agreed. Then they kissed, a first gentle kiss with their lips barely brushing and without touching each other.

Now I've got to bring this to some kind of ending. You think writers know how stories end before they write them, but that's not true. We're wracked with confusion and guilt about how things are going to end. And just as you're playing the role of Linda in this story, Michael is my alter ego. He even looks a little like me and he smokes the same kind of pipe. We all want this to end happily. If I were going to be realistic about this, I suppose I'd have to let them make love. Then, shaken with guilt and horror, Linda would go back and marry Gregg, and the doctor would go back to his practice. But I'm not going to do that. In the story from which I stole the plot, Michael turned out not to be a doctor at all, but a returned soldier who had always been in love with Linda. She recognized him as they kissed, because they had kissed as children, and even though they had grown up and changed, she recognized the flavour of wintergreen on his breath. That's no good. It brings in too many unexplained facts at the last minute.

I'm going to end it right here at the moment of the kiss. You can do what you want with the rest of it, except you can't make him a returned soldier, and you can't have them make love then separate forever. I've eliminated those options. In fact, I think I'll eliminate all options. This is where the story ends, at the moment of the kiss. It goes on and on forever while cities burn, nations rise and fall, galaxies are born and die, and the universe snuffs out the stars one by one. It goes on, the story, the brush of a kiss.

Women's Novels

MARGARET ATWOOD

For Lenore

1

MEN'S NOVELS ARE about men. Women's novels are about men too but from a different point of view. You can have a men's novel with no women in it except possibly the landlady or the horse, but you can't have a women's novel with no men in it. Sometimes men put women in men's novels but they leave out some of the parts: the heads, for instance, or the hands. Women's novels leave out parts of the men as well. Sometimes it's the stretch between the belly button and the knees, sometimes it's the sense of humour. It's hard to have a sense of humour in a cloak, in a high wind, on a moor.

Women do not usually write novels of the type favoured by men but men are known to write novels of the type favoured by women. Some people find this odd.

2

I like to read novels in which the heroine has a costume rustling discreetly over her breasts, or discreet breasts rustling under her costume; in any case there must be a costume, some breasts, some rustling, and, over all, discretion. Discretion over all, like a fog, a miasma through which the outlines of things appear only vaguely. A glimpse of pink through the gloom, the sound of breathing, satin slithering to the floor, revealing what? Never mind, I say. Never never mind.

3

Men favour heroes who are tough and hard: tough with men, hard with women. Sometimes the hero goes soft on a woman but this is always a mistake. Women do not favour heroines who are tough and hard. Instead they have to be tough and soft. This leads to linguistic difficulties. Last time we looked, monosyllables were male, still dominant but sinking fast, wrapped in the octopoid arms of labial polysyllables, whispering to them with arachnoid grace: *darling, darling.*

4

Men's novels are about how to get power. Killing and so on, or winning and so on. So are women's novels, though the method is different. In men's novels, getting the woman or women goes along with getting the power. It's a perk, not a means. In women's novels you get the power by getting the man. The man is the power. But sex won't do, he has to love you. What do you think all that kneeling's about, down among the crinolines, on the Persian carpet? Or at least say it. When all else is lacking, verbalization can be enough. *Love.* There, you can stand up now, it didn't kill you. Did it?

5

I no longer want to read about anything sad. Anything violent, anything disturbing, anything like that. No funerals at the end, though there can be some in the middle. If there must be deaths, let there be resurrections, or at least a Heaven so we know where we are. Depression and squalor are for those under twenty-five, they can take it, they even like it, they still have enough time left. But real life is bad for you, hold it in your hand long enough and you'll get pimples and become feeble-minded. You'll go blind.

I want happiness, guaranteed, joy all round, covers with nurses on them or brides, intelligent girls but not too intelligent, with regular teeth and pluck and both breasts the same size and no excess facial hair, someone you can depend on to know where the bandages are and to turn the hero, that potential rake and killer, into a well-groomed country gentleman with clean fingernails and the right vocabulary. *Always,* he has to say. *Forever.* I no longer want to read books that don't end with the word *forever.* I want to be stroked between the eyes, one way only.

6

Some people think a woman's novel is anything without politics in it. Some think it's anything about relationships. Some think it's anything with a lot of operations in it, medical ones I mean. Some think it's anything that doesn't give you a broad panoramic view of our exciting times. Me, well, I just want something you can leave on the coffee table and not be too worried if the kids get into it. You think that's not a real consideration? You're wrong.

7

She had the startled eyes of a wild bird. This is the kind of sentence I go mad for. I would like to be able to write such sentences, without embarrassment. I would like to be able to read them without embarrassment. If I could only do these two simple things, I feel, I would be able to pass my allotted time on this earth like a pearl wrapped in velvet.

She had the startled eyes of a wild bird. Ah, but which one? A screech owl, perhaps, or a cuckoo? It does make a difference. We do not need more literalists of the imagination. They cannot read *a body like a gazelle's* without thinking of intestinal parasites, zoos and smells.

She had a feral gaze like that of an untamed animal, I read. Reluctantly I put down the book, thumb still inserted at the exciting moment. He's about to crush her in his arms, pressing his hot, devouring, hard, demanding mouth to hers as her breasts squish out the top of her dress, but I can't concentrate. Metaphor leads me by the nose, into the maze, and suddenly all Eden lies before me. Porcupines, weasels, warthogs and skunks, their feral gazes malicious or bland or stolid or piggy and sly. Agony, to see the romantic *frisson* quivering just out of reach, a dark-winged butterfly stuck to an over-ripe peach, and not to be able to swallow, or wallow. *Which one?* I murmur to the unresponding air. *Which one?*

Blossom

DIONNE BRAND

Priestess of Oya, Goddess of Winds, Storms and Waterfalls

Blossom's was jumping tonight. Oya and Shango and God and spirit and ordinary people was chanting and singing and jumping the place down. Blossom's was a obeah house and speakeasy on Vaughan Road. People didn't come for the cheap liquor Blossom sell, though as night wear on, on any given night, Blossom, in she waters, would tilt the bottle a little in your favour. No, it wasn't the cheap liquor, even if you could drink it all night long till morning. It was the feel of the place. The cheap light revolving over the bar, the red shag covering the wall against which Blossom always sit, a line of beer, along the window sill behind, as long as she ample arms spread out over the back of a wooden bench. And, the candles glowing bright on the shrine of Oya, Blossom's mother Goddess.

This was Blossom's most successful endeavour since coming to Canada. Every once in a while, under she breath, she curse the day she come to Toronto from Oropuche, Trinidad. But nothing, not even snarky white people could keep Blossom under. When she first come it was to babysit some snot-nosed children on Oriole Parkway. She did meet a man, in a club on Henry Street in Port-of-Spain, who promise she to take care of she, if she ever was in Toronto. When Blossom reach, the man disappear and through the one other person she know in Toronto she get the work on Oriole.

Well Blossom decide long that she did never mean for this kinda work, steady cleaning up after white people, and that is when she decide to take a course in secretarial at night. Is there she meet Peg and Betty, who she did know from home, and Fancy Girl. And for two good years they all try to type; but their heart wasn't in it. So they switch to carpentry and upholstering. Fancy Girl swear that they could make a good business because she father was a joiner and white people was paying a lot of money for old-looking furniture. They all went along with this until Peg say she need to make some fast money because, where they was going to find white people who like old furniture, and who was going to buy old furniture from Black women anyway. That is when Fancy Girl come up with the pyramid scheme.

They was to put everybody name on a piece of paper, everybody was to find five people to put on the list and that five would find five and so on. Everybody on the list would send the first person one hundred dollars. In the end everybody was to get thousands of dollars in the mail and only invest one hundred, unless the pyramid break. Fancy Girl name was first and so the pyramid start. Lo and behold, Fancy Girl leave town saying she going to Montreal for a weekend and it was the last they ever see she. The pyramid bust up and they discover that Fancy Girl pick up ten thousand dollars clean. Blossom had to hide for months from people on the pyramid and she swear to Peg that, if she ever see Fancy Girl Munroe again, dog eat she supper.

Well now is five years since Blossom in Canada and nothing ain't breaking. She leave the people on Oriole for some others on Balmoral. The white man boss-man was a doctor. Since the day she reach, he eyeing she, eyeing she. Blossom just mark this down in she head and making sure she ain't in no room alone with he. Now one day, it so happen that she in the basement doing the washing and who come down there but he, playing like if he looking for something. She watching him from the corner of she eye and, sure as the day, he make a grab for she. Blossom know a few things, so she grab on to he little finger and start to squeeze it back till he face change all colour from white to black and he had to scream out. Blossom sheself start to scream like all hell, until the wife and children run downstairs too.

It ain't have cuss, Blossom ain't cuss that day. The wife face red and shame and then she start to watch Blossom cut eye. Well look at my cross nah Lord, Blossom think, here this dog trying to abuse me and she watching *me* cut eye! Me! a church-going woman! A craziness fly up in Blossom head and she start to go mad on them in the house. She flinging things left right and centre and cussing big word. Blossom fly right off the handle, until they send for the police for Blossom. She didn't care. They couldn't make she hush. It don't have no dignity in white man feeling you up! So she cuss out the police too, when they come, and tell them to serve and protect she, like they supposed to do and lock up the so-and-so. The doctor keep saying to the police, 'Oh this is so embarrassing. She's crazy, she's crazy.' And Blossom tell him, 'You ain't see crazy yet.' She run and dash all the people clothes in the swimming pool and shouting, 'Make me a weapon in thine hand, oh Lord!' Blossom grab on to the doctor neck, dragging him, to drown him. It take two police to unlatch Blossom from the man red neck, yes. And how the police get Blossom to leave is a wonder; but she wouldn't leave without she

33

pay, and in cash money too besides, she tell them. Anyhow, the police get Blossom to leave the house; and they must be 'fraid Blossom too, so they let she off down the street and tell she to go home.

The next day Blossom show up on Balmoral with a placard saying the Dr. So-and-So was a white rapist; and Peg and Betty bring a Black Power flag and the three of them parade in front of that man house whole day. Well is now this doctor know that he mess with the wrong woman, because when he reach home that evening, Blossom and Peg and Betty bang on he car, singing, 'We Shall Not Be Moved' and chanting, 'Doctor So-and-So is a Rapist.' They reach into the car and, well, rough up the doctor— grabbing he tie and threatening to cut off he balls. Not a soul ain't come outside, but you never see so much drapes and curtain moving and swaying up and down Balmoral. Police come again, but they tell Doctor So-and-So that the sidewalk is public property and as long as Blossom and them keep moving they wasn't committing no crime. Well, when they hear that, Blossom and them start to laugh and clap and sing 'We Shall Overcome.' That night, at Peg house, they laugh and they eat and they drink and dance and laugh more, remembering the doctor face when they was banging on he car. The next day Blossom hear from the Guyanese girl working next door that the whole family on Balmoral, Doctor, wife, children, cat and dog, gone to Florida.

After that, Blossom decide to do day work here and day work there, so that no white man would be over she and she was figuring on a way to save some money to do she own business.

Blossom start up with Victor one night in a dance. It ain't have no reason that she could say why she hook up with him except that in a dance one night, before Fancy Girl take off, when Peg and Betty and Fancy Girl was in they dance days, she suddenly look around and all three was jack up in a corner with some man.

They was grinding down the Trinidad Club and there was Blossom, alone at the table, playing she was groovin' to the music.

Alone. Well, keeping up sheself, working, working and keeping the spirits up in this cold place all the time ... Is not until all of a sudden one moment, you does see yourself. Something tell she to stop and witness the scene. And then Blossom decide to get a man. All she girl pals had one, and Blossom decide to get one too. It sadden she a little to see she riding partners all off to the side so. After all, every weekend they used to fête and insult man when they come to ask them to dance. They would fête all night in the middle of the floor and get tight on Southern Comfort. Then they would hobble down the steps out of the club on Church or 'Room at the Top,' high heels squeezing and waist in pain, and hail a taxi home to one house or the other. By the time the taxi reach wherever they was going, shoes would be in hand and stockings off and a lot of groaning and description of foot pain would hit the door. And comparing notes on which man look so good and which man had a hard on, they would cook, bake and salt fish, in the morning and laugh about the night before. If is one thing with Blossom, Peg and Betty and Fancy Girl, they like to have a good time. The world didn't mean for sorrow; and suffering don't suit nobody face, Blossom say.

So when she see girl-days done and everybody else straighten up and get man, Blossom decide to get a man too. The first, first man that pass Blossom eyes after deciding was Victor and Blossom decide on him. It wasn't the first man Blossom had, but it was the first one she decide to keep. It ain't have no special reason either; is just when Victor appear, Blossom get a idea to fall in love. Well, then start a long line of misery the likes of which Blossom never see before and never intend to see again. The only reason that the misery last so long is because Blossom was a stubborn woman and when she decide something, she decide. It wasn't even that Blossom really like Victor because whenever she sit down to count he attributes, the man was really lacking in kindness and had a streak of meanness when it come to woman. But she figure like and love not the same thing. So Blossom married to Victor that same summer, in the Pentecostal Church. Victor wanted to live together, but Blossom say she wouldn't be able to go to church no more if she living in sin and if Victor want any honey from she, it have to be with God blessing.

The wedding night, Victor disappear. He show up in a dance, in he white wedding suit and Blossom ain't see him till Monday morning. So Blossom take a sign from this and start to watch Victor because she wasn't a hasty woman by nature. He come when he want, he go when he want and vex when she ain't there. He don't bring much money. Blossom still working day work and every night of the week Victor have friends over drinking Blossom liquor. But Blossom love Victor, so she put up with this type of behaviour for a good few years; because love supposed to be hard and if it ain't hard, it ain't sweet, they say. You have to bear with man, she mother used to say, and besides, Blossom couldn't grudge Victor he good time. Living wasn't just for slaving and it seem that in this society the harder you work, the less you have. Judge not lest ye be judged; this sermon Blossom would give to Peg and Betty any time they contradict Victor. And anyway, Blossom have she desires and Victor have more than reputation between he legs.

So life go on as it supposed to go on, until Blossom decide not to go to work one day. That time, they was living on Vaughan Road and Blossom wake up feeling like an old woman. Just tired. Something tell she to stay home and figure out she life; because a thirty-six-year-old woman shouldn't feel so old and tired. She look at she face in the mirror and figure that she look like a old woman too. Ten years she here now, and nothing shaking, just getting older and older, watching white people live. She, sheself living underneath all the time. She didn't even feel like living with Victor anymore. All the sugar gone outa the thing. Victor had one scheme after another, poor thing. Everything gone a little sour.

She was looking out the window, towards the bus stop on Vaughan Road, thinking this. Looking at people going to work like they does do every morning. It make she even more tired to watch them. Today she was supposed to go to a house on Roselawn. Three bathrooms to clean, two living rooms, basement, laundry—God knows what else. Fifty dollars. She look at she short fingers, still water-laden from the day before, then look at the bus stop again. No, no. Not today. Not this woman. In the bedroom, she watch Victor lying in the bed, face peaceful as ever, young like a baby. Passing into the kitchen shaking she head, she think, 'Victor you ain't ready for the Lord yet.'

Blossom must be was sitting at the kitchen table for a hour or so when Victor get up. She hear him bathe, dress and come out to the kitchen. 'Ah, ah, you still here? Is ten o'clock you know!' She didn't answer. 'Girl, you ain't going to work today, or what?' She didn't answer. 'You is a happy woman yes, Blossom. Anyway,' as he put he coat on, 'I have to meet a fella.' Something just fly up in Blossom head and she reach for the bread knife on the table. 'Victor, just go and don't come back, you hear me?' waving the knife. 'Girl you crazy, or what?' Victor edged towards the door, 'What happen to you this morning?'

Next thing Blossom know, she running Victor down Vaughan Road screaming and waving the bread knife. She hear somebody screaming loud, loud. At first she didn't know who it is, and is then she realize that the scream was coming from she and she couldn't stop it. She dress in she nightie alone and screaming in the middle of the road. So it went on and on and on until it turn into cry and Blossom just cry and cry and cry and then she start to walk. That day Blossom walk. And walk and cry, until she was so exhausted that she find she way home and went to sleep.

She wake up the next morning, feeling shaky and something like spiritual. She was frightened, in case the crying come back again. The apartment was empty. She had the feeling that she was holding she body around she heart, holding sheself together, tight, tight. She get dressed and went to the Pentecostal Church where she get married and sit there till evening.

For two weeks this is all Blossom do. As soon as she feel the crying welling up inside she and turning to a scream, she get dressed and go to the Pentecost. After two weeks, another feeling come; one as if Blossom dip she whole head in water and come up gasping. She heart would pump fast as if she going to die and then the feeling, washed and gasping. During these weeks she could drink nothing but water. When she try to eat bread, something reach inside of she throat and spit it out. Two weeks more and Blossom hair turn white all over. Then she start to speak in tongues that she didn't ever learn, but she understand. At night, in Blossom cry dreams, she feel sheself flying round the earth and raging around the world and then, not just this earth, but earth deep in the blackness beyond sky. There, sky become further than sky and further than dream. She dream so much farther than she ever go in a dream, that she was awake. Blossom see volcano erupt and mountain fall down two feet away and she ain't get touch. She come to the place where legahoo and lajabless is not even dog and where soucouyant, the fireball, burn up in the bigger fire of an infinite sun, where none of the ordinary spirit Blossom know is nothing. She come to the place where pestilence mount good, good heart and good heart bust for joy. The place bright one minute and dark the next. The place big one minute, so big Blossom standing in a hole and the blackness rising up like long shafts above she and widening out into a yellow and red desert as far as she could see; the place small, next minute, as a pin head and only Blossom heart what shrink small, small, small, could fit in the world of it. Then she feel as if she don't have no hand, no foot and she don't need them. Sometimes, she crawling like mapeepee snake; sometimes she walking tall, tall, like a moco jumbie through desert and darkness, desert and darkness, upside down and sideways.

In the mornings, Blossom feel she body beating up and breaking up on a hard mud ground and she, weeping as if she mourning and as if somebody borning. And talking in tongues, the tongues saying the name, Oya. The name sound through Blossom into every layer of she skin, she flesh—like sugar and seasoning. Blossom body come hard like steel and supple like water, when she say Oya. Oya. This Oya was a big spirit Blossom know from home.

One night, Oya hold Blossom and bring she through the most terrifying dream in she life. In the dream, Oya make Blossom look at Black people suffering. The face of Black people suffering was so old and hoary that Blossom nearly dead. And is so she vomit. She skin wither under Suffering look; and she feel hungry and thirsty as nobody ever feel before. Pain dry out Blossom soul, until it turn to nothing. Blossom so 'fraid she dead that she take she last ball of spit, and stone Suffering. Suffering jump up so fast and grab the stone, Blossom shocked, because she did think Suffering was decrepit. Then Suffering head for Blossom with such a speed that Blossom fingernails and hairs all fall out. Blossom start to dry away, and melt away, until it only had one grain of she left. And Suffering still descending. Blossom scream for Oya and Oya didn't come and Suffering keep coming. Blossom was never a woman to stop, even before she start to dream. So she roll and dance she grain-self into a hate so hard, she chisel sheself into a sharp hot prickle and fly in Suffering face. Suffering howl like a beast and back back. Blossom spin and chew on that nut of hate, right in Suffering eyeball. The more Blossom spin and dance, the bigger Blossom get, until Blossom was Oya with she warrior knife, advancing. In the cold light of Suffering, with Oya hot and advancing, Suffering slam a door and disappear. Blossom climb into Oya lovely womb of strength and fearlessness. Full of joy when Oya show she the warrior dance where heart and blood burst open. Freeness, Oya call that dance; and the colour of the dance was red and it was a dance to dance high up in the air. In this dance Oya had such a sweet laugh, it make she black skin shake and it full up Blossom and shake she too.

Each night Blossom grow more into Oya. Blossom singing, singing for Oya to come,

'Oya arriwo Oya, Oya arriwo Oya, Oya kauako arriwo, Arripiti O Oya.'

Each night Blossom learn a new piece of Oya and finally, it come to she. She had the power to see and the power to fight; she had the power to feel pain and the power to heal. For life was nothing as it could be taken away any minute; what was earthly was fleeting; what could be done was joy and it have no beauty in suffering.

'Oya O Ologbo O de, Ma yak ba Ma Who! leh, Oya O Ologo O de, Ma yak ba Ma Who! leh, Oya Oh de arriwo, Oya Oh de cumale.'

From that day, Blossom dress in yellow and red from head to foot, the colour of joy and the colour of war against suffering. She head wrap in a long yellow cloth; she body wrap in red. She become a obeah woman, spiritual mother and priestess of Oya, Yuroba Goddess-warrior of winds, storms and waterfalls. It was

Oya who run Victor out and it was Oya who plague the doctor and laugh and drink afterwards. It was Oya who well up the tears inside Blossom and who spit the bread out of Blossom mouth.

Quite here, Oya did search for Blossom. Quite here, she find she.

Black people on Vaughan Road recognized Blossom as gifted and powerful by she carriage and the fierce look in she eyes. She fill she rooms with compelling powder and reliance smoke, drink rum and spit it in the corners, for the spirits who would enter Blossom obeah house in the night. Little by little people begin to find out that Blossom was the priestess of Oya, the Goddess. Is through Oya, that Blossom reach prosperity.

'Oya arriwo Oya, Oya arriwo Oya, Oya kauako arriwo, Arripiti O Oya.'

Each night Oya would enter Blossom, rumbling and violent like thunder and chant heroically and dance, slowly and majestically, she warrior dance against suffering. To see Oya dancing on one leg all night, a calabash holding a candle on she head, was to see beauty. She fierce warrior face frighten unbelievers. Then she would drink nothing but good liquor, blowing mouthfuls on the gathering, granting favours to the believers for an offering.

The offerings come fast and plentiful. Where people was desperate, Blossom, as Oya, received food as offering, boxes of candles and sweet oil. Blossom send to Trinidad for calabash gourds and herbs for healing, guided by Oya in the mixing and administering.

When Oya enter Blossom, she talk in old African tongues and she body was part water and part tree. Oya thrash about taking Blossom body up to the ceiling and right through the walls. Oya knife slash the gullets of white men and Oya pitch the world around itself. Some nights, she voice sound as if it was coming from a deep well; and some nights, only if you had the power to hear air, could you listen to Oya.

Blossom fame as a obeah woman spread all over, but only among those who had to know. Those who see the hoary face of Suffering and feel he vibrant slap could come to dance with Oya—Oya freeness dance.

'Oya O Ologbo O de, Ma yak ba Ma Who! leh, Oya O Ologo O de, Ma yak ba Ma Who! leh, Oya Oh de arriwo, Oya Oh de cumale.'

Since Oya reach, Blossom live peaceful. Is so, Blossom start in the speakeasy business. In the day time, Blossom sleep, exhausted and full of Oya warrior dance and laughing. She would wake up in the afternoon to prepare the shrine for Oya entrance.

On the nights that Oya didn't come, Blossom sell liquor and wait for she, sitting against the window.

Ann and Dan Got Married

DAVID BROMIGE

Life is a rose-garden. The petals
wilt and the thorns remain.
— Fritz Perls

Ann wants Daddy. But Mommy has beaten her to it.

ANN LIKED IT that Danny was older. Oh, not old enough to be her father. But he was promising material. She would make him into a fair replica of a father.

Ann would do this by acting younger than her age. By pretending not to understand what she was doing. She would invite this unhappily married man back to her flat for some classical music. She would be delightfully surprised to discover he was an amateur musician. Ann liked the way he played her piano. While he was thumping away, she would surrender herself to the seductive notion that he was thumping away just for her.

Ann never ceased to act girlish around Dan. At first, when she was nineteen, this was charming.

To Ann, acting girlish meant acting more grown-up than she was, the way her father had wanted her to act when she was really and truly a girl. It meant tippy-toeing around so as not to upset Daddy or the Daddy-substitute. It meant not letting Daddy see her true negative feelings. It came to mean paying the bills and driving the car and fending off visitors. It came to mean acting sophisticated about relationships during the seventies, a dangerous time to try that kind of a bluff. It came to grief.

———————

Dan *had* Mommy. Then Daddy kept coming back to take her away. But nevertheless, he had had her. It was Daddy he couldn't get to. So being handed a Daddy-role was attractive, possibly. Especially when the Daddy was really a big baby who got everything done for him.

Dan didn't like to make decisions. He liked to blame this on the Postmodern condition. But to everyone else it was apparent that this had more to do with Dan than with *Waiting for Godot* or a general confusion of social values. He should have to make the decisions *they* were faced with! Then he'd know Postmodern!

Actually, Dan was good at decisions about ends. He had decided to quit his unhappy marriage and live by himself. But women wouldn't leave him alone. It was simply that there were more of them than there was of him. He couldn't decide to begin anything, though, so he was spared most of these potential entanglements.

So Dan liked it that Ann acted so decisive around him. She decided they should take their socks off and then go to bed together. When she came back to Berkeley from the obligatory summer in La Jolla, she decided she should move in with Dan, rather than look for her own apartment. And when Dan's landlady gave him notice, on the grounds that his extra-marital arrangement would corrupt her young children who lived just over his head, Ann decided that she and Dan should find a place together. She would do the looking and the finding. All Dan had to do was to pack up his books.

Ann doted on Dan. So of course he told her that he loved her, too. But secretly this made him uneasy. There were so many meanings to the word. He suspected Ann meant it one way and that he meant it another way.

Part of the trouble was that Ann never would confront him. So he couldn't know what his feelings were. Ann didn't want him to know what his feelings were. She suspected he didn't really love her, not the way she loved him. She feared if he were to find this out that he might leave. Ann may not have been conscious of this, but Dan couldn't tell the difference anyway between people's conscious and unconscious motives. So he worried that he wasn't giving Ann enough reassurance. He felt like an ingrate, and redoubled his efforts. His charm cheered her up.

Ann and Dan had lots of fun. He would stand there talking to himself under his breath and Ann would come and dance around them both, the muttering one and the hearkening one, and fuse them with her high spirits and curious ways. As time went by, Dan came to identify with Ann. Without usually intending to, he impersonated her. This drove Ann wild with desire. She could make love to herself without feeling lonely!

Of course, Ann was resentful that Dan left everything practical up to her, even though or maybe just because she encouraged him to do so. She complained about it, but never to him. She complained about him to her friend Fran. She complained that Dan treated her like a little girl. This only increased Ann's pleasure. She got to be treated like a little girl and, like a little girl, all she could do was complain about it in secret to her girlfriend.

Fran replied that it looked to her like Dan treated Ann like she was his Mommy. This too gave Ann pleasure, for now she had replaced her own Mommy in a relationship with her Daddy-substitute. Ann found it was even more fun to complain about this to Fran. For as long as she was complaining about her relationship to Dan, that she was his daughter or that she was his Mommy, she was enjoying in a reflective way what she otherwise enjoyed in a half-conscious way. In order to complain she had to name, and she liked to find names for these binds. The binds gave her a sense of still being a child, for they were arrangements she felt powerless to alter, while naming them gave her a sense of power over her life.

Yes, for all that she was unliberated and unhappy, Ann was eating and having her cake, and very tasty she found it. All around Ann women were waking up and confronting the tyrants they had been brainwashed into marrying but Ann pooh-poohed all that. Secretly she was afraid of it, afraid of catching the infectious new spirit that threatened to carry off the persona she felt so secure in. Why, one heard of cases where the fellow actually started to listen to reason and stopped throwing dishes and started to do them instead! This was not for Ann. She had cast herself in a role that suited her to a 'T': she was one of those girl-heroines from Nineteenth-Century Literature whose mothers having died have Daddy all to themselves and pay the bills and the rent and keep the house so that Daddy can continue with his important work as an inventor of devices no one will ever see the use of except for the heroine herself.

This was the sort of Daddy Ann had made of Danny. It hadn't involved making him over entirely. Dan's mother and father and his first wife and the other women and men of his generation had all contributed. He could never have done it alone. Decades later, some men would claim that they had already been doing their share of the housework and childcare by this time in history, but usually they were lying, rewriting history to make themselves look better. They would claim that they had already stopped being promiscuous male chauvinists twenty years ago but this was just another line. They didn't say it to each other. They told it to women.

Dan was actually somewhat closer to seeing the light than many of his men friends during this the early-middle period of the relationship of Ann and Dan. While living alone he had gotten into doing the dishes and the laundry and messing around with food on his hotplate. However, after some years with Ann, who offered herself for each of these chores, he found it easier to backslide. If he *did* do the chores, Ann would invariably laugh at him, gently, and point out what was wrong with his methods. So it became easier to remain impractical.

When it came to childcare, though, Dan was almost in step with his time as it came later to be lyingly characterized. He saw his little son Van two or three times a week and would usually take him on a field trip of some kind, just the two of them. In fact Dan figured out that he spent more actual time with his son than *his* father had spent with him, although they had for the most part lived in the same house. Bit by bit Ann got herself included in these trips, and then, when Dan was under particular pressure because he had an opening coming up (for Dan's inventions were sculptures, and a handful of people found them interesting), Ann in the goodness of her heart would take charge of Van.

After Ann and Dan moved to the country, Ann would often drive to Berkeley to fetch or return Van to or from his mother's house. Dan couldn't drive; he abstained out of purely humanitarian motives, on the grounds that he was too absent-minded to be in charge of such a weapon. Ann let Dan get away

47

with this bullshit (which he believed) and so she had to do all the driving. But at least she had Dan where she wanted him and knew where he was at all times, unless someone else was taking him for a ride. Between his sculpting and his hobby, music, Dan had gotten to know a lot of people, and sometimes one of these good folk would come and fetch him in order to play with him.

But mostly he was at home, and usually Ann was there with him. They not only were together a lot, they did a lot of things together. They gardened together, they read Thomas Mann's mighty novel *Doktor Faustus* together, marvelling at the associations of music with the diabolical, they read the *Odyssey* together (Dan was moved to tears by the part about being wrecked on Calypso's isle), they went skinny-dipping in the hippie pond together, they made love under the sun and under the stars together, they made friends together, they played with Van and his friends together, and pretty soon, Ann decided they should sculpt together and she started to sculpt.

Dan's pieces weren't the simplest in the world, and it often took a few viewings to decide just where the representation was buried in them, but Ann's pieces were grotesques and immediately apprehensible as such. At first she did bats and lizards and bugs but then she started to do human figures—a person going to the bathroom, an acquaintance falling downstairs, Lot's Wife being turned into a pillar of salt unable to stop looking back. They were right for the times and Dan was among the first to see this. He wrote to the owner of the gallery which showed most of his own work and sent photographs of Ann's art. The man was not convinced so Dan wrote him a long letter pointing out how Ann's work worked. And then the man was convinced, and gave Ann her first show.

One curious fact about Ann as a sculptress was that she seldom could figure out how to finish a piece. To Dan it was usually quite obvious and he would tell her how to if she asked him to.

About this time Dan began composing songs. They weren't very good, although he had some terrific talents to help him. His favourite was about a man who is able through magical powers to shrink himself to a height of six inches and ride around in his wife's pocket. From time to time she slips her hand in there and feeds him pieces of chocolate. Then she has a bra specially made and carries him around in that, and when people come to call, she produces him and sets him on the table where he speaks in a thin voice barely within the range of human audition. But it doesn't matter that the neat American sentences he utters can't be decoded: it's enough that this diminutive figure speaks at all. Then she has a miniature piano made for him, and her friends enjoy watching him tickle its ivories.

As a song, it sank beneath the weight of its details, and Dan soon returned to sculpting. As a clue that the marriage was headed for trouble, it was indecipherable to those it most concerned.

Yes, Ann and Dan had finally married. Dan hadn't seen the need for it but Ann had shown him that once they moved to the country she could no longer pretend to her parents that she was living with a female roommate, as she had done during the Berkeley years. Besides, hadn't Dan complained about the inconvenience, having to move out whenever her folks came to town? He had had to go stay in Fran's flat while Fran and a large part of her wardrobe (enough to hide Dan's things in the closets) had to move into Dan and Ann's place. Dan let Ann know he thought it was dumb to go through this farce in the 1970s but Ann knew she could never let her parents know that she was living in sin no matter what decade they were in. They would think Ann was decadent.

First comes love, then comes marriage, then comes someone with a baby carriage. Ann repeated this truth to Dan until he got sick of hearing it. It didn't take long. He was convinced that he was inadequate parent material. He said that, like many cursed with the artistic temperament, he was childish and egocentric and had no room in his life for another baby. But Ann pointed out that he already had had another baby, whereas she, Ann, had not, and that this was unfair. Dan could sometimes be won over by an appeal to his sense of fair play.

But not on this matter. What would have been the upshot if Ann had told him, Either we have a child, or I'll leave you? Who can say? Ann did not have the nerve to find out. So something else happened instead.

What happened instead depends upon whether it is told by a friend of Ann or a friend of Dan. In one version, Ann sends a urine sample to a doctor friend who tests it on a rabbit and discovers Ann is pregnant. Ann retails this news to Dan who asks her to have an abortion. Ann just happens to have to go into hospital for this operation while Dan is away showing his art. When Dan phones that night, Ann tells him the doctors in the hospital found out it was a false pregnancy.

In the other version, Ann tries to bluff Dan into thinking she is pregnant, in the hope that he will be overjoyed at the news. Then Ann and Dan will copulate without further precautions and Ann *will* get pregnant.

Later, when they heard from Ann how miserable she had been in this marriage, how tired she had gotten of doing all the housework and of driving the car and of Dan's musical sessions, how tiresome had been his tantrums, how depressing his unwillingness to procreate, Ann and Dan's friends were quite startled. True, they had glimpsed problems, had understood that the marriage was not as ideal as Ann at the time had pretended;

but they had also watched Ann's pleasure in being with Dan, the pleasure she took in making his friends hers, the pleasure she took in Dan's art and her own, the pleasure she took in making music with Dan and friends; it was difficult, later, to hear that this show of pleasure was due solely to Ann's consummate ability as an actress. It looked more likely to be a case of history rewritten to gain sympathy *post facto* for the rewriter. Dan thought this was a great idea.

If Ann had learned from her marriage, these friends agreed, she would not have spoken of her new husband, Stan, as the Real Mr. Right. While this implied that Dan had been the False Mr. Right, it also implied Ann's continuing belief in the fiction of a Mr. Right. It had been Ann's belief in this fiction when applied to Dan that had helped destroy the relationship, some held, because it placed too great a burden on Dan's slender shoulders. Just as, however much broader Stan's frame, it placed too great a burden on him, which made Ann's friends worry about her.

No, Ann and Dan had had a great deal of fun together, and if Ann chose to regard this as misguided in her later incarnation, she couldn't quite erase that truth from her memory. Proof of this were the figures she was still making, ten years after the divorce, grotesques no doubt, but recognizably of Dan, keeping the connection to her past lover alive even while, in the apparent fury of their genesis, invoking his destruction.

When friends mentioned this to Dan, he agreed, saying that he himself often harked back to those days, which, if only that they preceded by some fifteen years the present in which the world was being turned into a labour camp, looked golden, thronged with friends who had nothing better to do than to hang out, play music, and talk sculpting. Ann was a remarkable woman and he wished her well. He thought her art had fallen off, her grotesques were no longer amusing but sentimental or

despairing, and they had an unfinished look about them. He felt
bad for the way he had used her life, given that she had later
complained of this; but she might have spoken up at the time,
Dan felt.

The trouble was, when Ann, egged on by new female
acquaintances, *did* begin to object to Dan, it was much too late;
he had become accustomed to an unobjecting mate. He could
only regard her novel ways as aberrant. He withdrew.

The last days were dismal enough. Dan no longer wanted to
play piano, or even blues harmonica. He didn't sculpt much any
more. Mostly he smoked—watched TV and smoked. He had
smoked so much that his neck had gotten just like a turkey's, the
way the necks of people who smoke a lot almost always do. And
he had circles under his eyes from his swim-goggles, for
swimming was another habit he indulged in at this time, even
persuading Ann to take it up. For a while it was good for her
figure, for which at the time Ann was grateful to Dan, as she had
been years before when he talked her into giving up her wiglet
and letting her hair grow out into a gorgeous aureole. But once
she gave up smoking, Ann, who did not give up being oral, put
on weight so that, if Dan resembled an old gobbler, Ann, whose
neck never had been of the longest, came to look like another
animal ritually slaughtered at holiday time.

It was only a matter of time before some fan of Dan's should
take Dan away from Ann. But within a year, Ann had met Stan.
And seeing that had turned out so well, it was a puzzle that, after
the initial pain and rancour dispersed, Ann had not become
grateful to Dan for seeing how to end it and freeing her to meet
the Real Mr. Right. But the paradox of the Fortunate Fall was
beyond her.

Also beyond Ann's powers of forgiveness were any claims Van
had on her love. She had become a good companion as well as a

fine stepmother to Van, but after Dan left she would have nothing more to do with his son. Dan could understand some of Ann's meanness after he left, just as he understood that those men who most wanted to leave their own wives, were those who most excoriated Dan for leaving his. (Later, these men left their wives.) He could understand those women who detested him in the name of sisterhood, just as he understood, later, when they called him up to ask how he was doing, and if he still missed Ann.

But Dan found harder to understand Ann's rejection of Van. When Van told Dan, Dan told Van it was probably that Ann needed to forget him (Dan) and that this probably had to mean forgetting Van too. But this was scarcely consolation for Van. Ann had been his friend. Now she treated him as if he were dead. Or as if she was.

So finally Dan determined to do a piece that would contain his feelings about Ann, and he went to work on it and worked for weeks, but he couldn't see how to finish it. Then he saw that it had to be done Ann-style, but with more charity.

While he was working on it, he went several times to see the latest retrospective of her work: figures he had helped Ann finish, and figures no one had. These latter had an odd consistency. In each, the Dan-figure, curiously distorted and maimed, is discovered in the act of making something. Some thought this something resembled an Ann-like figure; others, that it resembled nothing human. Others pointed out that it was simply present to prop the Dan-figure up. They drew attention to other male figures, which they called Stan-figures, which had identical ill-defined shapes under their hands, likewise serving (if not doubling) as props. Many said they missed a woman figure standing on its own two feet. But Dan said all the figures looked like Ann to him.

Then Dan took a trip. His sculpture was on show in a remote

town, so he went alone. He was put up at a motel and that night he called his wife, Penny, and let her sweet contralto soothe his nerves. As she spoke, he could picture her sitting at the phone table in the hallway. Her long brown hair flowed over her shoulders and her dazzling smile spoke into the mouthpiece. Or possibly she was mugging silent freakout at having to field his phone call while trying to get the kid to bed or work on her files or watch TV. Her big blue eyes would be bugging out and her mouth fixed in a comic-strip scream. After they said goodnight and hung up, he sat at the desk in his room, remembering.

Penny always sounded so sensible, she wore a mask easily and wisecracked with the best of them. But once in a while the persona would let slip a glimpse of need—tonight, in the final five seconds, when she said 'I love you, Daniel.' She couldn't be too vulnerable around him: he would walk right in and assume the ancient male prerogatives.

Dan lay down on his left side and, hugging the pillow that would have been hers had she been with him, fell fast asleep.

When he woke, he didn't know what time it was, only that it was still dark. He was hungry. He found a bar of chocolate, ate it, and went back to sleep.

There was a waterfall, a canal, a fountain, a golf course, a house. It was his house, his and his wife's. But the woman in it was Ann. She was as she had been the summer when she had been her slenderest. Sun-bleached curls, slender ankles, golden down on her thighs. Naked, she sprawled on the bed.

'You'll see,' she said to him, pouting, playful, 'I'm not so unlovable. You take me back, you'll have a good time—if you dare!'

He was awake again. Sweetness flooded his being. He felt like a man without a conscience. He actually felt around for Ann.

Not there. Of course. It was an impossible sweetness, full of chocolate and naked symbolism. The real Ann hated him. He didn't feel any too good about her, either. The real wife he loved was Penny.

But the dream said nothing was lost. Access was denied, yes. That was wisdom. But now he felt the 'So near, and yet so far' sensation. No wonder Ann still hated him. He who had known her so lovely, youthful, happy, had removed that image of herself. Dan had stolen years of Ann, locked them up where she couldn't get at them. The same went for him, with her. Dan and Ann would never sit in a room together again and say 'Remember when?' They would sculpt, separately. They were alone, together, them and the rest of the world.

When Dan got home, he looked at his piece about Ann and despaired. Her fault, his fault ... it was the fault of a society that didn't know what it wanted marriage to be: romantic imbroglio, business deal, kindergarten, buddy-system, duel to the death? Dan had learned that the one chance for a marriage to survive was if both parties abandoned every hope they had had of it, save that it persist.

He melted the piece down. He was left with a bicameral lump the size of two fists and weighing three pounds. Sentimental Ann would have thought it looked like a human heart, and then become disgusted at her own projection. But no heart was that big. Besides, the heart has four chambers, not two. Dan came to see it as a human brain. But Penny said it looked like a petrified piece of cake, inedible but deceptively alluring. And irredeemably lasting, Dan sighed.

A Literary History of Anton

MATT COHEN

Chapter 1. Anton is born

FROM THE MOMENT that Anton slid out of the bloody canal of his mother and into the world, he was obsessed with the most important question of his life: Who will love me? He cried and shrieked like an infantile prophet. His mother clasped him to her. Even through the fog of anesthetic and pain, she could recognize this voice as part of herself. While she held him, Anton felt his eyelids pressing wetly against his cheeks. For years he woke up this way, crying for no reason. When he was too old to go to his mother, he would lie in bed and wait for the morning to dry his skin.

'At least I was born,' he would say. Anton had developed a strange habit of reciting his life to himself, as if he was to be the best proof of his own existence. 'At least I was born,' he would say. Nothing could release him but the love of a beautiful woman.

Chapter 2. In the afternoon

In the afternoon, Anton liked to meditate upon his mind. He was cultivating that simple and direct clarity which he knew to be the mark of true genius. His eyes learned how to brush themselves in the mirror. Sometimes he dreamed eccentrically; and strolled about the city streets, giving out his innocent and generous smile.

'Anton,' his mother said. 'You're too old to live at home. It's time you moved out. Your father says you have to be a man.'

Anton sighed.

'Well?' his mother asked. 'What are you going to do?'

Anton moved to the room above the garage. He kept his curtains closed all the time and began to cultivate newspapers. He fell asleep for a week and no one noticed. When he woke up he inspected himself in the mirror. He spread his hands apart and held them in front of his eyes.

'At least I was born,' he said to himself. He dropped out of college and got a job driving a hearse. In the evenings he would go and visit with the inscrutable undertaker.

Chapter 3. Anton meets his destiny (Part One)

Without preamble, after all these years spent sleepwalking through the desert, Anton fell desperately in love. It was everything he had ever imagined: a vise clamping his insides; a symphony of pleasure; an endless trip to the bottom of the bottomless abyss. When he finally landed, there was a journalist waiting to interview him.

MC: Anton, please tell me, everyone wants to know. Is love worth it? Or is it just another game?

A: (Groaning) I think my leg is broken. (He feels it carefully, then staggers to his feet.) Where is she?

MC: Anton, I hate to tell you this—but she's gone.

A: Gone? (He clutches his chest and whimpers as he limps about in circles.) I hardly knew her.

MC: Alas, Anton, life is brief. (Takes out note pad and pen.) But you must remember something, all those golden timeless moments you shared together, the taste of her lips on your tongue, her warm breath on your neck ...

A: It began like this. How can I explain? Of those around me, no one but myself believed in love. Pure love. Redeeming love. The utter burning of selfless love. Love. True Love! I spent every day searching for the perfect woman. I didn't care who loved me, I only wanted to give. One day, when I was in a department store looking for some jewellery to give my poor lonely mother, I absent-mindedly stuffed a few pairs of socks in my coat pocket. (Sometimes, when I am driving at night, my feet begin to sweat.) As I was walking out of the store a premonition of change swept over me. At that very moment my arm was held by a small hand with an iron grip. I turned around. It was love at first sight.

Chapter 4. Intermission

You'll excuse me for interrupting. As you can see, Anton is the type of man who could talk about himself forever. Once started, he finds that his mouth moves with a will of its own, and he babbles compulsively without being able to remember why he began. Of course, self-expression is important. We are pleased to see that Anton is so free with words. But what is there about him that is particularly interesting? Why should we be persuaded that he is a hero of our times?

A hero is a man who is in the vanguard of his own life. He rides it with a kind of foolish resignation, charging bravely into history although it is made up of forces he can neither see nor understand. But Anton waits for his life to happen to him, like a man who has fallen asleep waiting for the bus. Poor Anton, we say, so simple and naïve. What else is there to know?

Chapter 5. Anton meets his destiny (Part Two)

We gazed into each other's eyes. She had grasped my soul, and I hers. We both shuddered at once; fate had crossed our lives, banging them together like two dry bones. During the entire interview with the police our faces were hot scarlet, as if we had been caught performing an obscene act behind the utensils section. Angela was her name.

She had eyes as blue as the sky at dawn. I saw my face reflected and I swam in them, like a fish in the sea.

Heat rose from our skins. Our bodies breathed together, breathed the night in and out. When we heard music, it was music played for us. When our souls joined, they swung together like the sun and the moon.

Chapter 6. The future as history

Looking back, we cannot judge Anton's passion. Although Anton himself is utterly insignificant, it could be that the love that he felt, the passion that briefly transformed him, was somehow universal—and that at least for a brief period Anton was redeemed. So it could be.

So it could be. But as for myself, I don't believe it. To tell the truth, I don't believe in anything about love anymore. Sitting here writing about Anton's ridiculous urge to life, I can't help looking out the window. Soon I'll go outside and walk through the streets. The cold concrete will reach up through my shoes, sucking out the warmth of my flesh as the ground beneath turns away from the sun.

What does my life mean? I ask myself. Who cares about Anton? Maybe someone else should be commissioned to write this story. After all, there are at least some interesting moments in his life. There was an incident, for example, that happened while he was working for the undertaker—a brief drama that revealed something about the very inner depths of Anton. It happened one night while they were up late talking.

'Pass the brandy,' the undertaker said. He was sitting on his usual casket, the one he used to save money on a couch.

'Of course,' Anton replied. He took a long draught from the flask and then passed it to his employer.

'You've worked here one whole year now,' the undertaker said. 'I want to make you an offer.' The undertaker was a tall, sallow man with a deep voice and a masklike face.

'Yes?'

'Suppose I guarantee to you that you will meet the perfect woman of your dreams. You will fall wildly in love with each other. For two weeks everything will be exactly as you have always wished. Even better. Then you will never see her again.'

Anton scratched his head. 'It sounds attractive—'

'Excellent.'

'But I was hoping for something better.'

They sat silent for a long time. 'You drive a hard bargain,' the undertaker finally said. He lit a cigar and puffed at it contemplatively, as if absorbing an unexpected defeat. 'You'd better be the one to set the terms.'

'A house, to begin with. And more than two weeks. Make it a lifetime, with children and trips to the ocean besides. And, to tell the truth, I've always wanted a sports car and a mistress.'

Chapter 7. The whole truth

I want to say first of all that there was no bargain, no deal, no contract or understanding—either under the table or otherwise. I admit that we had a conversation of sorts; it's only natural for people who work together to sometimes pass the day this way. I admit that sometimes the future comes true, but you know that in this and every other interview to the press I've constantly stressed the need—

You know what I mean.

Chapter 8. The interview concluded

MC: Anton?

A: Yes?

MC: I don't think they're coming to rescue us.

A: We're stuck here, then.

MC: When they find us, we'll be dead here at the bottom of the bottomless abyss. Our flesh will have rotted and the birds will have carried our bones away. Only this interview will remain. Do you have any final message? Touching last words?

A: (Groaning) There is something I'd like to say—just to you. Promise you won't write it down?

MC: It's getting too dark to see.

A: (Hesitantly) Maybe I should have been satisfied with her. I didn't really need a mistress and a sports car. If I would have just stayed at home, everything would have been all right. What do you think?

MC: Me?

A: Yes.

MC: I think you're losing your nerve, Anton. Millions of readers have eagerly followed your adventures, and now you're saying you would have rather stayed home?

A: Yes. That's it exactly.

MC: (After a long silence) Anton, the moon is coming up. Can you see the moon?

A: (Groaning) It's beautiful.

MC: I can write by the light of the moon, Anton. Now's the time to say it, to give one last message of hope.

A: I want to thank my parents ….

MC: (Reading) 'In his last, dying moments, the hero of love wished to thank his parents, his wife, and his mistress. He wished them to know that although he died of a broken heart, he suffered no pain, and was looking forward to the great beyond.'

Malcolm Lowry and the Trojan Horse

BRIAN FAWCETT

LET ME BEGIN with some declarative statements: The Trojan Horse was the most remarkable device built by the Mycenaean Greeks, and it is among the most devastating inventions in the history of language. Language is the most profound of all human inventions; the most flexible one, the most commonly used. It is also our most carelessly maintained invention, and because of that, it has always been the most dangerous one, both to its users and to the planet.

Wait a minute, I hear you saying. Never mind the grand generalities. The Trojan Horse wasn't a linguistic invention. It was a cunning technological device constructed by the Greeks in order to breach the walls of Troy and win the war; a piece of trickery. The only unusual linguistic element in the story was that the Greeks concealed inside it stopped arguing among themselves long enough to fool the Trojans into dragging the Horse inside the walls of the city.

Try looking at the Trojan Horse in a different way. First of all, it was the invention of Odysseus, the most cunning of the Greek warrior chieftains. To invent the Horse, he had to put his mind in two places at once. This had never been done before.

In those days, human beings still thought of themselves as part of nature. In order to conceive a trick like the Trojan Horse, Odysseus had to create (and operate) the concept that human consciousness is an entity distinct and separate from nature— outside its laws. By doing this, he transformed the gods that both the Greeks and Trojans worshipped. Instead of embodying aspects of nature, the gods became aspects of individual consciousness. Psychologisms—daemonic or educational. For Odysseus, the god represented by the Trojan Horse was a tool.

That may not sound very tricky to you, but to the Greeks and Trojans before Odysseus, it was, literally, unthinkable. And if you examine it carefully, you'll see how complicated it is. Everything Odysseus did involved the manipulation of abstractions: mind, divinity, the horse itself—things that were not at all abstract to his people. Again, easy for us. But for them, material reality— objects, processes, people—were inseparable in those days, part of a continuum linked by the metaphors of nature.

The Trojan Horse was therefore (at least initially) a philosophical invention, the first of its kind. It was dark and empty inside—rather like most modern philosophical inventions. As a physical object, the Horse may not have existed in the form and size to which legend has elevated it. Possibly the Greeks built a small and beautiful icon, or used a real horse and then approached the portals of Troy at a time of common festival rites and asked permission to offer sacrifice to the divinity. The Trojans, believing in the then-inviolable reality of metaphors drawn from nature, assented to the request, unable to imagine that the Greeks would be capable of collective blasphemy.

To the Trojans (and to the Greeks up to this point) blasphemy was possible by individual error or accident, or by willful perversity. But never in cold blood and never as a political tactic.

For the Ancients, political tactics were much more limited than they are now. There were the tactics of battlefield geometry, and the deceptions practised between one person and another that are as old as the human species. But nothing like this.

I'd dearly love to ask Homer about the Trojan Horse, but he's been dead for several thousand years and he spoke a language I don't understand. Besides, Homer himself (or *herself* as the case quite possibly is) is a metaphor for the uncounted oral transferences of the cultural myth of the Trojan War from one Greek to another, and for the much later act of writing down the collected intelligences of those voices.

That being the circumstance, I've looked around to find a modern and nearby equivalent of Homer. Luckily I've found one quite close to home: Malcolm Lowry, the Homer of alcoholic writing.

Again you complain. This time you accuse me of cruelty. Malcolm Lowry was a great writer, a tortured man.

No argument there. Malcolm Lowry was a great novelist. He wrote one great novel: *Under the Volcano*. He also wrote several very bad novels, all of them, like himself, beloved of hard drinkers across the English-speaking world and beyond. Lowry was also a first-rate drunk. Arguably, he was better at drinking than at writing. It's fair to say that he worked harder at drinking, and that in the end he was more loyal to that technology of altering consciousness than to those normally associated with imaginative writing. But since Lowry's capacities for both were magnificent, and because we are discussing both the alteration of consciousness and the possession of two minds, I decided he might have something interesting to say about the Trojan Horse. Several years ago, I began to search for him. Another howl of derision? Yes, I'm aware that he's been dead for years. So what? This is fiction, remember? I can do anything I want. If Kurt

Vonnegut can take us halfway across the galaxy for a few cheap intellectual party tricks, I can take you to Gabriola Island, which supplied part of both the title and the subject matter of Lowry's last novel, *October Ferry to Gabriola*.

Lowry's problem was that the impulses that made him write were the same ones that made him drink. Written English sentences probably offer greater possibilities for ambiguity than those of any language in human history. For sure, the sentences Lowry wrote were simultaneously opulent and labyrinthine. When they did what he intended them to do, they were symphonically sensuous. When they didn't, they were contraptive and occasionally hallucinogenic. Reading his best work is like riding a dragon's tail down to hell or up to paradise. You never know which it will be. His lesser works, are, well, simply a ride on the tail of a dragon—lots of movement, lots of dragon shit.

Lowry was helplessly attracted to the dragon. He rode his own sentences, and an essential part of him didn't care where they took him. By contrast, James Joyce, who rode a similar dragon, always knew where he was, even if his readers didn't (and don't). Henry James tamed the dragon and made it into a fine riding mare. Samuel Beckett, who understood dragons well and disliked them, wrote his sentences in French and then translated them into English to avoid the dragon's flight.

All kinds of metaphors to describe Lowry come to mind. He was a language drunk, and a cheap one. He was a classic drunk driver—capricious, irresponsible, self-pitying amid the wreckage. He didn't mean to run over those poor ideas and objects, he didn't know what he was doing. They're amusing metaphors, but that's all they are. The truth about Lowry is less dramatic.

He was a man who believed that self-control had a physical location, one that was outside himself. He thought it was a *place*. And for most of his life, he sought a sanitorial paradise where his impulse to write and drink could dry out enough for him to gain control over the daemons he believed controlled him. The trouble with that was that he also thought it would be a place where he could drink in peace, without hangovers and without remorse. Gabriola Island was to be one of those sanitoriums. The last, perhaps.

It just so happens that for the last ten years I've been spending part of each summer on Gabriola. The island is just off the east coast of Vancouver Island, close to a small city called Nanaimo, which used to be famous for its coal mines but is now famous for its unemployed loggers and its drunks. Both groups get together annually in order to hook outboard motors to the backs of old bathtubs and race the thirty or so miles across the Strait of Georgia to Vancouver. Thousands do it every year. Wealthy drunks come from all over the planet to compete against them. Who needs Kurt Vonnegut to make up things when there are places like Nanaimo.

For me Gabriola Island has been mainly a quiet place to write. I knew Lowry had written about it, and I assumed that because he had, he must have lived there at some point in his life. I had no idea where he'd stayed or how long. At first I didn't much give a damn. But by coincidence, the cabin I rented was among the oldest on the island, and that made me wonder who'd lived in it over the years. For a couple of summers I told myself that my cabin had once been Lowry's, but I let the fantasy idle in neutral. I was there to write, not to read biographies. I was also practising social isolation. For the first few summers I wrote, talked to no one, and didn't waste time trying to confirm the identity of my predecessors.

But as I grew older and became more interested in collecting materials for writing and less delighted with artistic privacy, I grew more curious about Lowry. I read *October Ferry to Gabriola*. I didn't learn anything specific from that, so I asked several of the local merchants if they knew which of the island's cabins Malcolm Lowry had lived in.

'Who?' they asked.

'Malcolm Lowry. You know.'

'Don't recall the name.'

'Malcolm Lowry. The writer. You know. Real famous guy.'

'Never heard of him. I don't read much myself. Too goddamn busy to read. What kind of stuff did this Lowdry write?'

'Lowry. Malcolm Lowry. English guy. He wrote fiction. Novels.'

'Oh yeah,' they would say after a moment's uncurious consideration. Then, if they were friendly, they might suggest someone else who might know. Most just grunted and walked away.

No one on the island knew where Lowry had lived. In fact, I couldn't even find anyone who knew who Malcolm Lowry was. No one wanted to know why I was curious about him, come to think of it. Guy comes around the island, drops a few bucks, doesn't talk much, how are they to know he's supposed to be a famous writer? And why should they have been curious? There's only two people on the island who know my name, and I've been around, off and on, for ten years.

Eventually I did find a man who knew about Lowry, and about his stay on the island. At least that's what I thought. His name was Barry Drylis. He's a doctor from Nanaimo. He owns a cabin a few hundred yards down the beach from the one I rent. No, he hadn't ever met Lowry. Barry is about my age, and he doesn't even drink. He just reads a few books now and then.

Barry wasn't clear about exactly where Lowry's cabin was. Someone had told him the name of the road, but he hadn't checked it out in person. Too busy working on his cabin, reading books, or looking into people's throats and ears and noses for that. But I pressed him, and one afternoon he came over to my cabin and told me he'd found the place where Lowry had lived.

'Let's go have a look,' I said.

Barry was into physical fitness, so at first he wanted us to ride bicycles to the spot, which he said was about two miles down the coast. I hate riding bicycles, so I talked him out of that plan, and into taking his expensive new Mercedes. He fell for it, but I had to swim back to his cabin with him. Then I had to sit on the hood of the Mercedes while he drove back to my cabin so I could get dry clothing. He wasn't going to let me sit in his new car in my wet bathing suit.

The ride on the hood of Barry's car didn't exactly put me in the best of moods. There was a certain sting to being made into a hood ornament for a guy who specializes in fixing broken noses. And all because of Malcolm Lowry. I lapsed into cynicism: what would we find at Malcolm Lowry's house, anyway? A spiritual redolence? A mountain of mouldering gin bottles?

I was still sulking when Barry pulled the Mercedes off the main road and onto a cedar-hedged lane that at a casual glance might have been in rural England. He let the big sedan drift into an alcove and shut off the motor. The transition from windswept Pacific coast to English country lane was an abrupt one, and for a moment I was taken in by it. Lowry must have liked it here, I decided. Then I realized that thirty years ago the hedges wouldn't have been there. They looked nursery-grown, and recently planted.

'Who told you about this,' I asked Barry as we climbed out of the car.

He evaded my question. 'Nice isn't it? A friend of mine owns it.'

'Did he plant the hedges?'

Barry didn't answer. He pushed open the new cedar gate and I followed him into a sheltered garden right out of *Better Homes and Gardens.*

'This is where Malcolm Lowry lived?' I asked, growing more sceptical by the moment.

Barry whirled around with an expansive gesture and pointed to a wooden plaque over the door of the house. 'That's what it says.'

It wasn't a cabin. It was a house; a very large, new, and expensive house. The plaque over the door read '#1 Malcolm Lowry Haven.' Beyond it were five more identical rooflines. They were condominiums, and they were brand-new.

I walked through the garden and out onto the beach the condos overlooked. Barry followed me, looking just a little sheepish. I glanced back at the roofline again, and saw one more item I hadn't been expecting. On the middle rooftop was a large latticed satellite receiving dish. I wasn't surprised to see it. The dishes were popping up all over the island. Last year the general store on the island scrapped its rack of paperback books and magazines and replaced it with a video cassette rental stall. The proprietors also installed an enormous dish on the store roof, and, according to Barry, were renting movie cassettes they'd taped from the dish.

'This is bullshit, Barry,' I said, pointing to the adjoining rooflines. 'These are brand new condominiums. Malcolm Lowry never lived here.'

He shrugged. 'So what?' he said neutrally. 'What's wrong with a little redevelopment?'

'I thought you were going to show me where Malcolm Lowry

lived. Instead, you show me some fucking tourist resort.'

'Hey! This is a tourist island,' he said. 'All there was here was a couple of dilapidated shacks and a lot of wind. Now people can buy into an authentic piece of local history and enjoy themselves at the same time. I think it's the way to go—capitalizing on the assets we've got.'

'I didn't come out here for a lecture on real-estate capitalism either, you dork,' I said, half under my breath. 'Let's go. This is depressing.'

Barry wanted to look around, and he was the one with the car. We checked out one of the other 'cabins,' and sure enough, it also had a plaque over its door: '#2 Malcolm Lowry Haven.' Like the other place, it was deserted. I checked out the dish. Like I'd expected, it was hooked into all five units.

While we were driving back I asked Barry who owned the condos.

'Dunno, exactly,' he admitted. 'They're all from Los Angeles. The one guy I know comes up for a couple of weeks during the summer, then rents it out to college professors during the winter. I think the others do the same. He says it's a hell of a tax write-off.'

―――――――

As it happened, Malcolm Lowry Haven was only a few hundred yards from my favourite clam bay. According to the sign nailed onto one of the wind-sculpted trees, the bay was supposed to be contaminated. But the sign was a homemade job, so I figured— correctly—that it was just somebody trying to keep the clams for themselves.

That evening, on an impulse, I drove my rusted-out Japanese stationwagon over to the bay to dig some clams and watch the sun go down. I shovelled out a small bucket of clams and stuck them in the back of the car. I'd brought along a thermos of coffee, and I poured out a cup and sat down on the rocks to enjoy the show. The tide was coming in quickly, and I began to idly scan the margins of the bay. I noticed something in the thick mat of beached seaweed and logging debris the tide was pushing up against the rocks.

I clambered across the rocks and found that the 'something' was the body of a man, lying face down, submerged to the waist in the water. He'd been quite large and stocky, and it looked as if he'd been in his late forties. The body wasn't bloated, so it hadn't been in the water long. I noticed, almost against my will, how extraordinarily short the arms and legs were, almost to the point of being misshapen. And he wasn't dead, because when I reached him, he groaned.

I turned him over onto his back. His eyes were closed, and his face was bloated enough to have been the face of a drowned man, except that the skin was ruddy, the cheeks starred by broken blood vessels. He seemed oddly familiar.

He opened his eyes and glared at me. 'Fuck you, arshhole,' he muttered. 'Lemme go back to shleep.'

Whoever he might be, he was dead drunk. He closed his eyes again and an irregular sigh rattled from his chest. I reached down and shook him. 'You're going to drown if you stay here,' I said. 'Let me give you a hand out of the water.'

His eyes opened again. Not a pretty sight. I grabbed his arms and tried to lever him onto his feet. I got him erect, and as I did he took a swing at me, lost his balance and fell backward into the slimy weeds. The water closed around his face, and he came up sputtering and cursing.

The dunking revived him, and he crawled out of the water on his hands and knees. This time I stood back and watched him clamber up onto the dry rocks and sit down. He shook his head to clear the cobwebs.

'Thank you,' he said after a moment, gazing at me blearily. His voice was now perfectly lucid, and his accent distinctly British. 'I owe you a drink for pulling me out of this.'

'I've got a thermos of coffee up on the rocks, ' I said. 'I think that might do you more good.'

He grimaced as he stood up and shook himself unsteadily. He looked like a dog that had just come out of the water after fetching a stick. 'After you,' he said, accepting my offer.

———————

'The name's Lowry,' he said, as he watched me pour the steaming coffee from the thermos. 'Malcolm. Where the hell are we, incidentally?'

'Sure you're Malcolm Lowry,' I said, not even trying to stifle my amusement. 'I'm Ernest Hemingway, and this is Pilot Bay.'

'You've lost weight,' he said, obviously prepared to carry on with the gag. 'Where is Pilot Bay, might I ask?'

'Gabriola Island. You should know that. You're supposed to have lived up on the point over there.' 'Over where?' he demanded, obviously startled. 'Gabriola Island? Are you certain?'

'Sure I'm certain. Who are you? I mean, really?'

The man got up without answering and stared across the bay at the point and the line of condominiums. He continued to stare for quite a long time, wavering gently back and forth on the balls of his feet. Then he sat down and gave me a piercing look.

'Jesus Lord Christ in Pandemonium,' he said. 'How did this happen to me? I must have died and gone to heaven.'

'I don't know about that, ' I said. 'I think you got drunk and fell off a boat. Who were you before you became Malcolm Lowry?'

'I've been quite a number of people,' he said quietly. 'But when I was drunk, and when I was writing, I was Malcolm Lowry. Every Godforsaken time. And this *is* Gabriola Island.'

'Where you lived,' I confirmed. 'Right over there where those nice dish-connected condos are.'

The man stared at me as if I were speaking gibberish. 'I didn't live here,' he said. 'I visited. Once. Stayed less than a day, actually, then went back to Dollarton.'

I saw his gaze darting between the condominiums and my car. 'That little automobile over there,' he said, with a mixture of confusion and awe in his voice. 'Is that yours? And that circular object on the roof of those buildings. What is that? What year is this?'

I decided to humour him. 'The year is 1985. Fourteenth of August. That wreck is mine, and the circular object is a satellite receiving dish. What about them?'

'It's a what?'

'It's a device that picks up television signals the American mega-stations bounce off, er, spacecraft circling the planet. Offers consumers a choice of up to seventy programs to watch.'

'You're serious, aren't you?' he said in a tone that made it clear that he was. 'This truly is 1985, and that device works as you say it does?' He swore again, this time more eloquently. 'I don't bloody believe it. Do you have a drink?'

'No,' I lied. I had a bottle of scotch back at the cabin, but there was no way I was taking this lunatic anywhere near the place. 'Listen, you're Malcolm Lowry and I'm Ernest Hemingway, and theoretically we're both dead as doornails. That being the case, this is probably an illusion that might all go up in a puff of smoke any second. So why don't we sit here while you sober up a little, and we can talk. I've got a few questions I'd like to ask you.'

He looked up towards the point again, then back at me.

'Okay. I might as well answer your questions. Lord only knows what this is all about.'

'What,' I said, 'can you tell me about the Trojan Horse?'

Lowry laughed. It was an eerie laugh. He let his head sink back and threw himself into it, like a hyena's hunting giggle. 'Let's see. The Trojan Horse. The great dildo of Pallas Athene. I take it you've read Homer.'

'In translation.'

'Ah, m'boy. You must read these things in the original. True beauty is always better in its birthday suit.'

'Stop bullying me with your British education. This is the 1980s. I can't even speak French, and it's an official language in this country.'

'I see you're something of a barbarian.'

'Something,' I agreed. 'Now what about the Trojan Horse?'

'Well,' Lowry said, both the arch-British accent and the drunken slur vanishing, 'being a barbarian you probably want the entire *Ars Poetica* explained to you. So let's begin by saying that the Trojan Horse was a metaphor. One that changed the world.'

'I've already got that far,' I said, more politely this time. 'But it was a metaphor that backfired, wasn't it? After the Trojan War, the Greek tribes collapsed into the isolation of individual self-occupation for nearly four hundred years.'

'Navel-gazing as the Dorian hordes overran them. Yes, I suppose it did backfire in the long run. But it did end the war.'

'Maybe not,' I said. 'The archaeological record indicates that the walls of Troy were probably breached by an earthquake and not by any military action.'

'That's as it may be,' Lowry said. 'Ancient history is largely conjecture. It's the metaphors it provides that count. So let me tell you about my personal Trojan Horse—the one I fell for, and most of my generation of writers fell for.'

'What was that?'

'The novel.'

'The novel?'

'Look at it. Any good novel creates a symbolic landscape in which metaphors can create emotions or release trapped ones. People need that. We're all of us far too repressed. A great novel releases great emotions, breaks open the walls of rational consciousness, just as the Trojan Horse broke open the walls of another kind of consciousness.'

'Times have changed,' I said. 'People now have most of their repressed emotions freed. So much so that they run around having emotions about things like laundry detergents and soft drinks. Great, profitable emotions, at least from the perspective of the corporate business sector. It's gotten so that emotion is the least authentic of human behaviours—you never know where the damned things come from. As often as not, they originate in some motivational research laboratory, and you've been fed them as subliminals on television.'

Lowry was interested. 'One generation's paradise is always the prison of the next. It's the natural result of the insurgence of any culture. But there's no denying what the novel meant for my generation: novelty, oddity of character, emotional metaphor. Those things were liberating.'

'Those are the things that hold my generation hostage,' I said. 'Even liberation is suspect. You hear about freedom and revolution more often in television commercials than anywhere else.'

'Television has become that powerful?' Lowry asked, ruminatively. 'Yes, I suppose. It wasn't much in my day, but even then one could see its potential for cheating idiots out of what little native sense they possessed.'

'How does the novel become a Trojan Horse?'

Lowry turned his back on me and gazed back at the condominiums and the satellite dish. 'Ah. Well, you know what Laocoön said: Beware of Greeks bearing gifts.'

'How so?'

He frowned. 'Well, the novel was a great gift to humanity. A democratic invention of enormous intellectual force. It provided a sense of individual complexity to a civilization caught up in a class structure—one that wanted to classify people according to who their ancestors were and how much wealth they possessed. Look at Zola and Balzac.'

'Let's look at you. All your central characters were cultured drunks who spoke in too-long sentences.'

'That's a trifle cruel of you.'

'You'll have to excuse me. I've spent my artistic life fighting against the confinements of character, plot, personality, sexuality. Writers of my generation are expected to engage those things and little else.'

'So?'

'So psychological minutiae and personal quirks aren't the complete constituents of human reality, however fascinating and complicated they may be. If we're going to continue on this planet, we have to find ways to register a more synchronic and detailed kind of intellectual and artistic attention. For the last thirty years there have been bombers flying over our heads twenty-four hours a day, each plane loaded to capacity with nuclear weapons, and a certain percentage never more than a few minutes to failsafe. And I'm expected to confine my artistic investigations to how people feel about their bodies or their disappointments over not getting a better job. The causalities open to examination are self-enclosing—our mothers forgot to clip our fingernails when we were children and now we suffer from an impulse to scratch our lovers while having sex. That sort of thing. I'm bored to shit with the daemonic. The novel has become part of the conspiracy of lies and irrelevance that is using up the planet and threatening daily to turn us all into a heap of radioactive debris.'

'I see,' Lowry said, quietly.

'No you don't. Right now, you're peeking up the beach towards those condominiums wondering if someone might be willing to serve you a martini. This is an important story here, to me at least, and I'd appreciate it if you'd damned well pay attention.'

'Let me turn this back on you,' Lowry said, gently. 'What's *your* metaphor? How would you want the novel to operate?'

'My metaphor is either the Global Village—or its progenitor, the Trojan Horse. I'm trying to see the one through the other. You don't know anything about the Global Village, so it isn't your problem. Be thankful for that. I'd explain it, but it's opaque because of the commercial rhetoric it's loaded with, sort of like a computer with a thatched straw cover on it. And it's assiduously kept from close scrutiny. That dish over there is one of its few coherent symbols.'

'Go on,' he said.

'Not here,' I answered. 'There's not enough time. But maybe I can explain the Trojan Horse in a more helpful way. We've more or less agreed that it wasn't, in essence, a physical contraption representing a horse. It's more than that, a new intellectual tool that appeared to free humanity, but in fact did the opposite. It created the prison of egocentric consciousness. In a minor way, the novel is the same thing, and for that reason I don't want it to operate at all. I want it dead, buried and forgotten—Freud-stained sailor suit and all.'

'Ah, you can't mean that, about the novel.'

'Why not? It's now a dangerous form of expression, at least given the limitations you accepted for it. More important, it's no longer an adequate form of human experience. It takes the writer out of his or her moral imagination—mostly these days into sociometric manipulations, and it takes the reader out of the social and intellectual structures that lead to change.'

'It doesn't have to,' Lowry said.

'That's like saying that nuclear physics doesn't have to lead to nuclear weapons. But it has, and now there are about 40,000 nuclear warheads kicking around the planet, enough to vaporize us all a thousand times over. Any productive force decays to its most venal possible use when a market economy overpowers both its cultural and political institutions, as it has done here. Imagination decays too, unless it builds in safeguards against that decay.'

'How is that done?'

'I don't know,' I admitted. 'I hoped you might.'

Lowry moved off the rock he'd been perched on, and slipped down, crab fashion, several rocks closer to the water. 'You might, ah, try to stay in the interzones,' he said, slowly, as if he were dragging the reluctant thoughts out of himself as he spoke. 'I always tried to write my way *out* of them—into hell, or into a paradise. But I lived in the interzones—in Dollarton I was literally atop the primeval ooze. I think that's why I was drawn back time and again. And I wrote from that vantage point, always.'

'Why did you stay there?' I asked, feeling less aggressive now. 'In Dollarton, I mean. And outside England.'

'I'm not sure,' he said unsteadily. 'There were reasons, of course. Family upbringing, the Imperial crush. I had cultural claustrophobia. But I had deeper instincts, you know. Strange ones, that told me to live in the interzone between the worn-out Cartesian universe and the wilderness. Gabriola Island was to be one of them, but it didn't work out. I had an uneasy soul, or something akin to one. And remember, I was a Christian. I was looking for mercy, expiation, paradise. I wasn't looking for social change.'

Lowry laughed his hyena laugh, but this time it was almost pleasant. 'So now you find me here, like the Orpheus head, and all the prophecy I can offer you is to tell you to go on doing what you're doing—beachcombing. What a world!'

I lay back on the rocks, and gave in to the soft night breezes moving off the uplands. In the dusky light I could feel the rocks giving up their stored heat. Above me there were stars, the familiar summer constellations beginning their evening traverse of the heavens. One of the stars was moving: a satellite. On a reflex, I glanced back at the dish. Yeah, I thought. What a world. Behind me I heard a cough, soft and apologetic, like an elderly man clearing his throat. I turned in the direction of the cough, but it was no old man. A cougar stood behind us, no more than a few yards away. I moved, slowly, slowly, until I was able to prod Lowry with my outstretched foot. He turned towards me, and when he saw the cougar, he smiled.

As if the animal knew him, it padded across the rocks past me and lay down beside him, in an heraldic pose.

'This is what metaphor gives us,' he said, stroking the cougar's tawny back. 'We still have this.'

Dreams

TIMOTHY FINDLEY

DOCTOR MENLO WAS having a problem: he could not sleep and his wife—the other Doctor Menlo—was secretly staying awake in order to keep an eye on him. The trouble was that, in spite of her concern and in spite of all her efforts, Doctor Menlo—whose name was Mimi—was always nodding off because of her exhaustion.

She had tried drinking coffee, but this had no effect. She detested coffee and her system had a built-in rejection mechanism. She also prescribed herself a week's worth of Dexedrine to see if that would do the trick. *Five mg at bedtime—* all to no avail. And even though she put the plastic bottle of small orange hearts beneath her pillow and kept augmenting her intake, she would wake half an hour later with a dreadful start to discover the night was moving on to morning.

Everett Menlo had not yet declared the source of his problem. His restless condition had begun about ten days ago and had barely raised his interest. Soon, however, the time spent lying awake had increased from one to several hours and then, on Monday last, to all-night sessions. Now he lay in a state of rigid apprehension—eyes wide open, arms above his head, his hands in fists—like a man in pain unable to shut it out. His neck, his back and his shoulders constantly harried him with cramps and spasms. Everett Menlo had become a full-blown insomniac.

Clearly, Mimi Menlo concluded, her husband was refusing to sleep because he believed something dreadful was going to happen the moment he closed his eyes. She had encountered this sort of fear in one or two of her patients. Everett, on the other hand, would not discuss the subject. If the problem had been hers, he would have said *such things cannot occur if you have gained control of yourself.*

Mimi began to watch for the dawn. She would calculate its approach by listening for the increase of traffic down below the bedroom window. The Menlos' home was across the road from the Manulife centre—corner of Bloor and Bay streets. Mimi's first sight of daylight always revealed the high, white shape of its terraced storeys. Their own apartment building was of a modest height and colour—twenty floors of smoky glass and polished brick. The shadow of the Manulife would crawl across the bedroom floor and climb the wall behind her, grey with fatigue and cold.

The Menlo beds were an arm's length apart, and lying like a rug between them was the shape of a large, black dog of unknown breed. All night long, in the dark of his well, the dog would dream and he would tell the content of his dreams the way victims in a trance will tell of being pursued by posses of their nameless fears. He whimpered, he cried and sometimes he howled. His legs and his paws would jerk and flail and his claws would scrabble desperately against the parquet floor. Mimi—who loved this dog—would lay her hand against his side and let her fingers dabble in his coat in vain attempts to soothe him. Sometimes, she had to call his name in order to rouse him from his dreams because his heart would be racing. Other times, she smiled and thought: *at least there's one of us getting some sleep.* The dog's name was Thurber and he dreamed in beige and white.

Everett and Mimi Menlo were both psychiatrists. His field was schizophrenia; hers was autistic children. Mimi's venue was the Parkin Institute at the University of Toronto; Everett's was the Queen Street Mental Health Centre. Early in their marriage they had decided never to work as a team and not—unless it was a matter of financial life and death—to accept employment in the same institution. Both had always worked with the kind of physical intensity that kills, and yet they gave the impression this was the only tolerable way in which to function. It meant there was always a sense of peril in what they did, but the peril— according to Everett—made their lives worth living. This, at least, had been his theory twenty years ago when they were young.

Now, for whatever unnamed reason, peril had become his enemy and Everett Menlo had begun to look and behave and lose his sleep like a haunted man. But he refused to comment when Mimi asked him what was wrong. Instead, he gave the worst of all possible answers a psychiatrist can hear who seeks an explanation of a patient's silence: he said there was *absolutely nothing wrong.*

'You're sure you're not coming down with something?'

'Yes.'

'And you wouldn't like a massage?'

'I've already told you: no.'

'Can I get you anything?'

'No.'

'And you don't want to talk?'

'That's right.'

'Okay, Everett ...'

'Okay, what?'

'Okay, nothing. I only hope you get some sleep tonight.'

Everett stood up. 'Have you been spying on me, Mimi?'

'What do you mean by *spying?*'

'Watching me all night long.'

'Well, Everett, I don't see how I can fail to be aware you aren't asleep when we share this bedroom. I mean—I can hear you grinding your teeth. I can see you lying there wide awake.'

'When?'

'All the time. You're staring at the ceiling.'

'I've never stared at the ceiling in my whole life. I sleep on my stomach.'

'You sleep on your stomach *if* you sleep. But you have not been sleeping. Period. No argument.'

Everett Menlo went to his dresser and got out a pair of clean pyjamas. Turning his back on Mimi, he put them on.

Somewhat amused at the coyness of this gesture, Mimi asked what he was hiding.

'Nothing!' he shouted at her.

Mimi's mouth fell open. Everett never yelled. His anger wasn't like that; it manifested itself in other ways, in silence and withdrawal, never shouts.

Everett was staring at her defiantly. He had slammed the bottom drawer of his dresser. Now he was fumbling with the wrapper of a pack of cigarettes.

Mimi's stomach tied a knot.

Everett hadn't touched a cigarette for weeks.

'Please don't smoke those,' she said. 'You'll only be sorry if you do.'

'And you,' he said, 'will be sorry if I don't.'

'But, dear ...' said Mimi.

'Leave me for Christ's sake alone!' Everett yelled.

Mimi gave up and sighed and then she said: 'all right. Thurber and I will go and sleep in the living room. Goodnight.'

Everett sat on the edge of his bed. His hands were shaking.

'Please,' he said—apparently addressing the floor. 'Don't leave me here alone. I couldn't bear that.'

This was perhaps the most chilling thing he could have said to her. Mimi was alarmed; her husband was genuinely terrified of something and he would not say what it was. If she had not been who she was—if she had not known what she knew—if her years of training had not prepared her to watch for signs like this, she might have been better off. As it was, she had to face the possibility the strongest, most sensible man on earth was having a nervous breakdown of major proportions. Lots of people have breakdowns, of course; but not, she had thought, the gods of reason.

'All right,' she said—her voice maintaining the kind of calm she knew a child afraid of the dark would appreciate. 'In a minute I'll get us something to drink. But first, I'll go and change ...'

Mimi went into the sanctum of the bathroom, where her nightgown waited for her—a portable hiding-place hanging on the back of the door. 'You stay there,' she said to Thurber, who had padded after her. 'Mama will be out in just a moment.'

Even in the dark, she could gauge Everett's tension. His shadow—all she could see of him—twitched from time to time and the twitching took on a kind of lurching rhythm, something like the broken clock in their living room.

Mimi lay on her side and tried to close her eyes. But her eyes were tied to a will of their own and would not obey her. Now she, too, was caught in the same irreversible tide of sleeplessness that bore her husband backwards through the night. Four or five times she watched him lighting cigarettes—blowing out matches, courting disaster in the bedclothes—conjuring the worst deaths for the three of them: a flaming pyre on the twentieth floor.

All this behaviour was utterly unlike him; foreign to his code of disciplines and ethics; alien to everything he said and believed. *Openness, directness, sharing of ideas, encouraging imaginative response to every problem. Never hide troubles. Never allow despair* ... These were his directives in everything he did. Now, he had thrown them over.

One thing was certain. She was not the cause of his sleeplessness. She didn't have affairs and neither did he. He might be ill—but whenever he'd been ill before, there had been no trauma; never a trauma like this one, at any rate. Perhaps it was something about a patient—one of his tougher cases; a wall in the patient's condition they could not break through; some circumstance of someone's lack of progress—a sudden veering towards a catatonic state, for instance—something that Everett had not foreseen that had stymied him and was slowly ... what? Destroying his sense of professional control? His self-esteem? His scientific certainty? If only he would speak.

Mimi thought about her own worst case: a child whose obstinate refusal to communicate was currently breaking her heart and, thus, her ability to help. If ever she had needed Everett to talk to, it was now. All her fellow doctors were locked in a battle over this child; they wanted to take him away from her. Mimi refused to give him up; he might as well have been her own flesh and blood. Everything had been done—from gentle holding sessions to violent bouts of manufactured anger—in her attempt to make the child react. She was staying with him every day from the moment he was roused to the moment he was induced to sleep with drugs.

His name was Brian Bassett and he was eight years old. He sat on the floor in the furthest corner he could achieve in one of the observation-isolation rooms where all the autistic children were placed when nothing else in their treatment—nothing of love or expertise—had managed to break their silence. Mostly, this was a signal they were coming to the end of life.

There in his four-square, glass-box room, surrounded by all that can tempt a child if a child can be tempted—toys and food and storybook companions—Brian Bassett was in the process, now, of fading away. His eyes were never closed and his arms were restrained. He was attached to three machines that nurtured him with all that science can offer. But of course, the spirit and the will to live cannot be fed by force to those who don't want to feed.

Now, in the light of Brian Bassett's utter lack of willing contact with the world around him—his utter refusal to communicate—Mimi watched her husband through the night. Everett stared at the ceiling, lit by the Manulife building's distant lamps, borne on his back further and further out to sea. She had lost him, she was certain.

When, at last, he saw that Mimi had drifted into her own and welcome sleep, Everett rose from his bed and went out into the hall, past the simulated jungle of the solarium, until he reached the dining room. There, all the way till dawn, he amused himself with two decks of cards and endless games of Dead Man's Solitaire.

Thurber rose and shuffled after him. The dining room was one of Thurber's favourite places in all his confined but privileged world, for it was here—as in the kitchen—that from time to time a hand descended filled with the miracle of food.

But whatever it was that his master was doing up there above him on the table-top, it wasn't anything to do with feeding or being fed. The playing cards had an old and dusty dryness to their scent and they held no appeal for the dog. So he once again lay down and he took up his dreams, which at least gave his paws some exercise. This way, he failed to hear the advent of a new dimension to his master's problem. This occurred precisely at 5:45 A.M. when the telephone rang and Everett Menlo, having rushed to answer it, waited breathless for a minute while he listened and then said: 'yes' in a curious, strangulated fashion. Thurber—had he been awake—would have recognized in his master's voice the signal for disaster.

For weeks now, Everett had been working with a patient who was severely and uniquely schizophrenic. This patient's name was Kenneth Albright, and while he was deeply suspicious, he was also oddly caring. Kenneth Albright loved the detritus of life, such as bits of woolly dust and wads of discarded paper. He loved all dried-up leaves that had drifted from their parent trees and he loved the dead bees that had curled up to die along the window sills of his ward. He also loved the spider webs seen high up in the corners of the rooms where he sat on plastic chairs and ate with plastic spoons.

Kenneth Albright talked a lot about his dreams. But his dreams had become, of late, a major stumbling block in the process of his recovery. Back in the days when Kenneth had first become Doctor Menlo's patient, the dreams had been overburdened with detail: 'over-cast,' as he would say, 'with characters' and over-produced, again in Kenneth's phrase, 'as if I were dreaming the dreams of Cecil B. De Mille.'

Then he had said: 'but a person can't really dream someone else's dreams. Or can they, Doctor Menlo?'

'No' had been Everett's answer—definite and certain.

Everett Menlo had been delighted, at first, with Kenneth Albright's dreams. They had been immensely entertaining—complex and filled with intriguing detail. Kenneth himself was at a loss to explain the meaning of these dreams, but as Everett had said, it wasn't Kenneth's job to explain. That was Everett's job. His job and his pleasure. For quite a long while, during these early sessions, Everett had written out the dreams, taken them home and recounted them to Mimi.

Kenneth Albright was a paranoid schizophrenic. Four times now, he had attempted suicide. He was a fiercely angry man at times—and at other times as gentle and as pleasant as a docile child. He had suffered so greatly, in the very worst moments of his disease, that he could no longer work. His job—it was almost an incidental detail in his life and had no importance for him, so it seemed—was returning reference books, in the Metro library, to their places in the stacks. Sometimes—mostly late of an afternoon—he might begin a psychotic episode of such profound dimensions that he would attempt his suicide right behind the counter and even once, in the full view of everyone, while riding in the glass-walled elevator. It was after this last occasion that he was brought, in restraints, to be a resident patient at the Queen Street Mental Health Centre. He had slashed his wrists with a razor—but not before he had also slashed and destroyed an antique copy of *Don Quixote*, the pages of which he pasted to the walls with blood.

For a week thereafter, Kenneth Albright—just like Brian Bassett—had refused to speak or to move. Everett had him kept in an isolation cell, force-fed and drugged. Slowly, by dint of patience, encouragement and caring even Kenneth could recognize as genuine, Everett Menlo had broken through the barrier. Kenneth was removed from isolation, pampered with food and cigarettes, and he began relating his dreams.

At first there seemed to be only the dreams and nothing else in Kenneth's memory. Broken pencils, discarded toys and the telephone directory all had roles to play in these dreams but there were never any people. All the weather was bleak and all the landscapes were empty. Houses, motor cars and office buildings never made an appearance. Sounds and smells had some importance; the wind would blow, the scent of unseen fires was often described. Stairwells were plentiful, leading nowhere, all of them rising from a subterranean world that Kenneth either did not dare to visit or would not describe.

The dreams had little variation, one from another. The themes had mostly to do with loss and with being lost. The broken pencils were all given names and the discarded toys were given to one another as companions. The telephone books were the sources of recitations—hours and hours of repeated names and numbers, some of which—Everett had noted with surprise—were absolutely accurate.

All of this held fast until an incident occurred one morning that changed the face of Kenneth Albright's schizophrenia forever; an incident that stemmed—so it seemed—from something he had dreamed the night before.

Bearing in mind his previous attempts at suicide, it will be obvious that Kenneth Albright was never far from sight at the Queen Street Mental Health Centre. He was, in fact, under constant observation; constant, that is, as human beings and modern technology can manage. In the ward to which he was ultimately consigned, for instance, the toilet cabinets had no doors and the shower rooms had no locks. Therefore, a person could not ever be alone with water, glass or shaving utensils.

(All the razors were cordless automatics.) Scissors and knives were banned, as were pieces of string and rubber bands. A person could not even kill his feet and hands by binding up his wrists or ankles. Nothing poisonous was anywhere available. All the windows were barred. All the double doors between this ward and the corridors beyond were doors with triple locks and a guard was always near at hand.

Still, if people want to die, they will find a way. Mimi Menlo would discover this to her everlasting sorrow with Brian Bassett. Everett Menlo would discover this to his everlasting horror with Kenneth Albright.

———————

On the morning of April 19th, a Tuesday, Everett Menlo, in the best of health, had welcomed a brand-new patient into his office. This was Anne Marie Wilson, a young and brilliant pianist whose promising career had been halted mid-flight by a schizophrenic incident involving her ambition. She was, it seemed, no longer able to play and all her dreams were shattered. The cause was simple, to all appearances: Anne Marie had a sense of how, precisely, the music should be and she had not been able to master it accordingly. 'Everything I attempt is terrible,' she had said—in spite of all her critical accolades and all her professional success. Other doctors had tried and failed to break the barriers in Anne Marie, whose hands had taken on a life of their own, refusing altogether to work for her. Now it was Menlo's turn and hope was high.

Everett had been looking forward to his session with this prodigy. He loved all music and had thought to find some means within its discipline to reach her. She seemed so fragile, sitting there in the sunlight, and he had just begun to take his first notes when the door flew open and Louise, his secretary, had said: 'I'm sorry, Doctor Menlo. There's a problem. Can you come with me at once?'

Everett excused himself.

Anne Marie was left in the sunlight to bide her time. Her fingers were moving around in her lap and she put them in her mouth to make them quiet.

———————————

Even as he'd heard his secretary speak, Everett had known the problem would be Kenneth Albright. Something in Kenneth's eyes had warned him there was trouble on the way: a certain wariness that indicated all was not as placid as it should have been, given his regimen of drugs. He had stayed long hours in one position, moving his fingers over his thighs as if to dry them on his trousers; watching his fellow patients come and go with abnormal interest—never, however, rising from his chair. An incident was on the horizon and Everett had been waiting for it, hoping it would not come.

Louise had said that Doctor Menlo was to go at once to Kenneth Albright's ward. Everett had run the whole way. Only after the attendant had let him in past the double doors, did he slow his pace to a hurried walk and wipe his brow. He didn't want Kenneth to know how alarmed he had been.

Coming to the appointed place, he paused before he entered, closing his eyes, preparing himself for whatever he might have to see. *Other people have killed themselves: I've seen it often enough,* he was thinking. *I simply won't let it affect me.* Then he went in.

The room was small and white—a dining room—and Kenneth was sitting down in a corner, his back pressed out against the walls on either side of him. His head was bowed and

94

his legs drawn up and he was obviously trying to hide without much success. An intern was standing above him and a nurse was kneeling down beside him. Several pieces of bandaging with blood on them were scattered near Kenneth's feet and there was a white enamel basin filled with pinkish water on the floor beside the nurse.

'Morowetz,' Everett said to the intern. 'Tell me what has happened here.' He said this just the way he posed such questions when he took the interns through the wards at examination time, quizzing them on symptoms and prognoses.

But Morowetz the intern had no answer. He was puzzled. What had happened had no sane explanation.

Everett turned to Charterhouse, the nurse.

'On the morning of April 19th, at roughly ten-fifteen, I found Kenneth Albright covered with blood,' Ms. Charterhouse was to write in her report. 'His hands, his arms, his face and his neck were stained. I would say the blood was fresh and the patient's clothing—mostly his shirt—was wet with it. Some—a very small amount of it—had dried on his forehead. The rest was uniformly the kind of blood you expect to find free-flowing from a wound. I called for assistance and meanwhile attempted to ascertain where Mister Albright might have been injured. I performed this examination without success. I could find no source of bleeding anywhere on Mister Albright's body.'

Morowetz concurred.

The blood was someone else's.

'Was there a weapon of any kind?' Doctor Menlo had wanted to know.

'No, sir. Nothing,' said Charterhouse.

'And was he alone when you found him?'

'Yes, sir. Just like this in the corner.'

'And the others?'

'All the patients in the ward were examined,' Morowetz told him.

'And?'

'Not one of them was bleeding.'

Everett said: 'I see.'

He looked down at Kenneth.

'This is Doctor Menlo, Kenneth. Have you anything to tell me?'

Kenneth did not reply.

Everett said: 'When you've got him back in his room and tranquilized, will you call me please?'

Morowetz nodded.

The call never came. Kenneth had fallen asleep. Either the drugs he was given had knocked him out cold, or he had opted for silence. Either way, he was incommunicado.

No one was discovered bleeding. Nothing was found to indicate an accident, a violent attack, an epileptic seizure. A weapon was not located. Kenneth Albright had not a single scratch on his flesh from stem, as Everett put it, to gudgeon. The blood, it seemed, had fallen like the rain from heaven: unexplained and inexplicable.

Later, as the day was ending, Everett Menlo left the Queen Street Mental Health Centre. He made his way home on the Queen streetcar and the Bay bus. When he reached the apartment, Thurber was waiting for him. Mimi was at a goddamned meeting.

That was the night Everett Menlo suffered the first of his failures to sleep. It was occasioned by the fact that, when he wakened sometime after three, he had just been dreaming. This, of course, was not unusual—but the dream itself was perturbing. There was someone lying there, in the bright white landscape of a hospital dining room. Whether it was a man or a woman could not be told, it was just a human body, lying down in a pool of blood.

Kenneth Albright was kneeling beside this body, pulling it open the way a child will pull a Christmas present open—yanking at its strings and ribbons, wanting only to see the contents. Everett saw this scene from several angles, never speaking never being spoken to. In all the time he watched—the usual dream eternity—the silence was broken only by the sound of water dripping from an unseen tap. Then, Kenneth Albright rose and was covered with blood, the way he had been that morning. He stared at Doctor Menlo, looked right through him and departed. Nothing remained in the dining room but plastic tables and plastic chairs and the bright red thing on the floor that once had been a person. Everett Menlo did not know and could not guess who this person might have been. He only knew that Kenneth Albright had left this person's body in Everett Menlo's dream.

Three nights running, the corpse remained in its place and every time that Everett entered the dining room in the nightmare he was certain he would find out who it was. On the fourth night, fully expecting to discover he himself was the victim, he beheld the face and saw it was a stranger.

But there are no strangers in dreams; he knew that now after twenty years of practice. *There are no strangers; there are only people in disguise.*

———————

Mimi made one final attempt in Brian Bassett's behalf to turn away the fate to which his other doctors—both medical and psychiatric—had consigned him. Not that, as a group, they had failed to expend the full weight of all they knew and all they could do to save him. One of his medical doctors—a woman whose name was Juliet Batemen—had moved a cot into his isolation room and stayed with him twenty-four hours a day for over a week. But her health had been undermined by this and when she succumbed to the Shanghai flu she removed herself for fear of infecting Brian Bassett.

The parents had come and gone on a daily basis for months in a killing routine of visits. But parents, their presence and their loving, are not the answer when a child has fallen into an autistic state. They might as well have been strangers. And so they had been advised to stay away.

Brian Bassett was eight years old—*unlucky eight,* as one of his therapists had said—and in every other way, in terms of physical development and mental capability, he had always been a perfectly normal child. Now, in the final moments of his life, he weighed a scant thirty pounds when he should have weighed twice that much.

Brian had not been heard to speak a single word in over a year of constant observation. Earlier—as long ago as seven months— a few expressions would visit his face from time to time. Never a smile—but often a kind of sneer, a passing of judgement, terrifying in its intensity. Other times, a pinched expression would appear—a signal of the shyness peculiar to autistic children, who think of light as being unfriendly.

Mimi's militant efforts in behalf of Brian had been exemplary. Her fellow doctors thought of her as *Bassett's crazy guardian angel.* They begged her to remove herself in order to preserve her health. Being wise, being practical, they saw that all her efforts would not save him. But Mimi's version of being a guardian angel was more like being a surrogate warrior: a hired gun or a samurai. Her cool determination to thwart the enemies of silence, stillness and starvation gave her strengths that even she had been unaware were hers to command.

Brian Bassett, seated in his corner on the floor, maintained a solemn composure that lent his features a kind of unearthly beauty. His back was straight, his hands were poised, his hair was so fine he looked the very picture of a spirit waiting to enter a newborn creature. Sometimes Mimi wondered if this creature Brian Bassett waited to inhabit could be human. She thought of all the animals she had ever seen in all her travels and she fell upon the image of a newborn fawn as being the most tranquil and the most in need of stillness in order to survive. If only all the natural energy and curiosity of a newborn beast could have entered into Brian Bassett, surely, they would have transformed the boy in the corner into a vibrant, joyous human being. But it was not to be.

On the 29th of April—one week and three days after Everett had entered into his crisis of insomnia—Mimi sat on the floor in Brian Bassett's isolation room, gently massaging his arms and legs as she held him in her lap.

His weight, by now, was shocking—and his skin had become translucent. His eyes had not been closed for days—for weeks—and their expression might have been carved in stone.

'Speak to me. Speak,' she whispered to him as she cradled his head beneath her chin. 'Please at least speak before you die.'

Nothing happened. Only silence.

Juliet Bateman—wrapped in a blanket—was watching through the observation glass as Mimi lifted up Brian Bassett and placed him in his cot. The cot had metal sides—and the sides were raised. Juliet Bateman could see Brian Bassett's eyes and his hands as Mimi stepped away.

Mimi looked at Juliet and shook her head. Juliet closed her eyes and pulled her blanket tighter like a skin that might protect her from the next five minutes.

Mimi went around the cot to the other side and dragged the

IV stand in closer to the head. She fumbled for a moment with the long plastic lifelines—anti-dehydrants, nutrients—and she adjusted the needles and brought them down inside the nest of the cot where Brian Bassett lay and she lifted up his arm in order to insert the tubes and bind them into place with tape.

This was when it happened—just as Mimi Menlo was preparing to insert the second tube.

Brian Bassett looked at her and spoke.

'No,' he said. 'Don't.'

Don't meant death.

Mimi paused—considered—and set the tube aside. Then she withdrew the tube already in place and she hung them both on the IV stand.

All right, she said to Brian Bassett in her mind, *you win.*

She looked down then with her arm along the side of the cot—and one hand trailing down so Brian Bassett could touch it if he wanted to. She smiled at him and said to him: 'not to worry. Not to worry. None of us is ever going to trouble you again.' He watched her carefully. 'Goodbye, Brian,' she said. 'I love you.'

Juliet Bateman saw Mimi Menlo say all this and was fairly sure she had read the words on Mimi's lips just as they had been spoken.

Mimi started out of the room. She was determined now there was no turning back and that Brian Bassett was free to go his way. But just as she was turning the handle and pressing her weight against the door—she heard Brian Bassett speak again.

'Goodbye,' he said.

And died.

Mimi went back and Juliet Bateman, too, and they stayed with him another hour before they turned out his lights. 'Someone else can cover his face,' said Mimi. 'I'm not going to do it.' Juliet agreed and they came back out to tell the nurse on duty that their ward had died and their work with him was over.

———

On the 30th of April—a Saturday—Mimi stayed home and made her notes and she wondered if and when she would weep for Brian Bassett. Her hand, as she wrote, was steady and her throat was not constricted and her eyes had no sensation beyond the burning itch of fatigue. She wondered what she looked like in the mirror, but resisted that discovery. Some things could wait. Outside it rained. Thurber dreamed in the corner. Bay Street rumbled in the basement.

Everett, in the meantime, had reached his own crisis and because of his desperate straits a part of Mimi Menlo's mind was on her husband. Now he had not slept for almost ten days. We *really ought to consign ourselves to hospital beds,* she thought. Somehow, the idea held no persuasion. It occurred to her that laughter might do a better job, if only they could find it. The brain, when over-extended, gives us the most surprisingly simple propositions, she concluded. *Stop,* it says to us. *Lie down and sleep.*

Five minutes later, Mimi found herself still sitting at the desk, with her fountain pen capped and her fingers raised to her lips in an attitude of gentle prayer. It required some effort to re-adjust and re-establish her focus on the surface of the window glass beyond which her mind had wandered. Sitting up, she had been asleep.

Thurber muttered something and stretched his legs and yawned, still asleep. Mimi glanced in his direction. *We've both been dreaming,* she thought, *but his dream continues.*

Somewhere behind her, the broken clock was attempting to strike the hour of three. Its voice was dull and rusty, needing oil.

Looking down, she saw the words BRIAN BASSETT written

on the page before her and it occurred to her that, without his person, the words were nothing more than extrapolations from the alphabet—something fanciful we call a 'name' in the hope that, one day, it will take on meaning.

She thought of Brian Bassett with his building blocks—pushing the letters around on the floor and coming up with more acceptable arrangements: TINA STERABBS ... IAN BRETT BASS ... BEST STAB *the* RAIN: a sentence. He had known all along, of course, that BRIAN BASSETT wasn't what he wanted because it wasn't what he was. He had come here against his will, was held here against his better judgement, fought against his captors and finally escaped.

But where was here to Ian Brett Bass? Where was here to Tina Sterabbs? Like Brian Bassett, they had all been here in someone else's dreams, and had to wait for someone else to wake before they could make their getaway.

Slowly, Mimi uncapped her fountain pen and drew a firm, black line through Brian Bassett's name. *We dreamed him,* she wrote, *that's all. And then we let him go.*

———

Seeing Everett standing in the doorway, knowing he had just returned from another Kenneth Albright crisis, she had no sense of apprehension. All this was only as it should be. Given the way that everything was going, it stood to reason Kenneth Albright's crisis had to come in this moment. If he managed, at last, to kill himself then at least her husband might begin to sleep again.

Far in the back of her mind a carping, critical voice remarked that any such thoughts were *deeply unfeeling and verging on the barbaric.* But Mimi dismissed this voice and another part of her brain stepped forward in her defence. *I will weep for Kenneth*

Albright, she thought, *when I can weep for Brian Bassett. Now, all that matters is that Everett and I survive.*

Then she strode forward and put out her hand for Everett's briefcase, set the briefcase down and helped him out of his topcoat. She was playing wife. It seemed to be the thing to do.

For the next twenty minutes Everett had nothing to say, and after he had poured himself a drink and after Mimi had done the same, they sat in their chairs and waited for Everett to catch his breath.

The first thing he said when he finally spoke was: 'finish your notes?'

'Just about,' Mimi told him. 'I've written everything I can for now.' She did not elaborate. 'You're home early,' she said, hoping to goad him into saying something new about Kenneth Albright.

'Yes,' he said. 'I am.' But that was all.

Then he stood up—threw back the last of his drink and poured another. He lighted a cigarette and Mimi didn't even wince. He had been smoking now three days. The atmosphere between them had been, since then, enlivened with a magnetic kind of tension. But it was a moribund tension, slowly beginning to dissipate.

Mimi watched her husband's silent torment now with a kind of clinical detachment. This was the result, she liked to tell herself, of her training and her discipline. The lover in her could regard Everett warmly and with concern, but the psychiatrist in her could also watch him as someone suffering a nervous breakdown, someone who could not be helped until the symptoms had multiplied and declared themselves more openly.

Everett went into the darkest corner of the room and sat down hard in one of Mimi's straight-backed chairs: the ones inherited from her mother. He sat, prim, like a patient in a doctor's office, totally unrelaxed and nervy; expressionless. Either he had come to receive a deadly diagnosis, or he would get a clean bill of health.

Mimi glided over to the sofa in the window, plush and red and deeply comfortable; a place to recuperate. The view—if she chose to turn only slightly sideways—was one of the gentle rain that was falling onto Bay Street. Sopping-wet pigeons huddled on the window sill; people across the street in the Manulife building were turning on their lights.

A renegade robin, nesting in their eaves, began to sing.

Everett Menlo began to talk.

'Please don't interrupt,' he said at first.

'You know I won't,' said Mimi. It was a rule that neither one should interrupt the telling of a case until they had been invited to do so.

Mimi put her fingers into her glass so the ice cubes wouldn't click. She waited.

Everett spoke—but he spoke as if in someone else's voice, perhaps the voice of Kenneth Albright. This was not entirely unusual. Often, both Mimi and Everett Menlo spoke in the voices of their patients. What was unusual, this time, was that, speaking in Kenneth's voice, Everett began to sweat profusely—so profusely that Mimi was able to watch his shirt front darkening with perspiration.

'As you know,' he said, 'I have not been sleeping.'

This was the understatement of the year. Mimi was silent.

'I have not been sleeping because—to put it in a nutshell—I have been afraid to dream.'

Mimi was somewhat startled by this. Not by the fact that Everett was afraid to dream, but only because she had just been thinking of dreams herself.

'I have been afraid to dream, because in all my dreams there have been bodies. Corpses. Murder victims.'

Mimi—not really listening—idly wondered if she had been one of them.

'In all my dreams, there have been corpses,' Everett repeated. 'But I am not the murderer. Kenneth Albright is the murderer, and, up to this moment, he has left behind him fifteen bodies: none of them people I recognize.'

Mimi nodded. The ice cubes in her drink were beginning to freeze her fingers. Any minute now, she prayed, they would surely melt.

'I gave up dreaming almost a week ago,' said Everett, 'thinking that if I did, the killing pattern might be altered; broken.' Then he said tersely; 'it was not. The killings have continued ...'

'How do you know the killings have continued, Everett, if you've given up your dreaming? Wouldn't this mean he had no place to hide the bodies?'

In spite of the fact she had disobeyed their rule about not speaking, Everett answered her.

'I know they are being continued because I have seen the blood.'

'Ah, yes. I see.'

'No, Mimi. No. You do not see. The blood is not a figment of my imagination. The blood, in fact, is the only thing not dreamed.' He explained the stains on Kenneth Albright's hands and arms and clothes and he said: 'It happens every day. We have searched his person for signs of cuts and gashes—even for internal and rectal bleeding. Nothing. We have searched his quarters and all the other quarters in his ward. His ward is locked. His ward is isolated in the extreme. None of his fellow patients was ever found bleeding—never had cause to bleed. There were no injuries—no self-inflicted wounds. We thought of animals. Perhaps a mouse—a rat. But nothing. Nothing. Nothing ... We also went so far as to strip-search all the members of the staff who entered that ward and I, too, offered myself for this experiment. Still nothing. Nothing. No one had bled.'

Everett was now beginning to perspire so heavily he removed his jacket and threw it on the floor. Thurber woke and stared at it, startled. At first, it appeared to be the beast that had just pursued him through the woods and down the road. But, then, it sighed and settled and was just a coat; a rumpled jacket lying down on a rug.

Everett said: 'we had taken samples of the blood on the patient's hands—on Kenneth Albright's hands and on his clothing and we had these samples analyzed. No. It was not his own blood. No, it was not the blood of an animal. No, it was not the blood of a fellow patient. No, it was not the blood of any members of the staff ....'

Everett's voice had risen.

'Whose blood was it?' he almost cried. 'Whose the hell was it?'

Mimi waited.

Everett Menlo lighted another cigarette. He took a great gulp of his drink.

'Well ...' He was calmer now; calmer of necessity. He had to marshal the evidence. He had to put it all in order—bring it into line with reason. 'Did this mean that—somehow—the patient had managed to leave the premises—do some bloody deed and return without our knowledge of it? That is, after all, the only possible explanation. Isn't it?'

Mimi waited.

'Isn't it?' he repeated.

'Yes,' she said. 'It's the only possible explanation.'

'Except there is no way out of that place. There is absolutely no way out.'

Now, there was a pause.

'But one,' he added—his voice, again, a whisper.

Mimi was silent. Fearful—watching his twisted face.

'Tell me,' Everett Menlo said—the perfect innocent, almost the perfect child in quest of forbidden knowledge. 'Answer me this—be honest: is there blood in dreams?'

Mimi could not respond. She felt herself go pale. Her husband—after all, the sanest man alive—had just suggested something so completely mad he might as well have handed over his reason in a paper bag and said to her, *burn this*.

'The only place that Kenneth Albright goes, I tell you, is into dreams,' Everett said. 'That is the only place beyond the ward into which the patient can or does escape.'

Another—briefer—pause.

'It is real blood, Mimi. Real. And he gets it all from dreams. *My dreams.*'

They waited for this to settle.

Everett said: 'I'm tired. I'm tired. I cannot bear this any more. I'm tired ...'

Mimi thought, *good. No matter what else happens, he will sleep tonight.*

He did. And so, at last, did she.

Mimi's dreams were rarely of the kind that engender fear. She dreamt more gentle scenes with open spaces that did not intimidate. She would dream quite often of water and of animals. Always, she was nothing more than an observer; roles were not assigned her; often, this was sad. Somehow, she seemed at times locked out, unable to participate. These were the dreams she endured when Brian Bassett died: field trips to see him in some desert setting; underwater excursions to watch him floating amongst the seaweed. He never spoke, and, indeed, he never

107

appeared to be aware of her presence.

That night, when Everett fell into his bed exhausted and she did likewise, Mimi's dream of Brian Bassett was the last one she would ever have of him and somehow, in the dream, she knew this. What she saw was what, in magical terms, would be called a disappearing act. Brian Bassett vanished. Gone.

———————

Sometime after midnight on May Day morning, Mimi Menlo awoke from her dream of Brian to the sound of Thurber thumping the floor in a dream of his own.

Everett was not in his bed and Mimi cursed. She put on her wrapper and her slippers and went beyond the bedroom into the hall.

No lights were shining but the street lamps far below and the windows gave no sign of stars.

Mimi made her way past the jungle, searching for Everett in the living room. He was not there. She would dream of this one day; it was a certainty.

'Everett?'

He did not reply.

Mimi turned and went back through the bedroom.

'Everett?'

She heard him. He was in the bathroom and she went in through the door.

'Oh,' she said, when she saw him. 'Oh, my God.'

———————

Everett Menlo was standing in the bathtub, removing his pyjamas. They were soaking wet, but not with perspiration.

They were soaking wet with blood.

For a moment, holding his jacket, letting its arms hang down across his belly and his groin, Everett stared at Mimi, blank-eyed from his nightmare.

Mimi raised her hands to her mouth. She felt as one must feel, if helpless, watching someone burn alive.

Everett threw the jacket down and started to remove his trousers. His pyjamas, made of cotton, had been green. His eyes were blinded now with blood and his hands reached out to find the shower taps.

'Please don't look at me,' he said. 'I ... Please go away.'

Mimi said: 'no.' She sat on the toilet seat. 'I'm waiting here,' she told him, 'until we both wake up.'

Dog Attempts to Drown Man in Saskatoon

DOUGLAS GLOVER

M Y WIFE AND I decide to separate, and then suddenly we are almost happy together. The pathos of our situation, our private and unique tragedy, lends romance to each small act. We see everything in the round, the facets as opposed to the flat banality that was wedging us apart. When she asks me to go to the Mendel Art Gallery Sunday afternoon, I do not say no with the usual mounting irritation that drives me into myself. I say yes and some hardness within me seems to melt into a pleasant sadness. We look into each other's eyes and realize with a start that we are looking for the first time because it is the last. We are both thinking, Who is this person to whom I have been married? What has been the meaning of our relationship? These are questions we have never asked ourselves; we have been a blind couple groping with each other in the dark. Instead of saying to myself, Not the art gallery again! What does she care about art? She has no education. She's merely bored and on Sunday afternoon in Saskatoon the only place you can go is the old sausage-maker's mausoleum of art! Instead of putting up arguments, I think, Poor Lucy, pursued by the assassins of her past, unable to be still. Perhaps if I had her memories I also would be unable to stay in on a Sunday afternoon. Somewhere that cretin Pascal says that all our problems stem from not being able to sit quietly in a room alone. If Pascal had had Lucy's mother, he would never have written anything so foolish. Also, at the age of nine, she saw her younger brother run over and killed by a highway roller. Faced with that, would Pascal have written anything? (Now I am defending my wife against Pascal! A month ago I would have used the same passage to bludgeon her.)

———————

Note. Already this is not the story I wanted to tell. That is buried, gone, lost—its action fragmented and distorted by inexact recollection. Directly it was completed, it had disappeared, gone with the past into that strange realm of suspended animation, that coat rack of despair, wherein all our completed acts await, gathering dust, until we come for them again. I am trying to give you the truth, though I could try harder, and only refrain because I know that that way leads to madness. So I offer an approximation, a shadow play, such as would excite children, full of blind spots and irrelevant adumbrations, too little in parts; elsewhere too much. Alternately I will frustrate you and lead you astray. I can only say that, at the outset, my intention was otherwise; I sought only clarity and simple conclusions. Now I know the worst—that reasons are out of joint with actions, that my best explanation will be obscure, subtle and unsatisfying, and that the human mind is a tangle of unexplored pathways.

———————

'My wife and I decide to separate, and then suddenly we are almost happy together.' This is a sentence full of ironies and lies. For example, I call her my wife. Technically this is true. But now that I am leaving, the thought is in both our hearts: Can a marriage of eleven months really be called a marriage? Moreover, it was only a civil ceremony, a ten-minute formality performed at City Hall by a man who, one could tell, had been drinking heavily over lunch. Perhaps if we had done it in a cathedral surrounded by robed priests intoning Latin benedictions we would not now be falling apart. As we put on our coats to go to the art gallery, I mention this idea to Lucy. 'A year,' she says. 'With Latin we might have lasted a year.' We laugh. This is the most courageous statement she has made since we became aware of our defeat, better than all her sour tears. Usually she is too self-conscious to make jokes. Seeing me smile, she blushes and becomes confused, happy to have pleased me, happy to be happy, in the final analysis, happy to be sad because the sadness frees her to be what she could never be before. Like many people, we are both masters of beginnings and endings, but founder in the middle of things. It takes a wise and mature individual to manage that which intervenes, the duration which is a necessary part of life and marriage. So there is a sense in which we are not married, though something *is* ending. And therein lies the greater irony. For in ending, in separating, we are finally and ineluctably together, locked as it were in a ritual recantation. We are going to the art gallery (I am guilty of over-determining the symbol) together.

It is winter in Saskatoon, to my mind the best of seasons because it is the most inimical to human existence. The weather forecaster gives the temperature, the wind chill factor and the number of seconds it takes to freeze exposed skin. Driving between towns one remembers to pack a winter survival kit (matches, candle, chocolate, flares, down sleeping bag) in case of a breakdown. Earlier in the week just outside the city limits a man disappeared after setting out to walk a quarter of a mile from one farmhouse to another, swallowed up by the cold prairie night. (This is, I believe, a not unpleasant way to die once the initial period of discomfort has been passed.) Summer in Saskatoon is a collection of minor irritants: heat and dust, blackflies and tent caterpillars, the nighttime electrical storms that leave the unpaved concession roads impassable troughs of gumbo mud. But winter has the beauty of a plausible finality. I drive out to the airport early in the morning to watch jets land in a pink haze of ice crystals. During the long nights the *aurora borealis* seems to touch the rooftops. But best of all is the city itself which takes on a kind of ghostliness, a dreamlike quality that combines emptiness (there seem to be so few people) and the mists rising from the heated buildings to produce a mystery. Daily I tramp the paths along the riverbank, crossing and re-crossing the bridges, watching the way the city changes in the pale winter light. Beneath me the unfrozen parts of the river smoke and boil, raging to become still. Winter in Saskatoon is a time of anxious waiting and endurance; all that beauty is alien, a constant threat. Many things do not endure. Our marriage, for example, was vernal, a product of the brief, sweet prairie spring.

Neither Lucy nor I was born here; Mendel came from Russia. In fact there is a feeling of the camp about Saskatoon, the temporary abode. At the university there are photographs of the town—in 1905 there were three frame buildings and a tent. In a bar I nearly came to blows with a man campaigning to preserve a movie theatre built in 1934. In Saskatoon that is ancient history, that is the cave painting at Lascaux. Lucy hails from an even newer settlement in the wild Peace River country where her father went to raise cattle and ended up a truck mechanic. Seven years ago she came to Saskatoon to work in a garment factory (her left hand bears a burn scar from a clothes press). Next fall she begins law school. Despite this evidence of intelligence, determination and ability, Lucy has no confidence in herself. In her mother's eyes she will never measure up, and that is all that is important. I myself am a proud man and a gutter snob. I wear a ring in my left ear and my hair long. My parents migrated from a farm in Wisconsin to a farm in Saskatchewan in 1952 and still drive back every year to see the trees. I am two courses short of a degree in philosophy which I will never receive. I make my living at what comes to hand, house painting when I am wandering; since I settled with Lucy, I've worked as the lone overnight editor at the local newspaper. Against the bosses, I am a union man; against the union, I am an independent. When the publisher asked me to work days, I quit. That was a month ago. That was when Lucy knew I was leaving. Deep down she understands my nature. Mendel is another case: he was a butcher and a man who left traces. Now on the north side of the river there are giant meat-packing plants spilling forth the odours of death, guts and excrement. Across the street are the holding pens for the cattle and the rail lines that bring them to slaughter. Before building his art gallery Mendel actually kept his paintings in this sprawling complex of buildings, inside the slaughterhouse. If you went to his office, you would sit in a waiting room with a Picasso or a Rouault on the wall. Perhaps even a van Gogh. The gallery is downriver at the opposite end of the city, very clean and modern.

But whenever I go there I hear the panicky bellowing of the death-driven steers and see the streams of blood and the carcasses and smell the stench and imagine the poor beasts rolling their eyes at Gauguin's green and luscious leaves as the bolt enters their brains.

We have decided to separate. It is a wintry Sunday afternoon. We are going to the Mendel Art Gallery. Watching Lucy shake her hair out and tuck it into her knitted hat, I suddenly feel close to tears. Behind her are the framed photographs of weathered prairie farmhouses, the vigorous spider plants, the scarred child's school desk where she does her studying, the brick-and-board bookshelf with her meagre library. (After eleven months there is still nothing of me that will remain.) This is an old song; there is no gesture of Lucy's that does not fill me instantly with pity, the child's hand held up to deflect the blow, her desperate attempts to conceal unworthiness. For her part she naturally sees me as the father who, in that earlier existence, proved so practiced in evasion and flight. The fact that I am now leaving her only re-inforces her intuition—it is as if she has expected it all along, almost as if she has been working towards it. This goes to show the force of initial impressions. For example I will never forget the first time I saw Lucy. She was limping across Broadway, her feet swathed in bandages and jammed into her pumps, her face alternately distorted with agony and composed in dignity. I followed her for blocks—she was beautiful and wounded, the kind of woman I am always looking for to redeem me. Similarly, what she will always remember is that first night we spent together when all I did was hold her while she slept because, taking the bus home, she had seen a naked man masturbating in a window. Thus she had arrived at my door, laughing hysterically, afraid to stay at her own place alone, completely undone. At first she had played the temptress because she thought that was what I wanted. She kissed me hungrily and unfastened my shirt buttons. Then she ran into the bathroom and came out crying because she had dropped and broken the soap dish. That was when I put my arms around her and comforted her, which was what she had wanted from the beginning.

An apology for my style. I am not so much apologizing as invoking a tradition. Heraclitus whose philosophy may not have been written in fragments but certainly comes to us in that form; Kierkegaard who mocked Hegel's system-building by writing everything as if it were an afterthought, *The Unscientific Postscript;* Nietzsche who wrote in aphorisms or what he called 'attempts,' dry runs at the subject matter, even arguing contradictory points of view in order to see all sides; Wittgenstein's *Investigations*, his fragmentary response to the architectonic of the earlier *Tractatus*. Traditional story writers compose a beginning, a middle and an end, stringing these together in continuity as if there were some whole which they represented. Whereas I am writing fragments and discursive circumlocutions about an object that may not be complete or may be infinite. 'Dog Attempts to Drown Man in Saskatoon' is my title, cribbed from a facetious newspaper headline. Lucy and I were married because of her feet and because she glimpsed a man masturbating in a window as her bus took her home from work. I feel that in discussing these occurrences, these facts (our separation, the dog, the city, the weather, a trip to the art gallery) as constitutive of a non-system, I am peeling away some of the mystery of human life. I am also of the opinion that Mendel should have left the paintings in the slaughterhouse.

———————

The discerning reader will by now have trapped me in a number of inconsistencies and doubtful statements. For example, we are not separating—I am leaving my wife and she has accepted that fact because it reaffirms her sense of herself as a person worthy of being left. Moreover it was wrong of me to pity her. Lucy is a quietly capable woman about to embark on what will inevitably be a successful career. She is not a waif nor could she ever redeem me with her suffering. Likewise she was wrong to view me as forever gentle and forbearing in the sexual department. And finally I suspect that there was more than coincidence in the fact that she spotted the man in his window on my night off from the newspaper. I do not doubt that she saw the man; he is a recurring nightmare of Lucy's. But whether she saw him that particular night, or some night in the past, or whether she made him up out of whole cloth and came to believe in him, I cannot say. About her feet, however, I have been truthful. That day she had just come from her doctor after having the stitches removed.

———————

Lucy's clumsiness. Her clumsiness stems from the fact that she was born with six toes on each foot. This defect, I'm sure, had something to do with the way her mother mistreated her. Among uneducated folk there is often a feeling that physical anomalies reflect mental flaws. And as a kind of punishment for being born (and afterwards because her brother had died), Lucy's feet were never looked at by a competent doctor. It wasn't until she was twenty-six and beginning to enjoy a new life that she underwent a painful operation to have the vestigial digits excised. This surgery left her big toes all but powerless; now they flop like stubby, white worms at the ends of her feet. Where she had been a schoolgirl athlete with six toes, she became awkward and ungainly with five.

———————

Her mother, Celeste, is one of those women who make feminism a *cause célèbre*—no, that is being glib. Truthfully, she was never any man's slave. I have the impression that after the first realization, the first inkling that she had married the wrong man, she entered into the role of submissive female with a strange, destructive gusto. She seems to have had an immoderate amount of hate in her, enough to spread its poison among the many people who touched her in a kind of negative of the parable of loaves and fishes. And the man, the father, was not so far as I can tell cruel, merely ineffectual, just the wrong man. Once, years later, Lucy and Celeste were riding on a bus together when Celeste pointed to a man sitting a few seats ahead and said, 'That is the one I loved.' That was all she ever said on the topic and the man himself was a balding, petty functionary type, completely uninteresting except in terms of the exaggerated passion Celeste had invested in him over the years. Soon after Lucy's father married Celeste he realized he would never be able to live with her—he absconded to the army, abandoning her with the first child in a drover's shack on a cattle baron's estate. (From time to time Lucy attempts to write about her childhood—her stories always seem unbelievable—a world of infanticide, blood feuds and brutality. I can barely credit these tales, seeing her so prim and composed, not prim but you know how she sits so straight in her chair and her hair is always in place and her clothes are expensive if not quite stylish and her manners are correct without being at all natural; Lucy is composed in the sense of being made up or put together out of pieces, not in the sense of being tranquil. But nevertheless she carries these *cauchemars* in her head: the dead babies found beneath the fence row, blood on sheets, shotgun blasts in the night, her brother going under the highway roller, her mother's cruel silence.) The father fled as I say. He sent them money orders, three-quarters of his pay, to that point he was responsible. Celeste never spoke of him and his infrequent visits home were always a surprise to the children; his visits and the locked bedroom door and the hot, breathy silence of what went on behind the door; Celeste's rising vexation and hysteria; the new pregnancy; the postmarks on the money orders. Then the boy died. Perhaps he was Celeste's favourite, a perfect one to hold over the tall, already beautiful, monster with six toes and (I conjecture again) her father's look. The boy died and the house went silent—Celeste had forbidden a word to be spoken— and this was the worst for Lucy, the cold parlour circumspection of Protestant mourning. They did not utter a redeeming sound, only replayed the image of the boy running, laughing, racing the machine, then tripping and going under, being sucked under— Lucy did not even see the body, and in an access of delayed grief almost two decades later she would tell me she had always assumed he just flattened out like a cartoon character. Celeste refused to weep; only her hatred grew like a heavy weight against her children. And in that vacuum, that terrible silence accorded all feeling and especially the mysteries of sex and death, the locked door of the bedroom and the shut coffin lid, the absent father and the absent brother, somehow became inextricably entwined in Lucy's mind; she was only nine, a most beautiful monster, surrounded by absent gods and a bitter worship. So that when she saw the naked man calmly masturbating in the upper storey window, framed as it were under the cornice of a Saskatoon rooming house, it was for her like a vision of the centre of the mystery, the scene behind the locked door, the corpse in its coffin, God, and she immediately imagined her mother waiting irritably in the shadow just out of sight with a towel to wipe the sperm from the windowpane, aroused, yet almost fainting at the grotesque denial of her female passion.

Do not, if you wish, believe any of the above. It is psychological jazz written *en marge;* I am a poet of marginalia. Some of what I write is utter crap and wishful thinking. Lucy is not 'happy to be sad'; she is seething inside because I am betraying her. Her anger gives her the courage to make jokes; she blushes when I laugh because she still hopes that I will stay. Of course my willingness to accompany her to the art gallery is inspired by guilt. She is completely aware of this fact. Her invitation is premeditated, manipulative. No gesture is lost; all our acts are linked and repeated. She is, after all, Celeste's daughter. Also do not believe for a moment that I hate that woman for what she was. That instant on the bus in a distant town when she pointed out the man she truly loved, she somehow redeemed herself for Lucy and for me, showing herself receptive of forgiveness and pity. Nor do I hate Lucy though I am leaving her.

My wife and I decide to separate, and then suddenly we are almost happy together. I repeat this crucial opening sentence for the purpose of reminding myself of my general intention. In a separate notebook next to me (vodka on ice sweating onto and blurring the ruled pages) I have a list of subjects to cover: 1) blindness (the man the dog led into the river was blind); 2) a man I know who was gored by a bison (real name to be withheld); 3) Susan the weaver and her little girl and the plan for us to live in Pelican Narrows; 4) the wolves at the city zoo; 5) the battlefields of Batoche and Duck Lake; 6) bridge symbolism; 7) a fuller description of the death of Lucy's brother; 8) three photographs of Lucy in my possession; 9) my wish to have met Mendel (he is dead) and be his friend; 10) the story of the story or how the dog tried to drown the man in Saskatoon.

Call this a play. Call me Orestes. Call her mother Clytemnestra. Her father, the wandering warrior king. (When he died accidentally a year ago, they sent Lucy his diary. Every day of his life he had recorded the weather; that was all.) Like everyone else, we married because we thought we could change one another. I was the brother-friend come to slay the tyrant Celeste; Lucy was to teach me the meaning of suffering. But there is no meaning and in the labyrinth of Lucy's mind the spirit of her past eluded me. Take sex for instance. She is taller than I am; people sometimes think she must be a model. She is without a doubt the most beautiful woman I have been to bed with. Yet there is no passion, no arousal. Between the legs she is as dry as a prairie summer. I am tender, but tenderness is no substitute for biology. Penetration is always painful. She gasps, winces. She will not perform oral sex though sometimes she likes having it done to her, providing she can overcome her embarrassment. What she does love is for me to wrestle her to the living-room carpet and strip her clothes off in a mock rape. She squeals and protests and

122

then scampers naked to the bedroom where she waits impatiently while I get undressed. Only once have I detected her orgasm—this while she sat on my lap fully clothed and I manipulated her with my fingers. It goes without saying she will not talk about these things. She protects herself from herself and there is never any feeling that we are together. When Lucy's periods began, Celeste told her she had cancer. More than once she was forced to eat garbage from a dog's dish. Sometimes her mother would simply lock her out of the house for the night. These stories are shocking: Celeste was undoubtedly mad. By hatred, mother and daughter are manacled together for eternity. 'You can change,' I say with all my heart. 'A woman who only sees herself as a victim never gets wise to herself.' 'No,' she says, touching my hand sadly. Ah! Ah! I think, between weeping and words. Nostalgia is form; hope is content. Lucy is an empty building, a frenzy of restlessness, a soul without a future. And I fling out in desperation, Orestes-like, seeking my own Athens and release.

———————

More bunk! I'll let you know now that we are not going to the art gallery as I write this. Everything happened some time ago and I am living far away in another country. (Structuralists would characterize my style as 'robbing the signifier of the signified.' My opening sentence, my premise, is now practically destitute of meaning, or it means everything. Really, this is what happens when you try to tell the truth about something; you end up like the snake biting its own tail. There are a hundred reasons why I left Lucy. I don't want to seem shallow. I don't want to say, well, I was a meat-and-potatoes person and she was a vegetarian, or that I sometimes believe she simply orchestrated the whole fiasco, seduced me, married me, and then refused to be a wife—yes, I would prefer to think that I was guiltless, that I didn't just wander off fecklessly like her father. To explain this, or for that matter to explain why the dog led the man into the river, you have to explain the world, even God—if we accept Gödel's theorem regarding the unjustifiability of systems from within. Everything is a symbol of everything else. Or everything is a symbol of death, as Levi-Strauss says. In other words, there is no signified and life is nothing but a long haunting. Perhaps that is all that I am trying to say …) However, we *did* visit the art gallery one winter Sunday near the end of our eleven-month marriage. There were two temporary exhibitions and all of Mendel's slaughterhouse pictures had been stored in the basement. One wing was devoted to photographs of grain elevators, very phallic with their little overhanging roofs. We laughed about this together; Lucy was kittenish, pretending to be shocked. Then she walked across the hall alone to contemplate the acrylic prairie-scapes by local artists. I descended the stairs to drink coffee and watch the frozen river. This was downstream from the Idylwyld Bridge where the fellow went in (there is an open stretch of two or three hundred yards where a hot-water outlet prevents the river from freezing over completely) and it occurred to me that if he had actually drowned, if the current had dragged him under the ice, they wouldn't have found his body until the spring breakup. And probably they would have discovered it hung up on the weir which I could see from the gallery window.

Forget it. A bad picture: Lucy upstairs 'appreciating' art, me downstairs thinking of bodies under the ice. Any moment now she will come skipping towards me flushed with excitement after a successful cultural adventure. That is not what I meant to show you. That Lucy is not a person, she is a caricature. When legends are born, people die. Rather let us look at the place where all reasons converge. No. Let me tell you how Lucy is redeemed: preamble and anecdote. Her greatest fear is that she will turn into Celeste. Naturally, without noticing it, she is becoming more and more like her mother every day. She has the financial independence Celeste no doubt craved, and she has been disappointed in love. Three times. The first man made himself into a wandering rage with drugs. The second was an adulterer. Now me. Already she is acquiring an edge of bitterness, of why-me-ness. But, and this is an Everest of a but, the woman can dance! I don't mean at the disco or in the ballroom; I don't mean she studied ballet. We were strolling in Diefenbaker Park one summer day shortly after our wedding (this is on the bluffs overlooking Mendel's meat-packing plant) when we came upon a puppet show. It was some sort of children's fair: there were petting zoos, pony rides, candy stands, bicycles being given away as prizes, all that kind of thing in addition to the puppets. It was a famous troupe which had started in the sixties as part of the counter-culture movement—I need not mention the name. The climax of the performance was a stately dance by two giant puppets perhaps thirty feet tall, a man and a woman, backwoods types. We arrived just in time to see the woman rise from the ground, supported by three puppeteers. She rises from the grass stiffly then spreads her massive arms towards the man and an orchestra begins a reel. It is an astounding sight. I notice that the children in the audience are rapt. And suddenly I am aware of Lucy, her face aflame, this crazy grin and her eyes dazzled. She is looking straight up at the giant woman. The music, as I say, begins and the puppet sways and opens her arms towards her partner (they are both very stern, very grave) and Lucy begins to sway and spread her arms. She lifts her feet gently, one after the other, begins to turn, then swings back. She doesn't know what she is doing; this is completely unselfconscious. There is only Lucy and the puppets and the dance. She is a child again and I am in awe of her innocence. It is a scene that brings a lump to my throat: the high, hot, summer sun, the children's faces like flowers in a sea of grass, the towering, swaying puppets, and Lucy lost in herself. Lucy, dancing. Probably she no longer remembers this incident. At the time, or shortly after, she said, 'Oh no! Did I really? Tell me I didn't do that!' She was laughing, not really embarrassed. 'Did anyone see me?' And when the puppeteers passed the hat at the end of the show, I turned out my pockets, I gave them everything I had.

I smoke Gitanes. I like to drink in an Indian bar on 20th Street near Eaton's. My nose was broken in a car accident when I was eighteen; it grew back crooked. I speak softly; sometimes I stutter. I don't like crowds. In my spare time, I paint large pictures of the city. Photographic realism is my style. I work on a pencil grid using egg tempera because it's better for detail. I do shopping centres, old movie theatres that are about to be torn down, slaughterhouses. While everyone else is looking out at the prairie, I peer inward and record what is merely transitory, what is human. Artifice. Nature defeats me. I cannot paint ripples on a lake, or the movement of leaves, or a woman's face. Like most people, I suppose, my heart is broken because I cannot be what I wish to be. On the day in question, one of the coldest of the year, I hike down from the university along Saskatchewan Drive overlooking the old railway hotel, the modest office blocks, and the ice-shrouded gardens of the city. I carry a camera, snapping end-of-the-world photos for a future canvas. At the Third Avenue Bridge I pause to admire the lattice of I-beams, black against the frozen mist swirling up from the river and the translucent exhaust plumes of the ghostly cars shuttling to and fro. Crossing the street, I descend the wooden steps into Rotary Park, taking two more shots of the bridge at a close angle before the film breaks from the cold. I swing round, focusing on the squat ugliness of the Idylwyld Bridge with its fat concrete piers obscuring the view upriver, and then suddenly an icy finger seems to touch my heart: out on the river, on the very edge of the snowy crust where the turbid waters from the outlet pipe churn and steam, a black dog is playing. I refocus. The dog scampers in a tight circle, races towards the brink, skids to a stop, barks furiously at something in the grey water. I stumble forward a step or two. Then I see the man, swept downstream, bobbing in the current, his arms flailing stiffly. In another instant, the dog leaps after him, disappears, almost as if I had dreamed it. I don't quite know what I am doing, you understand. The river is no man's land. First I am plunging through the knee-deep snow of the park. Then I lose my footing on the bank and find myself sliding on my seat onto the river ice. Before I have time to think, There is a man in the river, I am sprinting to intercept him, struggling to untangle the camera from around my neck, stripping off my coat. I have forgotten momentarily how long it takes exposed skin to freeze and am lost in a frenzy of speculation upon the impossibility of existence in the river, the horror of the current dragging you under the ice at the end of the open water, the creeping numbness, again the impossibility, the alienness of the idea itself, the dog and the man immersed. I feel the ice rolling under me, throw myself flat, wrapped in a gentle terror, then inch forward again, spread-eagled, throwing my coat by a sleeve, screaming, 'Catch it! Catch it!' to the man whirling towards me, scrabbling with bloody hands at the crumbling ledge. All this occupies less time than it takes to tell. He is a strange bearlike creature, huge in an old duffel coat with its hood up, steam rising around him, his face bloated and purple, his red hands clawing at the ice shelf, an inhuman 'awing' sound emanating from his throat, his eyes rolling upwards. He makes no effort to reach the coat sleeve trailed before him as the current carries him by. Then the dog appears, paddling towards the man, straining to keep its head above the choppy surface. The dog barks, rests a paw on the man's shoulder, seems to drag him under a little, and then the man is striking out wildly, fighting the dog off, being twisted out into the open water by the eddies. I see the leather hand harness flapping from the dog's neck and suddenly the full horror of the situation assails me: the man is blind. Perhaps he understands nothing of what is happening to him, the world gone mad, this freezing hell. At the same moment, I feel strong hands grip my ankles and hear another's laboured breathing. I look over my shoulder. There is a raw-cheeked policeman with a thin yellow moustache stretched on the ice behind me. Behind him, two teenage boys are in the act of dropping to all fours, making a chain of bodies. A fifth person, a young woman, is running towards us. 'He's blind,' I shout. The policeman nods: he seems to comprehend everything in an instant. The man in the water has come to rest against a jutting point of ice a few yards away. The dog is much nearer, but I make for the man, crawling on my hands and knees, forgetting my coat. There seems nothing to fear now. Our little chain of life reaching towards the blind drowning man seems sufficient against the infinity of forces which have culminated in this moment. The crust is rolling and bucking beneath us as I take his wrists. His fingers, hard as talons, lock into mine. Immediately he ceases to utter that terrible, unearthly bawling sound. Inching backward, I somehow contrive to lever the dead weight of his body over the ice lip, then drag him on his belly like a sack away from the water. The policeman turns him gently on his back; he is breathing in gasps, his eyes rolling frantically. 'T'ank you. T'ank you,' he whispers, his strength gone. The others quickly remove their coats and tuck them around the man who now looks like some strange beached fish, puffing and muttering in the snow. Then in the eerie silence that follows, broken only by the shushing sound of traffic on the bridges, the distant whine of a siren coming nearer, the hissing river and my heart beating, I look into the smoky water once more and see that the dog is gone. I am dazed; I watch a drop of sweat freezing on the policeman's moustache. I stare into the grey flux where it slips quietly under the ice and disappears. One of the boys offers me a cigarette. The blind man moans; he says, 'I go home now. Dog good. I all right. I walk home.' The boys glance at each other. The woman is shivering. Everything seems empty and anticlimactic. We are shrouded in enigma. The policeman takes out a notebook, a tiny symbol of rationality, scribbled words against the void. As an ambulance crew skates a stretcher down the riverbank, he begins to ask the usual questions, the usual, unanswerable questions.

This is not the story I wanted to tell. I repeat this *caveat* as a reminder that I am willful and wayward as a storyteller, not a good storyteller at all. The right story, the true story, had I been able to tell it, would have changed your life—but it is buried, gone, lost. The next day Lucy and I drive to the spot where I first saw the dog. The river is once more sanely empty and the water boils quietly where it has not yet frozen. Once more I tell her how it happened, but she prefers the public version, what she hears on the radio or reads in the newspaper, to my disjointed impressions. It is also true that she knows she is losing me and she is at the stage where it is necessary to deny strenuously all my values and perceptions. She wants to think that I am just like her father or that I always intended to humiliate her. The facts of the case are that the man and dog apparently set out to cross the Idylwyld Bridge but turned off along the approach and walked into the water, the man a little ahead of the dog. In the news account, the dog is accused of insanity, dereliction of duty and a strangely uncanine malevolence. 'Dog Attempts to Drown Man,' the headline reads. Libel law prevents speculation on the human victim's mental state, his intentions. The dog is dead, but the tone is jocular. *Dog Attempts to Drown Man.* All of which means that no one knows what happened from the time the man stumbled off the sidewalk on Idylwyld to the time he fell into the river and we are free to invent structures and symbols as we see fit. The man survives, it seems, his strange baptism, his trial by cold and water. I know in my own mind that he appeared exhausted, not merely from the experience of near-drowning, but from before, in spirit, while the dog seemed eager and alert. We know, or at least we can all agree to theorize, that a bridge is a symbol of change (one side to the other, hence death), of connection (the marriage of opposites), but also of separation from the river of life, a bridge is an object of culture. Perhaps man and dog chose together to walk through the pathless snows to the water's edge and throw themselves into uncertainty. The man was blind as are we all; perhaps he sought illumination in the frothing waste. Perhaps they went as old friends. Or perhaps the dog accompanied the man only reluctantly, the man forcing the dog to lead him across the ice. I saw the dog swim to him, saw the man fending the dog off. Perhaps the dog was trying to save its master, or perhaps it was only playing, not understanding in the least what was happening. Whatever is the case my allegiance is with the dog; the man is too human, too predictable. But man and dog together are emblematic—that is my impression at any rate—they are the mind and spirit, the one blind, the other dumb; one defeated, the other naïve and hopeful, both forever going out. And I submit that after all the simplified explanations and crude jokes about the blind man and his dog, the act is full of a strange and terrible mystery, of beauty.

My wife and I decide to separate, and then suddenly we are almost happy together. But this was long ago, as was the visit to the Mendel Art Gallery and my time in Saskatoon. And though the moment when Lucy is shaking down her hair and tucking it into her knitted cap goes on endlessly in my head as does the reverberation of that other moment when the dog disappears under the ice, there is much that I have already forgotten. I left Lucy because she was too real, too hungry for love, while I am a dreamer. There are two kinds of courage: the courage that holds things together and the courage that throws them away. The first is more common; it is the cement of civilization; it is Lucy's. The second is the courage of drunks and suicides and mystics. My sign is impurity. By leaving, you understand, I proved that I was unworthy. I have tried to write Lucy since that winter—her only response has been to return my letters unopened. This is appropriate. She means for me to read them myself, those tired, clotted apologies. I am the writer of the words; she knows well enough they are not meant for her. But my words are sad companions and sometimes I remember ... well ... the icy water is up to my neck and I hear the ghost dog barking, she tried to warn me; yes, yes, I say, but I was blind.

Butterfly on a Pin

CLAIRE HARRIS

IN SUCH DREAM quickened dark
        everything looms   streetlights
corner bank   drugstore   even small houses in small
gardens gather their skirts   lean
in their intent night-windows a scythe-moon
glitters   and this is where a poem begins   innocent
insistent   *she finds herself at the corner*   dream
sense of stifled horror   how doom swirls   to know
once and for all what it is that eludes
and teases   in such a space the night is wet   dank
streetlights are blue / orange / red in pavement   a wind
a plastic bag that lifts and skids and blows
gleams   *ghostly as flimsy as i in the schoolyard*
twirling   twirling to music that not even the dream
reveals   what is a dream *without revelation*
i watch as from a great distance above how *she*
comes face to face with her self   that other that
in the dream *is glimmering*   trailing   not always
there   not all there   sudden as dreams are sudden

the city glows in her forehead
her eyes are islands   dark Caribbean seas
a yellow light on her face   deft peculiar grace
my mouth opens straining to fit in to   reach what
is there   on that street corner in Calgary below
the bluffs and dry poplars   *to fit into*
infiltrated by the bitter orange glow of midnight streets
to reach what there is teasing beyond the edges and
heaven's bruised light spilt i am crying   *i am Enid*
Thomas   my voice rising i think it is my voice   *i am*
Enid Thomas   voice as if my hands were tied behind
my back as if someone were denying me
a name *i am Enid Thomas*

She wakes. She is not. Not Enid Thomas. Let's make that clear.
She is Patricia Williams. Patricia Whittaker-Williams. Narrator of
her own story. And Patricia has never met, never even heard of
Enid Thomas. As if she didn't have problems enough. What with
a principal trying to get rid of her. And a publisher (m)ucking up
her book. If she smoked this would be a good time for a cigarette.
Bars of moonlight across the bed. The cross from her father's
coffin handed to her mother before the mattress and the
shovelfuls of earth and stone. Now, since her mother's death,
passed on to her. Mysterious in grey-blue light. She is hot, throat
sore, dry. The secret dream-life as strenuous as other rebellions.

The bed is a ghostly galleon floating the moonlit sea
Enid Thomas comes sailing   sailing

sailing
Enid Thomas comes sailing up to the old Bounty

When she wakes for the second time, grey light fills the room like an unwanted visitor. Her head is stuffed, bulging with the night's images. Walking about the room she touches everything, claims the bright spines of detective fiction, the Inca head, the Warri beads. She runs her hands over the television screen, the Brecht, the Spaniards. Reads the titles of all the Africans. Then stands shivering before the open window trying to pierce the storm-driven torment of snow to the bluffs and sentinel towers. As if to reassure herself. As if some vital truth of herself, some proof susceptible to the hand, the eye, lingered on the surface of things. So could bear witness.

When she first come to tell me this story, she say, 'Great Aunt, what happen here? What it is that really happen?' Is a question Patricia always asking, as if she suspicious, she want the whole world to have meaning. She is a child that never believe in accident, in chance. She tell me she read somewhere 'God don't play dice.' Well, if it ain't dice He playing, is card He pulling. But she can't believe that yet. It going to come. She got some more living to do.

Well to go back to the beginning. The whole trouble start with this dream she have. Simple as that. Patricia have a dream. Everybody have nightmares, but hers have to be dramatic! They have to have atmosphere! Is a worse thing: they have to have meaning! So she set like a comet on somebody path. She got to interfere with Enid Thomas. While she standing there at that

135

window, pretending that everything she see is hers ... she seeing changing it, you understand ... laser eyes ... that poor woman, Jocelyn, who don't even know her, who is getting out of bed, pushing those heavy blankets back, pulling her pink brushed nylon nightgown up over her head, and struggling a little, seeing as she forget the buttons at the neck, and liking how it soft, and how she smell she own sweetish warm scent, and wondering if is so Lloyd does smell it when he sleep over, and how she got to get that Ashley out of bed, and the porridge on the stove; that woman who don't believe in this cornflakes thing, and the child only picking up, picking up from that damn TV, but porridge does stick to the ribs, and she going to put an egg in it, no child of hers going to school hungry, and blast! the child have a dentist appointment this morning, she hope Marylyn, since she owe her one, going to cover when she take Ashley ... that place so far, is the LRT she going to have to take and then a bus, it go take two hours, if she go early and use the lunch hour perhaps sourface Garth ain't going to mind, but is a kind dentist, she talk real soft and she Black, and not stuck-up because she professional, but is so damn far; that woman who don't have no time for water trouble now, so is what wrong with the tap ... is only hot water coming, she ain't got time for this fiddling fiddling this morning, she really got to get in early ... ah is now the water coming good; that woman who stand under the shower who throw she head back who let water fall on she face like rain on the banks of the Lopinot river, the water pockmarked the cocoa trees darkening and glistening in the rain and the sound of it like a kind of thunder ... you see what I mean this Jocelyn who thinking like a normal person about what is real: what happen already, what she know going to happen again because it happen already, whose life ain't no fantasy, that woman going to have to deal all unexpected with Patricia who think she and God in this together. Together they creating everything she see, everything she

touch. I tell you life ain't no equal contest. Just think how no Carib,
no Iroquois, could ever imagine that somebody could leave their
own place, come thousands of miles to this place and think to take
he land from him, think he have a right to take he land, not only
he land, he world, he very self. And calling he 'Indian.' In the same
way this poor woman who once call she self Enid Thomas can't
even imagine what go happen to she, can't even prepare she self for
this thing what coming.

This morning she puts on the loose floating African gown she
affects, then drifts into the kitchen. From the door of the broom
closet she takes the huge barbecue apron and fastens it on. This is
an egg morning. There is the unexpected school holiday, the
snow on the balcony banked up against her glass wall, the soft
muffling sound of sky slanting into heavy white drifts, wind-
howl rising every now and again to penetrate the triple windows.
As if it were a whisper, a secret breathed in her ear, she begins to
hear words, phrases, the poem she dreamt last night. She
connects the blanks, begins to design the whole, to lay the poem
out in her head.

While the water for her poached egg boils, she cuts the crusts
off wholewheat slices. That done, she drops creamy Danish
butter into the small china jar, breaks an egg into the butter,
hesitates over thyme, a drop of tabasco, a sprinkle of cheese; or
salt, white pepper, a dusting of paprika. She decides on a plain
egg, but at the last moment fishes the jar out of the boiling water,
unscrews the stainless cover and adds a twist of black pepper to
the orange-yellow yolk. One part of her quietly enjoys the
breakfast ritual, the silence, the other part of her works furiously
at the poem she intends to write.

I can see Patricia sitting there now prim as prim, looking like she mother and planning something. The next thing you know she pick up the phone. She tell me it have twenty-three E. Thomas in the phone book, one E.J. Thomas, one Edwin Thomas, one Ethelridge Thomas, one Edgar, one Eulah. She figure it have to be one of the E. Thomases, but Ethelridge sound like a West Indian name so she try there first. Well, is an English man answer, she ask for Enid anyhow, but she knew was a waste of time. In she mind, Enid single. I have to tell you she ain't think twice about any of this. She have a writing plan, nothing else matter. I know how this shaping up it sound bad for my girl. You have to remember what they teach she there. Is a big country is Canada, is advanced, people there think theory matter more than human being. She learn a writer have a right to write anything, do anything for the writing. Never matter who life it bruise, who life rough up. Is freedom of speech all the way. If words does kill, she ain't grow enough to know that. Bull in a china shop. I tell you now, is so people delicate. Is easy to mangle them, and words does mangle better than iron. It ain't have no cripple like a soul-cripple, and no one so dangerous. But she ain't think so far yet. Patricia like a child. She want every life she see, every life she dream. She ain't want to live it, no, just to lay it out on paper, like a butterfly on a pin.

'Hello.'
   'May I speak to Enid Thomas, please?'
   'It don't have no Enid Thomas here.'
   'Is this Eulah Thomas?'
   'Yes. Whom am I speaking to, please?'

'I represent the Heritage school. It runs on Saturdays at the Multicultural Centre from 9:30 to 3:30 P.M. Its purpose is to put African and Caribbean children in touch with their heritage and themselves.'

'Well, we don't have any kids in this house. But it sound like a good idea.'

'Please tell your friends: we rely on word of mouth.'

She writes down the dialogue for nuance and flavour. Then continues the long trek through the E. Thomases.

'Hello.'

'May I speak to Enid Thomas, please?'

'I'm sorry, you must have the wrong number.'

'Oh, I'm sorry.'

'Goodbye.'

The brisk Northern formula speeds things up, but there are no more West Indians, no possible Enid Thomas.

The slender dark-skinned woman with the high cheekbones and great dark eyes is not present in any voice she has heard. Yet she knows she is there somewhere. And a great story with her. It has taken one and a half hours to phone. If she is to get anything done today she must hurry. She calls the various West Indian associations, she calls a few 'spokepersons,' she calls the food bank, the battered women's shelters (who incidentally would give out no information). She calls the Remand Centre, the hospitals, Unemployment Insurance. In all these places she is trying to get in touch with her cousin who came to Calgary and vanished. Sometimes she is surprised and cheered by the helpfulness. But she cannot find Enid Thomas. She has a cup of tea and decides to phone Immigration. Somebody must have a record of a West Indian woman, a recent immigrant to this country. Outside the snow has stopped. Blue, blue sky, white and cold. 'Bone-chilling' the radio says. She is so keyed up, so excited by the search, that her hands are trembling as she dials the Department. Somehow the very elusiveness of her dream-woman makes the search more important, the possible story looms fantastic in her mind. It never for one moment occurs to her that Enid Thomas may not exist. That she may be simply the figment of her dream, a name she once heard and last night put to a use of her own. Normally brimming with the psychological imperative, she does not recognize it now.

The Immigration Department is cautious; she is put on hold, then a man comes to the phone. Brennan wants to know where last she saw Miss Thomas. When she tells him Trinidad, he begins to suggest places she might check. They are chatting, getting on quite famously, reviewing various possibilities when she suggests the Multicultural Centre. He tells her they've moved to larger quarters, gives her the new address. She thanks him and is about to ring off when he says 'You will of course let us know if you find her.' When she hesitates, he tells her withholding information is a criminal offence. She has not of course given them her real name. Ethelready Thomas, she had said. Now outraged by the menacing tone, she simply puts down the receiver. 'Her own status may be in jeopardy.' She notes the weasel words as she writes it down. It is clear she will be able to find use for it.

———

If it had stop there, if only. Ain't those the saddest words. And every story have them, even if they ain't said aloud. But no, she had to put on she coat. In spite of all that snow and cold and wind, all what it had for weather, she cover she face with ski mask. Patricia don't ski, but she have ski mask to mind poor Jocelyn business. She put on big high boots and go down to the Multicultural Centre. She say she think perhaps somebody there could tell her something. All this because of a dream. Life is something, yes! Somebody dream and you life mash-up! Patricia tell me it was only eight blocks from her, and she couldn't call a taxi, so she walk. This is the same girl, everybody have to leave whatever they doing to come with the car and carry she wherever she want to go. That was when she in Trinidad, and she wasn't walking no place. Now she leave she warm house to walk eight blocks in ice. The same distance as from here to the river. I remember how I used to see Jocelyn coming there to the ledge, every Thursday with that boy from town ... Burri. Everybody know he was no good. Woman get under he skin and he jumpy. First one flower, then another, then another. When he get in that accident, the only person surprise was he. Jocelyn mother send she to she aunt in Calgary. Was for a visit: to have the child in secrecy. When she never come back, the poor mother tell everybody she going university. I don't know who believe that! By the time Jocelyn leave here, the child rounding she arms and thing, she hair thick and shining. A pretty-pretty girl ... They say if you don't trouble trouble, trouble wouldn't trouble you ... is a long penance that girl pay and paying still and for what ... she young, she innocent, she trust where she love.

———

Sheets of steel blow off the Bow river. Patricia is thrust forward with each gust, and in the end the wind carries her along the icy pavement at a half trot. Today ice frosts the mouth holes of ski masks, forms icicles on beards and moustaches. Normally noisy with the bustle of Adult Vocational Students on the way to class, the streets are lonely. Only the cars sweep by in the blue cold, and the heavy trucks grind past. Many of those who are out, red-faced and smiling, carry a jaunty air. Below the din of the asthmatic traffic, they exchange quick amused glances with her. There is an air of secret triumph, of camaraderie, as if this were an adventure. She smiles absent-mindedly at everyone who glances at her, and while part of her mind notes every stance and gesture, she is busy plotting the discovery of Enid Thomas. She expects the centre will have employment records, volunteer lists, mailing lists. If she can only get a lead, she is certain she will find Thomas. In any case, someone there may have heard of her. It's such a relief to escape the cold that she finds her way through the maze of corridors and security doors where her back door entry has led her, with ease. Finally, she comes to a hall enlivened with the bright, clear art of children. She passes through a half-opened door to a small reception room furnished with green plastic chairs, mustard walls, with posters of functions both past and future. On the receptionist's desk there is a brave croton. The person at the desk is about fifty, well-groomed. With great poise and assurance, Patricia introduces herself as a writer who has lived in the city for many years.

———————

'I have been asked by my aunt, quite old actually, to get in touch with a cousin, Enid Thomas.' The lie trips off her tongue, dances in the air. 'We know she's in the city, but no one has heard from her for years. Such a pity when families drift apart, don't you think?'

The receptionist agrees, 'Family is really important to ethnic people. We have gathering with children every Sunday. First the Mass, then the big dinner.'

'Do you really? Where are you from? Are you Latvian?'

The woman is surprised.

'How you know?'

'A friend whose father is Latvian. They farm outside of Beiseker. When I lived in the islands, we did the gatherings. I miss it now. I wonder if I could see your mailing lists? Perhaps my cousin is on them?'

'Today, everything is on computer.'

'Is the manager of the Centre in?'

'Oh yes! She got in early.'

Half an hour later Patricia sits at a long table in the bare conference room beyond. Through the open door she can hear and see what is obviously the multicultural daycare centre. No doubt because of the storm, there is an unusually wide age range of child painters happily attacking large sheets of brown paper tacked up on the walls of the corridor. She has already gone carefully through the mailing lists. No Enid, no E. Thomas. She has begun to work her way through a varied list of volunteers, paid workers, and possible volunteers.

'We update this list every three years. So anyone who has done anything here, even attending a meeting, is on this. We haven't done the deletions yet.'

Patricia is halfway through the list, and still certain that she will find Thomas, when she becomes aware that a woman is standing in the doorway of the daycare centre arguing with a furious small girl. The girl is about eight, and is making her feelings clear about staying in a daycare for toddlers. Something about the child's eyes, the diamond slant of her face, trigger a memory. Eight years old and still Pat to all and sundry, she is standing on the verandah of the house at Lopinot, staring horrified at a girl she doesn't know. A girl her own age, who, eyes glazed with admiration, is holding out a gift, two firm, plump mangoes, a spray of hibiscus. A girl, whose face marked with the same awe, the same suppressed excitement she has seen on the faces of the white girls chosen to present flowers to the Governor's wife, she never forget. She is told the girl's name is Jocelyn, Jocelyn Romero. And Jocelyn's shy smile comes and goes, but she stands there her hands rooted to her sides, making no effort to take the fruit from her. Finally, mother pushes her forward, she takes the fruit, says a low 'thank you.' Jocelyn runs back to her mother smiling hugely. Mrs. Romero smiles at her parents on the verandah, and with her daughter continues on their way to the village. But she stands staring after them, tears pouring down her cheeks. She has begun to sob uncontrollably.

That was the first time she meet Jocelyn, far as I know, was the only time they ever talk, if you can call it talk. Jocelyn give her the fruit, and she stand there bawling like somebody do her an injury. Embarrass everybody that child. Is not one cry she cry you know. After the mother take her inside, and she can't stop the child crying, I go in after them. I tell the mother leave her with me. I get a glass of cold water, a wash rag, and a towel. I pick her up off the pillows, and make her stand up. I wash she face and make her drink the glass well slow. And I ain't talk at all. Then I hold she hands by she side, and I make her breathe with me. Slow-slow breathing. Then we wash the face again. I say to her 'Tell me the truth, what take you so?' She look like a misery, but she ain't say nothing. I hold both she soft little hands in my cocoa hands, an I say 'So tell me, just tell me how it come.' She say Jocelyn just like she. 'What you mean? You is a girl, Jocelyn is a girl. All-you-two the same age. How you mean that?' She say it ain't have no difference. She could be Jocelyn, Jocelyn could be she. She look in Jocelyn eye and feel she self Jocelyn.

What if she wake up one morning and find she Jocelyn? She ain't want to be poor. What it have to say to child like that? Everybody know it have rich and poor in the world. She eight years old and she see is accident. Come to think of it, must be that what make her decide God don't play dice! Is a idea she don't want to risk. Anyway, I hold she hard-hard in my arms, rocking she. She say she ain't no 'royal personage.' Is so she used to talk. Plenty-plenty words. Read too much. I know right then that child go see trouble. The world is a hard place for them what see further than the eye. And for who have to live with them.

And is that same seeing that lead her to Jocelyn. For is Jocelyn self was there standing in the doorway with Ashley. Jocelyn who once, just once, call she self Enid Thomas.

Is when Burri leave she pregnant by the river and go he way. The mother know one time was disgrace. A child with no name for she one daughter. And she proud. She sit down and write she sister in Canada. Just as they getting everything together, the registry office burn down in Arouca. Well! The government announce how anybody could replace their papers with two sign pictures, and two important signatures, in any registry office in the area. They see they chance, Jocelyn and she mother. They seize it.

Is so it start, this Enid Thomas thing, so easy-easy. First, they take pictures with she hair crimp and comb up in a big Afro. Then they fool the headmaster to sign is Enid Thomas. You can't expect the man to remember everybody what pass through a district school. Children coming from everywhere. Next, they went quite Port-of-Spain to a real fashionable hairdresser to get it straighten and so. With that they take pictures and get the priest to sign is Jocelyn Romero. Is so she get the two identification, and the two passport to go to Canada. Once she pass in the country, was a easy thing to burn up Enid Thomas. She just go back to being she. The mother say she go to school nights. She bear a real pretty-pretty girlchild, that one, and intelligent for so. With nobody to help she. Is so when you too proud. They ain't even apply for immigration. Just sneak in the people country. Live like a thief. Always frighten-frighten. Prouder than pocket! It don't pay. Then one day Jocelyn look up and see my great-niece.

The two of them just start moving towards each other. They hold out their hands and they move across the room. Like is a magnet. Like they can't stop. They on track and they can't stop. People say thing like that is God's will. If I was God, lightning and thunder! That is slander, yes! Think about it. Something lead to blood and guts in the street, and you saying is God's will! What kind of God is that? Such a God! Too much like people for people to be safe. If He was wanting her to dead, you ain't think He could let her dead in bed. Private like! With some dignity! God! My foot! You ain't think is time priest come up with a reason what better than that?

They are laughing, their hands still clasped together, all of home in their palms, when she feels Jocelyn stiffen, sees her face go rigid. Ashley too is still, her eyes wide. She looks over her shoulders, sees two men hurrying down the long hallway towards them. Perhaps it's their slight swagger. She knows immediately. Immigration! Immigration! Immig …. Jocelyn grabs Ashley, races down that long hall.

'STOP! STOP! IMMIGRATION! ENID THOMAS! ENID THOMAS! STOP! IMMIGRATION!'

Shouldering Patricia aside, sweeping her against the wall, they run past. Startled, horrified beyond belief, she stands for a moment, and sees Jocelyn, her dark green coat flying out behind her, half dragging Ashley as she tugs at the heavy doors. The child struggles with her red backpack as she runs.

At the door, Ashley looks back, her small face intent, terrified. Patricia begins to run now, through halls that seem to narrow inexplicably, are dark, towards the brilliant patch of light at the door. She pushes the door open and finds that she is on Sixth Avenue, where cars and trucks come pounding through to the overpass, sweep over the Langevin to Memorial. As she reaches the curb, Patricia sees Jocelyn's scarf on the street, and looks wildly around. Then in the gap left between two trucks, she sees Jocelyn herself on the median. Such a look on her face! Together, their mouths widen into a scream. When the trucks move on she sees the Immigration officers on the opposite sidewalk, their lips shaped in an O, their eyes wide and staring. At first she does not see Ashley. And always afterwards Patricia is to believe she called 'Jocelyn come back! This way! Come back!' but she can never be sure what if anything she says before the tableau is complete.

On the far side of the far lane, a brown car has caught the child. She cannot see her head, her face; only the one arm lifted, a red rag of coat, a foot like a doll's in a white stocking. There is blood and mud. The snow clots and burns. Cars, trucks, buses are grinding to abrupt halt. The shrieks of tires, bang, jangle, crash of metal is repeated again and again as cars crash into the backs of cars. It seems to her that Jocelyn falls in slow motion to her knees in the snow; that the wind picks up, sends loose-leaf sheets whirling into the air; that the sky begins to fall in thick white drifts; that the distance between her curb and Jocelyn is all the years between that girl on the verandah, and the woman who dreamt.

Cement Woman

J.B. JOE

I'M GOING TO dress all in greys today. Grey socks under grey boots, grey pantyhose under my grey panties, grey bra under grey slip, grey sweater over a long, grey skirt ... grey blouse.

This is my grey day.

There's just a silver of purple light squeezing through a critch in my purple blinds. The dawn has arrived. I lie on my narrow cot, holding the edge of my quilt just under my chin. My body is perfectly straight, my toes aligned. I can feel my body settle into nothingness. In the far corner of the room a spider is preparing a web. She's a big, black spider, with red-gold tinges underneath her belly. Could be she's pregnant. I narrow my eyelids to slits, my pupils get large and the web becomes blue and dust flies from it as she works. There are sparks flying every which way, slowly becoming more and more blue until the room is filled with blue dust. Blue sparks from a pregnant spider. Outside giant ravens clink-clink together as they swoop over the river. I blink and the room returns to its normal hue. My body is in stillness underneath the quilt. I hear the stream running quickly and rippling along the jagged edges of yellow grasses clinging to the shore. A raven lets out a long screech.

There is always time to fling away the everyday.

I would hold the ashtray just under Wustenaxsun's chin. He would tell me to fling away the everyday. He was too weak to hold up his head, and sometimes to blink. He would lay there on his deathbed, telling me over and over again. There is always time to fling away the everyday. Always time. Always. I would flick the ashes from his cigarette with a long-handled paintbrush (number seven) as he sighed into his sleep. He wouldn't take long drags, just little intakes of breath to smell the smoke. He lay on his bed for four weeks like that. People came, but only to the doorway. He would not allow anyone else in the room.

The spider continues to work slowly and precisely. I get up from the cot and pick up my drum. The drum holds a new song for today and I beat it slowly, slowly, taking turns about the room. The light from the blinds follows as I beat the drum. I beat faster. I place my knees wide apart and spread my legs. I can feel pulls from deep in my stomach. I take small steps, increasing the speed of the drumming. The song is about a woman who learns all the ways of the hunt. She studies stories about Raven and his trickster ways to hunt. She studies how the air changes when a big animal enters her territory. She studies how her own body slips into the very breezes until she smells like her prey. Pieces of flesh line her bag. Flesh of the deer, the bear, the bait. She kills and recovers life for the old and for the children. The veins in my arms stick out like blue ribbons on the back of a garter snake. I can feel the pull in my stomach becoming almost unbearable. I continue to drum and to move about the room, with the new knowledge that the pain I feel is a signal. I feel myself falling forward and I stumble, but do not miss a beat. I feel the importance building and building. The song turns to high notes that last and last, my head tilts further and further back, and I can feel my hair brushing the small of my back. The song tells of the woman hunter entering the body of the deer. She feels his fear; she feels her blood rushing from one end of her body to the other in flashes of hot, lightning-like rushes. I kneel further back until the back of my head touches the floor and my pelvis is arched upward. I stay that way, letting the drum fall.

The song is ended and I get up slowly and I see that I have left blood on the floor. I go over to my dresser and open the top drawer. Inside is my jar of *tumulth*. I spread the red cream on my face until I see only my brown eyes. I go to my full-length mirror and proceed to spread *tumulth* all over myself. There is a soft coolness all over my body as the cream mixes with my sweat.

I walk like that, through my kitchen and then through my small living room and out the door. Outside it is cool and the sun is shedding its first light. The light hits the tips of the trees and casts long, thin lines of white dust-lines between the trees and among the branches of cedar. I place my feet into the stream. The yellow grasses tickle my feet. I enter slowly and walk to the middle of the stream until I am submerged. I close my eyes and I can feel my pupils filling everything.

I open my eyes and I am in a cave filled with the old ones and a golden light surrounds them. They have red bodies and all are naked. Their hair flies about their faces in a beautiful slow motion as they dance around a fire. I can feel Wustenaxsun. He is near. Oh, dear, dear Wustenaxsun. My husband. I see him. He is coming to me. I know that smile. I enter his eyes and we laugh together. He is restored to youth and he is strong again.

The flames from the fire light the cave until it is as bright as daylight, only, with a golden glow. The old ones come to Wustenaxsun and me and they kiss the tips of our fingers. They float away and continue dancing. They begin to chant, 'The Mother of All Things waits,' over and over again. There is a new knowledge for me. The Mother is waiting for me. I feel that knowledge very strongly. It tells me that if I turn to the entrance of the cave, she will be there. I am filled with the desire to see her and I turn. She is not there. I turn back to the fire and I find myself walking into the flames. Wustenaxsun lets me go and I can see him walking away as the flames wrap themselves around me. The *tumulth* crumbles from my body. I hear the chanting become faster and then all I hear is the whu-whu-whu over and over again. The flames unwrap themselves and I step out of the fire.

From deep inside of me I feel steel glowing red-hot and hardening all in the same instant. There is a movement of time that hits me. It feels like slow motion and decides itself into FLASHES OF FRACTIONS OF SECONDS! I scream. My pupils grow inside my eyes, filling everything. The steel becomes hard and cold. I align my toes and make my body still. The steel helps me. I close my eyes.

When I open them, I am in a shopping mall. There are people hurrying by me and they are grim-faced. Some of them pull angry babies. I look down and I am pulling my own angry baby. I have all grey clothes on and I turn to a man with powerfully built arms and legs. I smile at him. He wears soft, rich woollen clothes and he picks me up by the waist. The child falls on his face and screams. I scream. Blood falls from my eyes and I push the man away. He disappears and I close my eyes.

I open them and I am on a large, white ship and I am ordering *Oncorhynchus kisutch* from a waiter. I use only my eyes to place the order. He scampers away yelling, 'The lady wants coho!' I wear a gold dress. The dress has no top and my breasts rest on top of the table. There are eyes sitting on the edges of the table and I glare back at them. Blood begins to fall from their sockets and I drink it from cups placed at exactly measured intervals around the table, which turns from square, to oblong, to round as I pick up each cup. I find an eyeball in the cup, too late. It slips down my throat. I yell, 'Take a number!' and it pops back out. I pick up a fork and poke at it. It winks at me and wobbles away. I reach down to pick it up and the gold from my dress falls from my body like dust and scatters underneath the table and then it changes into the entrails of a deer. I put my face into the entrails and enter a room of spinning lights.

I fly and weave in and out of shadows. There are pinpricks of lights in my eye and they annoy me. I look down and I see that I have wings. They flutter only at the tips. They carry me about not by my power, not my power. It is the power of this room. Tears drop from my eyes and my pupils grow into everything. The dancing lights fade and everything is white and then darker shapes form themselves. The shapes are the people in the cave and they have stopped their blood. Time does not move. The shadows are still against the white walls. I breathe and my breath comes out in streams of pink and blue and orange and turquoise and purple and red and green and yellow.

I know she is here. I feel her blinking at me. The blinks are slow and steady, like a heartbeat. I turn away from the shadows and see an entrance. I hear the whu-whu-whu and it becomes more and more insistent, yet not louder. She stands there. She is blinking slowly, slowly. Blue air surrounds her. She sighs and her breath, too, is pink and blue and orange and turquoise and purple and red and green and yellow. I see my colours blending with her breath. She sits down, cross-legged.

I fly over and land just to her right. She turns to me and I enter her eyes. 'I am the Mother of All Things,' she says with her blink. Lights from our breath dance around our bodies and twinkle in the pupils of her eyes.

I tremble and she blinks that we, she and I are mothers. We

are mothers of gods. Indeed, she says, you are the mother of Wustenaxsun, who is himself a god. She said she was the fire and the water and the coloured air. She saw me before I was born. She told me I existed in the fire and the water and the air. I told her I was lonely all my life. I told her Wustenaxsun came and made me a whole new life. She said yes, he did that. She blinked that I, too, made my new life. She told me my new life was my own wish. It was the wish to become who I am. It was the wish of the cave-dancers. It was the wish of the Mother of All Things. It was my own wish. We are one. We are one with our wishes. She blinked these words at me and I sighed into her breath.

I blinked that I lived with the cement people. They wished me to be one of them and I lived as one of them. I lived a life in the cold streets. I performed before them, dancing in the dimness of a beaten-down old beer hall. I made them put dollars into my clothing. I closed my eyes. She said you do not live among the cement people, now. I opened my eyes and she blinked my life. She blinked that I live in the mountains. I live in the forest. I live in the house beside the stream. I live with the ravens. The steel bends inside and I am sad. She emits a long stream and her breath captures my breath. She closes her eyes and fades away. The coloured streams turn back to white.

I close my eyes, feeling the tears dropping onto my breasts. I open them and I am back in the cave. The fire is no longer burning and I see Wustenaxsun's image on the cave wall. I see images of the old ones on the cave wall, their hair flying in graceful folds in the hard rock of the cave. I fly back to the shopping mall, through the hurrying crowd of grim-faced people and back to the white ship and back to the stream. I walk out of the stream and go back into my house.

There is always time to fling away the everyday.

Wustenaxsun would sit in the chair and tell me over and over that our life together would not be ordinary. He told me he would see that I would not miss the cement people. I would assure him that I did not miss anything of the town, the long roads, the noise of the traffic. We would go to the stream and bathe while he sang the songs. He would sing and the ravens would clink-clink in the trees. He made our song about our meeting. It told of a dying man who wished to have a wife. It told of a young woman living in the land of cement. She was dancing for money in a run-down beer hall and he sang how he, Wustenaxsun, travelled into the land of cement and found her. The song told about how she struggled with her past life after she moved into his house. Wustenaxsun sang about how her past belonged with the crumbled rocks at the bottom of the ocean.

I go and take my grey clothes from my closet. They fit me perfectly and I pick up my rattle and, suddenly, I hear the Mother of All Things. She tells me to put aside fear. She tells me the steel remains and keeps me strong in the face of real substances. The substances that make up the cement, the fire and the water and the coloured air, are also the substances that make up my own self, the same substances that make up the Mother of All Things. She is in the cement. She is all. She is one. We are one.

I shake the rattle and I see my future. It contains my children. Their faces are smiling and round, their heads shining from their bathwater. They run and hide among the tress and count petals that fall from their fingertips. My children. I am a mother. I am a child.

I put away the rattle and the steel inside remains stronger than ever. I will go and find my future. I will go and find my husband who waits in the land of the cement people. Wustenaxsun found me. I will find my husband. I already picture him in my mind. He has brown hair and brown skin, golden from the sun, and his eyes have pupils that never narrow down.

Who knows but the wind and the rain that the man is not blonde? I am at the centre of the universe. I place the rattle in a soft cloth bag.

Twins

ERIC McCORMACK

PEOPLE SWARM FROM north and south, abandon the rituals of Saturday afternoon shopping expeditions and ball-game attendances, in favour of him. One thing: no children. He demands no admission fee, so he is entitled to say 'No children.' ('Say' won't do. Even that woman, his mother, the crutch on which he has limped his eighteen years, can never be sure of what he 'says.' He, therefore, writes. And has written, with his right hand, and with his left hand, 'NO CHILDREN.') For children are always the enemy: they suspect something, frown at him, tire of his performances, spoil everything. (As for dogs, they are wary too when they see him out walking. They sheath their tails. They slink growling to the opposite side of the road.) But, ah! The adults! The benches of the old church hall sag under the weight of their veneration. His devotees. How they admire him, how they nod their approval of his enigmatic sermons. He bestows upon them tears perhaps of gratitude, howls perhaps of execration. Either way, his votaries (the tall man with the blue eyes sits among them) are content.

The name of the one they come to hear? Malachi. That, at

least, is sure. He has a sickness (is there a name for it?). His sickness attracts them. He is the one who speaks with two voices, two different voices, at the same time. One of the voices trolls smoothly from the right side of his mouth. The other crackles from the left corner. How memorable, how remarkable, the sound of those two voices emanating from that one flexible mouth.

————————

Is his affliction, then, a miracle? No matter, it certainly complicates his life. It might be easier to bear if the two voices would speak in turns. But whenever he wants to say something, both voices chime in, overlap, each using an exactly equal number of syllables. Without euphony. There is discord in the sounds, there is dissent in the things said. What allures is the eerieness of it. The right-side voice thanks the tall man with the blue eyes for a gift he has brought:

'Thanks a lot.'
But the left-side voice remarks simultaneously:
'You're a fool.'
(Or is it vice versa? Often it is hard to tell.) The hearing is a difficult experience. Words sometimes twine together, like this—

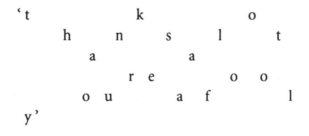

—braided like two snakes. Or a discrepancy in timing produces a long alien word: *'thyaounksreaalfoolot.'* Or exact synchronization causes a triple grunt: *'thyaounksreaalfootol.'* Leaving the hearer to rummage among fragments of words, palimpsests of phrases. Did he hear, 'you're a lot,' 'thanks a fool,' 'yanks a lol,' 'thou're a foot'?

A disease of words. When Malachi was a child, nobody was willing to diagnose his problem. No father to turn to. His mother never revealed who fathered him in the bed of her clapboard house, imitation brick, a mile north of town. Malachi squirmed out of the womb, purple. Let loose his inhuman shrieks. It was presumed his brain was not right.

See him at the age of ten. A boy unable to cope with anything scholastic. No one understands his noises, the drooling, the maddening grunts. Then, lying on the floor on a Sunday morning in June, in his mother's presence, tiger stripes of sun through the shutters on his prone body, he who has never written a word, picks up two pencils, one in each hand, and writes two messages simultaneously on a sheet of paper. With his right hand, a neat firm line:

'Help me, Mother.'

With his left hand a scrawl:

'Leave me alone.'

She stares at the paper, squints at his mouth, understands at last.

The why of it? How can such a thing have happened to her son? She expounds her theory to the tall man. (He has blue eyes, fine lines web the corners.) Malachi, she says, is meant to be twins, but somehow the division has not occurred, and he has been born, two people condemned to one body. Reverse Siamese twins. When she speaks of her theory in Malachi's presence, his face seems to confirm it. The right side blooms smooth, an innocent boy's. The left side shimmers with defiance. His head becomes unsteady, wobbles like an erratic planet with orbiting satellite eyes.

The German pastor is the force behind the audiences. He has spoken at some length to the tall man with the unflinching blue eyes. The pastor suggests to the mother that it will be good for the boy's confidence to exhibit himself. Is the pastor concerned about therapy or theology? Is he convinced that ultimately one voice or the other will prevail in open combat? Is he enthusiastic because he himself marvels at the sight? (Understands something?) He never misses an audience, sits rapt, engrossed in the turmoil in the face, the voice, of Malachi.

───────────

A sudden change. In the middle of the eighteenth year, tranquility. The harsh voice silent, the soft voice alone emerges from the twisted mouth, unencumbered. The left side of the mouth still curls, the left cheek still twitches, the left eye still glares. People still cringe ready for the snarl. But they wait in vain. And Malachi appears one morning wearing a black cloth patch over the left side of his face. A black triangle.

They ask him, 'What has happened to your other voice?'

He seems surprised at the question, as though unaware of the years of struggle. Soon, no one asks him any more, everyone becomes used to his masked face. They admire it, a portentous half moon. Malachi is a kind-hearted boy. His long illness is forgotten.

Three years later, he dies. At the age of twenty-one, he is sucked into the spirals of the river on a dark night. The verdict at the inquest: death by accident. The pathologist does not fail to take note of Malachi's remarkable tongue, wide as two normal tongues, linked by a membrane of skin. It must have made breathing difficult in those final moments. Malachi's mother attends the inquest, too distraught to be called as a witness. Afterwards, in the car park, the tall man catches up to her. He is about her age. (He has blue eyes. Fine lines web the corners.) He is silent. The sun beats down, mid-July, a day that ridicules mourning. She is still a woman of some beauty.

'It would have happened long ago,' she says, 'but for a pact. Three years ago I made them agree to it. One voice was to be in command all day, then after dark the other would take over. They just shifted the patch. But the girl drove them against each other again. They were jealous over her. They couldn't share her any longer. They needed to fight it out. But there was only the one body to hurt.'

She can no longer control herself. She sobs, and begs the man to leave her alone. A neighbour takes her by the arm to a waiting car. The man with blue eyes watches her go. He knows what must be done.

He drives to where the girl lives, a country motel, a run-down place, peeling green paint. She greets him solemnly, invites him up to her room. A lank-haired girl, not beautiful. He savours her quiet voice.

'He was a good friend to me,' telling of Malachi. 'I could trust him. On sunny days, we just sat by the river and talked. He said everything was under control. I was not to worry about his moods at night. I told him I liked him just as much at night when he switched the patch and changed his voice. At night, he would drink and drink, and make love. I told him how much I loved the feel of his tongue on my body. I suppose he didn't believe me.'

She asks the man with the blue eyes to wait with her for a while. He stays, consoles her. It is dark when he leaves.

————————

Ten years have passed. I am on an assignment to this country town. It is a pleasant summer's morning with, strangely, an arc of moon still visible in the bright sky like a single heelprint on glare ice. I am here to observe two children. They are twins, I am told. I am a little afraid of what I may find. I have a fear of children.

They don't look especially alike. One is fair, composed, the other is dark and fidgety. They are ten years old. They speak in a babble no one has been able to understand. Aside from themselves, that is, for they seem to understand each other.

I am here with the other observers because of a curious development. The twins have discovered how to communicate with the world. When they wish to be understood by others, we are told, they join hands and speak in unison. The sounds blend together and produce words that are intelligible.

The twins do not seem happy to meet our group of linguists, philologists, semanticists, etymologists, cynics, believers. Amongst us, the tall man with blue eyes. Fine lines web the corners. He seems anxious.

At length the boys' mother, who has not changed much over the years, asks them to speak to us. They hesitate, resolve to please her. They join hands. The two solo voices that, separately, are incomprehensible to the audience, blend together in a curious duet:

'Please help us, Father,' they cry.

This evokes great delight on the part of the other observers. They demand more. But the two little boys stand firm, hand-in-hand. They look directly at me. They repeat, for me, their shy, angry chant:

'Please help us, Father,' they plead.

They are staring directly at the man with blue eyes. He glances around fearfully, understands that the boys are making their appeal only to him. He looks at me in desperation. He can no longer refuse to acknowledge me. I, for my part, am ready to acknowledge him. I try to control my terror. I extend my hand to him. I find I am alone. Alone, for the first time, with my children.

Hiroko Writes a Story

DAVID McFADDEN

*I had one special reader and that was you .... I published
the book and I didn't give a damn for the critics. You did
me a great service. You gave me a confidence in myself that
I shouldn't have had alone .... If you thought something
was good, then it was fine as far as I was concerned.*
> — *Jean-Paul Sartre, in conversation*
> *with Simone de Beauvoir*

THE PROBLEM WITH this story is its lack of motivation. I'm
writing it, that is, merely because Hiroko wants me to. She
ordered it, like a dinner. I'm writing it by candlelight, having just
finished, speaking of dinner, a wonderful meal of fresh-caught
rainbow trout, capped with Hawaiian coffee and Courvoisier.
Hiroko is facing me as I type. She's typing on her own
typewriter, on the floor, facing me. The candlelight is in her eyes
and the moonlight sweeping through the windows is adorning
her hair as she sits tapping out her own version of what
happened earlier this evening, before we ate, before we came

165

home with that fresh-caught rainbow trout and cooked it, with green onions, mushrooms, tomatoes, oyster and soya sauce, rice, Jamaican hot sauce, washed down with Italian white wine, Japanese beer and the aforementioned cognac and coffee.

We were arguing. I called her a hypocrite, that is I didn't actually use that word, but I suggested she was being hypocritical for being critical of the kid who caught the fish. (I had to be careful to keep it light because a week or so earlier I lost my temper during an argument we were having about journalistic ethics in which she was being particularly stubborn and I told her I had absolutely no respect for her intelligence.) You pay people to kill your food, I said, like Peter Demeter paying some unknown goon to kill his wife, and Hiroko said that was irrelevant. She knew that, she said, that's not what she was talking about. She was sickened by the kid, she said, the way he spoke of the squaws and chubs, the fish he caught inadvertently when he was trying to catch the beautiful rainbow trout, the squaws and chubs he'd take from his hook angrily and bash against the docks until they were senseless, the fish he'd toss out into the green waters of Kootenay Lake for the gulls to swoop down on and gobble up.

'It's like a gardener weeding, pulling out the unwanted shoots,' I said, and I reminded her that the Japanese term for abortion was thinning-the-bamboo-shoots, the polite Japanese term, although that was obviously a red herring, as was the Demeter remark. 'Those chubs and squaws are useless as food,' I said, 'yet they eat thousands of young rainbow trout that would otherwise grow up like the one we just finished eating.'

'I know that,' she said, 'but didn't you hear what he was saying, the way he was talking? I asked him if he'd ever eaten squawfish or whatever you call them and he said he hated them, they tasted like mud, he hated them, didn't you hear him say that? He sounded positively evil, fanatic.'

'I thought he said he hated the taste of them,' I said. 'That's different. I thought that he probably had never tasted them, but had been merely repeating what his father had told him, and his father had probably never tasted them either.' And I told her about my childhood on the Grand River in Southern Ontario, how black families from Buffalo would come up the sacred and wondrous river in huge rowboats and ask if we had any catfish we didn't want. They'd say things like, 'I have a cat that just loves catfish,' and my brother—

'Is that why they're called catfish?' said Hiroko.

'What do you mean?'

'Because cats eat them?' She seemed serious.

'Could be.' I didn't smile. 'But cats like all fish so maybe it's more because they've got whiskers like cats—'

'Catfish?'

'Yes, and there's the dogfish that looks something like a dog—'

'Damp nose?'

'Very damp nose.'

And I told her we'd give these Negro families the catfish we'd caught and killed, the catfish that ate the young of the game fish we wanted to catch. And we knew these black families would take them home and make catfish stew not for their cats but for themselves. And maybe catfish were good to eat, but the idea of it made us sick. I didn't know, I'd never tasted one, my brother hadn't, my dad had never tasted one. Maybe it was just that they were so ugly and their skin was so smooth and unappetizing. They didn't have scales like ordinary fish, just smooth skin like soft patent leather, slightly slimy. Maybe that was why we never ate them. And they were too bony, we used to say. I have no idea what they tasted like. For all I knew they were better than rainbow trout. This was before white folks discovered the wonderful taste of catfish and chains of catfish restaurants began forming all over the southern United States. You eat them with honey.

'Soul food,' said Hiroko in the dim light. 'Ugly but delicious.' There were coloured rays coming out of her eyes, it made my stomach ache. She had her green-rimmed sunglasses pushed up over her long black hair and she was so lovely in her white sweater, tight beige pants that showed the slit between her legs, like the gill of a fish, and her white socks and high-heeled sandals.

'We were poor ourselves—'

'But proud.'

'Hm, yes.'

'Too proud to eat catfish.'

'Most definitely.'

'You weren't poor.'

'Maybe not.'

She had been coming home with groceries just as I pulled up in my car. We put the groceries away and opened a bottle of wine. I'd been thinking of getting together some fishing gear and going down there and fishing for an hour or two. Maybe I could make a routine of it. Get up an hour earlier in the morning, or fish for an hour after work and catch a rainbow or Kokanee for dinner. At any rate just relaxing, getting in touch with my childhood, so much of which in memory at least revolved around fishing.

You could see the government wharf from my place. There was someone on the dock, possibly a fisherman. I asked Hiroko if she wanted to take a walk down there before dinner and she said, 'Would you rather walk down there by yourself?' Such a beautifully sensitive woman.

'No. Come with me.'

As we approached the dock Hiroko stopped to watch some ducks floating in their pocket of paradise and I kept walking to the end where a kid was standing fishing. He was about sixteen, had a little moustache like Hitler, was serious-looking but overweight. He had an expensive-looking spinning outfit and was fishing with long thin worms. Casting out and reeling in slowly. 'Caught any yet?' I said, after standing there in silence for a minute to prove my sincerity. He walked across the dock to show his catch. He picked it up. A sixteen-inch rainbow wrapped in a plastic bag. 'Boy, does that ever look good,' I said. 'How much do you want for it?'

'It's not for sale,' he said in a peculiarly calm voice.

'Why not?'

'I'm going to take it home and have it for supper.'

'Just you?'

'Me and my mom.'

Hiroko took a break from her typing and poured us another Courvoisier. She was smiling. I figured her story was going well. I wondered what she was writing, how it was different from mine. I wondered if I'd be embarrassed, if she'd make me look uh naked perhaps.

The mountains. There were mountains all around the lake, the spot on the lake where we were standing. Elephant Mountain right in front of us, I could feel the eyes of bears staring down at us from three thousand feet, angrily. And far off in the distance, Kokanee Glacier sitting up there against the sky so impossibly high and cold and ancient, the same Kokanee Glacier you see on the label of Kokanee beer, the same Kokanee Glacier after which the Kokanee salmon was named.

'What's a Kokanee?' said Hiroko.

'It's a salmon,' I said, without certainty, 'a special freshwater salmon hybrid.'

The kid was saying he fished there all the time, winter, fall, all seasons. He usually used a wedding ring, he said, and I wondered where he got the wedding ring, he was too young to be married, thinking of a real wedding ring, had it belonged to someone now divorced, someone who didn't mind if you used it for bait?

But no, of course he was talking about a special kind of artificial lure, wittily called a wedding ring. 'And I load it up with maggots,' he said. There was a LIVE MAGGOTS sign in the window of the sporting goods store on Baker Street. 'Just cast out as far as you can and reel it in slowly. You can catch your limit of rainbows and Kokanees any day right from this dock.' As he spoke he was dangling his line in the water, bouncing it up and down, and he didn't have a wedding ring on the end, just a small weight, a small hook, and a bit of worm.

'What's a squaw?' I said.

'Oh, they're ugly things, really ugly. One this big,' he said, 'would have a mouth this big.' Holding his two hands curved as if he were holding a football.

'Yech.'

'I'll try to catch you one so you can see for yourself.' Just then his rod bent and he gave a yank. 'I got one,' he said.

He pulled it up. It wasn't exactly an ugly fish. It was white and silver, about six inches long, a nicely proportioned little fish. It looked good enough to eat.

At that point a strange thing happened to me: I grabbed the fish, popped it in my mouth and swallowed it whole, still flipping. I looked at the kid. He was standing there with his eyes spinning. 'Are you crazy?' he said, stammering, taking a step backwards.

'That was good. Catch me another one.'

Hey, I was kidding. I didn't really eat the fish. I didn't even think about it till now, typing out this story. What really happened, the kid just held the fish in his hand and said, matter-of-factly, maybe solemnly, 'It's a chub.'

'Not a squaw?'

'No, squaws are brown and ugly. Usually bigger. This is just a chub. They eat baby rainbows. This little one probably ate hundreds of baby rainbows already today. I always kill 'em.' With that he took the chub from the line and bashed its head against the wooden dock, then tossed it out into the lake about thirty feet. 'Let the gulls have it,' he said.

Hiroko turned to me with a sick look on her face. 'Let's go,' she said.

'Okay, just a minute.' I turned to the kid. 'I'll give you two bucks for that rainbow,' I said.

'I was going to cook it for supper.'

'I know. You already told me that. Three bucks and not a penny more.' I would have given him ten but it didn't seem right, I didn't want to spoil him.

'Okay.' He took the three dollars and the fish was mine.

We took it home and cooked it. You know all that.

Dinner conversation: Hiroko said she thought the kid was full of violence and repressed sexuality. I disagreed.

'I'll admit there is something sexual about the sport of fishing,' I said. 'Something wiggling on the end of your line.' When I was a kid I'd catch a fish then throw it back in without taking it off the hook, and pull it in again and again, trying to recapture the thrill of the catch, gradually becoming ashamed of myself. I didn't say anything about that though. Until now.

I thought about my friend Zip who was a commercial fisherman on Lake Huron until he drowned one miserable day in January while trying to take a fishing boat down to Kincardine for winter storage, drowned when a sudden storm came up and they turned around to head back to Southampton and struck an ancient submerged pier right in front of the beach where I'd first met him five years earlier, walking along the beach in his wet jeans, a Pentax around his neck, and he stopped and said he wanted to take a picture of me. Sweet Zip, a total innocent, a member of the Bahai faith, who complained only mildly about his landlady when she insisted he keep his door open when his girlfriend visited which wasn't often, sweet foul-smelling Zip, clothes always smelling of dead and rotting fish, and he was drowned along with the owner of the fleet, the boss, dying with the guy he was always complaining about, the boss, his stinginess, and their dying voices being recorded on tape by the owner's wife on her two-way radio, a transcript of the tape running on the front page of the local weekly a few weeks later. And the time I went fishing for whitefish with him, all the nets were full of suckers that day, and the crew had special hooks, ugly-looking spikes with wooden handles, and they'd shove the spike into the eye of each sucker and deep into the brain, pull the fish with its sucking little mouth out of the net and throw it overboard for the gulls, just like farmers weeding the crops. To save the whitefish stock, whitefish, my favourite fish, even better than fresh rainbow or Kokanee, although most of the catch on Lake Huron ends up in plants in New York for processing as frozen fish sticks.

Maybe I'd missed an important point. I didn't know. Writing was hard work. My typewriter was sitting on the coffee table. I was sitting on the sofa, typing. There was a candle burning away on each side of the typewriter, the smell of Black Sobranie cigarettes in the air, Hiroko sitting on the floor in front of me, facing me, her typewriter almost in her lap. She took a sip of Courvoisier then a puff of her Russian cigarette. There was a rock station from Spokane on the FM band and I realized I hadn't heard it all the time I'd been typing. Then I heard it. John and Yoko. They always played John and Yoko.

We'd been planning to go to the hot springs at Ainsworth to

soak in the hot water and listen to the Doukhobors singing hymns in the steaming caves. But suddenly in the middle of our conversation about the fisherman, Hiroko said she thought it'd be fun to write a story each about the meeting with the kid.

'Okay,' I said, tired, innocent as Zip, not looking forward to the long drive to Ainsworth. And Hiroko had an unpleasant memory or three connected with the hot springs, or rather pleasant memories it would be unpleasant to have to remember at this point, you know the sort of thing. And of course she had me convinced I had it in me, to write.

'What page are you on?'

She looked. 'Two,' she said, slightly drunk, her sunglasses fallen back down over her eyes.

'Double spaced?'

She looked again. 'No, single.'

'—' (as a character in Malcolm Lowry might say).

'I'm almost finished. Are you almost finished?'

'Yes, I think I am finished.'

'Well, give me just another five minutes will you? I'm not as fast a typist as you are. Besides, I can hardly see—'

'Then why don't you take off your sunglasses?'

'Oh! No wonder! Silly me! I could hardly read my own typing ... I actually spelled unburied "u-n-b-e-e-r-i-e-d."'

'Unburied?'

But she had taken off her glasses, placed them on the floor and was typing again.

Hiroko's Story

I am standing on the dock, leaning on the railing, looking down into the water. There are strange weeds growing almost up to the surface, stunted trees unable to reach for oxygen, unnatural forms, trees underwater. I remember swimming through them when I was a girl ... probably some lake in Japan ... terrified that they would imprison me and claim me as unnatural too. I wondered what lived in their depths. I still wonder.

Are these the kind of algae that are clogging the lakes in the Okanagan, I silently ask Walter.

Walter has gone on ahead, has left me to contemplate whatever. I didn't see him go down the stairs to the end of the dock, but I know that's where he has gone, partly because that's the only place left to go and partly because I think he felt the same magical pull to the end, to the end of the dock and somehow it is improper to stop halfway.

I know that I won't turn around now and return to the house up the hill, I know that I will also walk to the end, hidden at the base of the stairway, before I return. But for the moment I indulge at the halfway mark and gaze at the weeds and watch the ducks playing on the surface. I am struck by how at home they seem in an environment that is uncomfortable for me. The weeds! But once again it is just the surface. They skirt this way and that, but only surrender half of their bodies in ridiculous duck dives to only the very tops of the weeds.

Later when I ask Walter if ducks can breathe underwater he says of course not, they don't have gills, they're like whales. Did you know that whales can't breathe underwater? Yes, I reply, whales have to sound. And I feel as if I have passed an exam. But I probably only know that from reading *Moby Dick*. Literature is good for something.

But now I am watching the ducks weave along the surface of the weeds. Walter calls it a duck's paradise, and

Walter has already descended the rough wooden staircase to the point of the dock where the wooden platform is level with the water—or almost.

I am tired of waiting for him to come back to me so that I can ask him all the questions I have. When I was little I always got points for asking questions, but I think less for asking than for displaying my ignorance and making everyone around me feel secure. It's a habit I've never quite outgrown. Especially with men.

I walk cautiously to the edge and pace myself carefully down the stairway. Walter is standing at the end. I am aware of rotting boards under my feet. Save me, I scream, inwardly. Save me from the weeds.

But I arrive safely and Walter is excited. There is a boy. Later we agree at sixteen for his age. He is holding a fishing rod. I notice that the end of the fishing rod is pointed directly at Walter's penis and that as he points it Walter lifts his hands in the air above his head. I am in a land of gods.

Look, look what he's got, Walter says, and I stare at a plastic bag and the dead eyes of a fish gazing through and I think of the weeds. At the same time I remember the delicious fish I ate last week at Audrey's and I ask, 'What kind of fish is this?' A rainbow trout, Walter replies with envy. Later he tells me he wanted to ask the kid to sell it to him for our supper. Even there on the dock, looking at the plastic bag, I know that Walter is thinking of eating it and I'm hoping he won't ask because I don't think I should eat it, so shocked am I by the fact of its death. And I know that if I say anything about this I will be confronted with my gluttony at Audrey's the week before. How I raved about that fish and how I enjoyed it. And how later Audrey and I got in a nasty argument about Margaret Atwood. So to remain credible I have to be consistent now, but in fact I am caught directly in the contradiction and I feel slightly nauseous. Later when I mention my repulsion, Walter replies, 'But you certainly eat fish.' And I am caught wriggling.

The young boy is talking about a bride's ring. For a moment I think he wants to borrow my ring to attract the fish and I imagine all those diamonds, rubies and white gold at the bottom of the lake, or swimming in the stomach of the rainbow trout. I am almost ready to give it to him. I don't think either Walter or the boy notice my fingers go nervously to the ring on my finger and play with it, turn it, twist it until the diamonds are out of sight. But at the same time I wonder at the beauty of a fish who is attracted to brides' rings. There is a moment of indecision. Robin Blaser and the metaphysics of light.

I have already seen the young man in action. I heard him first as I was coming down the rotting stairway. I heard a dull thumping. A hollow sound on the wood. And looked up in time to see a silver flash of beauty in his hand. A silver you could look through forever. When the dull sound stopped he threw the silver flash back in the lake where it floated, unable to sink down into the weeds. It floated now—like us—on the surface. It seemed indecent. And I thought of Antigone. I thought of the unburied brothers. And I averted my eyes.

But now he is threading something, a worm, on his line. It looks like a worm but later he tells Walter he uses maggots as bait. I am shocked at the ease with which he puts a hook through the worm. The way I butter bread. He is all anticipation.

Walter asks the boy if he will catch another rainbow.

Walter too earned points by asking questions. Nope, replies the boy, I'll probably catch another chub or squaw. But Walter also earned points by knowing things, unlike me, and he points to a place where he saw a big fish jumping at the far end of the dock. There is a slight moment of indecision but the young fisherman disposes of Walter's report. Probably squaws, he says, with a sneer. I seen some sixty pounds. I ask if they are edible, hoping for their sake that they are. You can always tell a squaw, he says. Pull one out of the water and you can tell by the size of their mouth, great big, and he opens his hands a span wide. Then he laughs. You going to catch another rainbow? asks Walter. Nope, probably catch a chub or a squaw, and he casts his line with ease and grace and then pulls it slowly, up and down, through the surface of the water. I am holding my breath. I am silently praying that the next fish will be a rainbow, then I won't have to watch another dockside execution for its own sake. I can still hear the sound of the hollow wood.

Are squaws edible? I ask. Nope, wouldn't eat them, they taste like mud. I hate them, says the boy. They eat the trout, Walter explains. All this time my eyes are glued to the end of the line. When it finally surfaces I almost scream in frustration as I see another silver streak, a chub, squirming, flashing brilliantly in the evening light—a sea star? Then the young man turns and takes the fish off the line and bends to smash its head, unconscious, dead, before he throws it back to the gulls for food. Let's go, I hiss at Walter, and turn my back. I fly up the stairs, my ears plugged.

Later Walter, as we munch on cream cheese and tomato sandwiches, says in answer to one of my questions, yes, there is something sexual about having a fish on the end of your line, squirming.

The next morning Hiroko edited and retyped our manuscripts, incorporating her story into mine just as you see it now. 'You've got a publishable story here, congratulations,' she said and I could feel myself blushing but she didn't seem to notice, and she seemed pleased with herself, as if she'd given birth to me, and she suggested I try to sell it as my own to a magazine, under my own name, and I said I felt a little embarrassed by the discrepancies between her story and mine and I felt I'd be exposed as a liar, if not worse.

'Everyone knows writers lie,' she said. 'They're expected to. It's okay. Better than being boring. And the discrepancies are what make the story fascinating. Reality through different eyes.' She said she was the one who should be embarrassed but she wasn't. I looked at her. Her face had grown solemn, dark, old like the glacier.

'Turn your head and look at the picture on the wall,' I said. She turned. It was a framed reproduction of a fresco found ten years ago in a three-thousand-year-old villa during excavations on a small volcanic island in the Aegean. It showed a naked, brown-skinned boy, about sixteen, a string of green and gold fish in each hand.

Bardon Bus

ALICE MUNRO

I THINK OF BEING an old maid, in another generation. There
were plenty of old maids in my family. I come of straitened
people, madly secretive, tenacious, economical. Like them, I
could make a little go a long way. A piece of Chinese silk folded
in a drawer, worn by the touch of fingers in the dark. Or the one
letter, hidden under maidenly garments, never needing to be
opened or read because every word is known by heart, and a
touch communicates the whole. Perhaps nothing so tangible,
nothing but the memory of an ambiguous word, an intimate,
casual tone of voice, a hard, helpless look. That could do. With
no more than that I could manage, year after year as I scoured
the milk pails, spit on the iron, followed the cows along the
rough path among the alder and the black-eyed Susans, spread
the clean wet overalls to dry on the fence, and the tea towels on
the bushes. Who would the man be? He could be anybody. A
soldier killed at the Somme or a farmer down the road with a
rough-tongued wife and a crowd of children; a boy who went to
Saskatchewan and promised to send for me, but never did, or the
preacher who rouses me every Sunday with lashings of fear and

promises of torment. No matter. I could fasten on any of them, in secret. A lifelong secret, lifelong dream-life. I could go round singing in the kitchen, polishing the stove, wiping the lamp chimneys, dipping water for the tea from the drinking-pail. The faintly sour smell of the scrubbed tin, the worn scrub cloths. Upstairs my bed with the high headboard, the crocheted spread, and the rough, friendly-smelling flannelette sheets, the hot-water bottle to ease my cramps or be clenched between my legs. There I come back again and again to the centre of my fantasy, to the moment when you give yourself up, give yourself over to the assault which is guaranteed to finish off everything you've been before. A stubborn virgin's belief, this belief in perfect mastery; any broken-down wife could tell you there is no such thing.

Dipping the dipper in the pail, lapped in my harmless craziness, I'd sing hymns, and nobody would wonder.

'He's the Lily of the Valley,
The Bright and Morning Star.
He's the Fairest of Ten Thousand to my Soul.'

2

This summer I'm living in Toronto, in my friend Kay's apartment, finishing a book of family history which some rich people are paying me to write. Last spring, in connection with this book, I had to spend some time in Australia. There I met an anthropologist whom I had known slightly, years before, in Vancouver. He was then married to his first wife (he is now married to his third) and I was married to my first husband (I am now divorced). We both lived in Fort Camp, which was the married students' quarters, at the university.

The anthropologist had been investigating language groups in northern Queensland. He was going to spend a few weeks in the city, at a university, before joining his wife in India. She was there on a grant, studying Indian music. She is the new sort of wife with serious interests of her own. His first wife had been a girl with a job, who would help him get through the university, then stay home and have children.

We met at lunch on Saturday, and on Sunday we went up the river on an excursion boat, full of noisy families, to an animal preserve. There we looked at wombats curled up like blood puddings, and disgruntled, shoddy emus, and walked under an arbour of brilliant unfamiliar flowers and had our pictures taken with koala bears. We brought each other up to date on our lives, with jokes, sombre passages, buoyant sympathy. On the way back we drank gin from the bar on the boat, and kissed, and made a mild spectacle of ourselves. It was almost impossible to talk because of the noise of the engines, the crying babies, the children shrieking and chasing each other, but he said, 'Please come and see my house. I've got a borrowed house. You'll like it. Please, I can't wait to ask you, please come and live with me in my house.'

'Should I?'

'I'll get down on my knees,' he said, and did.

'Get up, behave!' I said. 'We're in a foreign country.'

'That means we can do anything we like.'

Some of the children had stopped their game to stare at us. They looked shocked and solemn.

3

I call him X, as if he were a character in an old-fashioned novel, that pretends to be true. X is a letter in his name, but I chose it also because it seems to suit him. The letter X seems to me expansive and secretive. And using just the letter, not needing a name, is in line with a system I often employ these days. I say to myself, 'Bardon Bus, No. 144,' and I see a whole succession of scenes. I see them in detail; streets and houses. LaTrobe Terrace, Paddington. Schools like large, pleasant bungalows, betting shops, frangipani trees dropping their waxy, easily bruised, and highly scented flowers. It was on this bus that we rode downtown, four or five times in all, carrying our string bags, to shop for groceries at Woolworths, meat at Coles, licorice and chocolate ginger at the candy store. Much of the city is built on ridges between gullies, so there was a sense of coming down through populous but half-wild hill villages into the central part of town, with its muddy river and pleasant colonial shabbiness. In such a short time everything seemed remarkably familiar and yet not to be confused with anything we had known in the past. We felt we knew the lives of the housewives in sun hats riding with us on the bus, we knew the insides of the shuttered, sun-blistered houses set up on wooden posts over the gullies, we knew the streets we couldn't see. This familiarity was not oppressive but delightful, and there was a slight strangeness to it, as if we had come by it in a way we didn't understand. We moved through a leisurely domesticity with a feeling of perfect security—a security we hadn't felt, or so we told each other, in any of our legal domestic arrangements, or in any of the places where we more properly belonged. We had a holiday of lightness of spirit without the holiday feeling of being at loose ends. Every day X went off to the university and I went downtown to the research library, to look at old newspapers on the microfilm reader.

One day I went to the Toowong Cemetery to look for some graves. The cemetery was more magnificent and ill-kempt than cemeteries are in Canada. The inscriptions on some of the splendid white stones had a surprising informality. 'Our

Wonderful Mum,' and 'A Fine Fellow.' I wondered what this meant, about Australians, and then I thought how we are always wondering what things mean, in another country, and how I would talk this over with X.

The sexton came out of his little house, to help me. He was a young man in shorts, with a full-blown sailing ship tattooed on his chest. *Australia Felix* was its name. A harem girl on the underside of one arm, a painted warrior on top. The other arm decorated with dragons and banners. A map of Australia on the back of one hand; the Southern Cross on the back of the other. I didn't like to peer at his legs, but had an impression of complicated scenes like a vertical comic strip, and a chain of medallions wreathed in flowers, perhaps containing girls' names. I took care to get all these things straight, because of the pleasure of going home and telling X.

He too would bring things home: conversations on the bus; word derivations; connections he had found.

We were not afraid to use the word love. We lived without responsibility, without a future, in freedom, with generosity, in constant but not wearying celebration. We had no doubt that our happiness would last out the little time required. The only thing we reproached ourselves for was laziness. We wondered if we would later regret not going to the Botanical Gardens to see the lotus in bloom, not having seen one movie together; we were sure we would think of more things we wished we had told each other.

4

I dreamed that X wrote me a letter. It was all done in clumsy block printing and I thought, that's to disguise his handwriting, that's clever. But I had great trouble reading it. He said he wanted us to go on a trip to Cuba. He said the trip had been offered to him by a clergyman he met in a bar. I wondered if the clergyman might be a spy. He said we could go skiing in Vermont. He said he did not want to interfere with my life but he did want to shelter me. I loved that word. But the complications of the dream multiplied. The letter had been delayed. I tried to phone him and I couldn't get the telephone dial to work. Also it seemed I had the responsibility of a baby, asleep in a dresser drawer. Things got more and more tangled and dreary, until I woke. The word shelter was still in my head. I had to feel it shrivel. I was lying on a mattress on the floor at Kay's apartment at the corner of Queen and Bathurst streets at eight o'clock in the morning. The windows were open in the summer heat, the streets full of people going to work, the streetcars stopping and starting and creaking on the turn.

This is a cheap, pleasant apartment with high windows, white walls, unbleached cotton curtains, floorboards painted in a glossy grey. It has been a cheap temporary place for so long that nobody ever got around to changing it, so the wainscoting is still there, and the old-fashioned perforated screens over the radiators. Kay has some beautiful faded rugs, and the usual cushions and spreads, to make the mattresses on the floors look more like divans and less like mattresses. A worn-out set of bedsprings is leaning against the wall, covered with shawls and scarves and pinned-up charcoal sketches by Kay's former lover, the artist. Nobody can figure a way to get the springs out of here, or imagine how they got up here in the first place.

Kay makes her living as a botanical illustrator, doing meticulous drawings of plants for textbooks and government handbooks. She lives on a farm, in a household of adults and children who come and go and one day are gone for good. She keeps this place in Toronto, and comes down for a day or so every couple of weeks. She likes this stretch of Queen Street, with its taverns and secondhand stores and quiet derelicts. She doesn't stand much chance here of running into people who went to Branksome Hall with her, or danced at her wedding. When Kay married, her bridegroom wore a kilt, and his brother officers made an arch of swords. Her father was a brigadier-general; she made her debut at Government House. I often think that's why she never tires of a life of risk and improvisation, and isn't frightened by the sound of brawls late at night under these windows, or the drunks in the doorway downstairs. She doesn't feel the threat that I would feel, she never sees herself slipping under.

Kay doesn't own a kettle. She boils water in a saucepan. She is ten years younger than I am. Her hips are narrow, her hair long and straight and dark and streaked with grey. She usually wears a beret and charming, raggedy clothes from the secondhand stores. I have known her six or seven years and during that time she has often been in love. Her loves are daring, sometimes grotesque.

On the boat from Centre Island she met a paroled prisoner, a swarthy tall fellow with an embroidered headband, long grey-black hair blowing in the wind. He had been sent to jail for wrecking his ex-wife's house, or her lover's house; some crime of passion Kay boggled at, then forgave. He said he was part Indian and when he had cleared up some business in Toronto he would take her to his native island off the coast of British Columbia, where they would ride horses along the beach. She began to take riding lessons.

During her breakup with him she was afraid for her life. She found threatening, amorous notes pinned to her nightgowns and underwear. She changed her locks, she went to the police, but she didn't give up on love. Soon she was in love with the artist, who had never wrecked a house but was ruled by signs from the spirit world. He had gotten a message about her before they met, knew what she was going to say before she said it, and often often saw an amorous blue fire around her neck, a yoke or a ring. One day he disappeared, leaving those sketches, and a lavish horrible book on anatomy which showed real sliced cadavers, with innards, skin, and body hair in their natural colours, injected dyes of red or blue illuminating a jungle of blood vessels. On Kay's shelves you can read a history of her love affairs: books on prison riots, autobiographies of prisoners, from the period of the parolee; this book on anatomy and others on occult phenomena, from the period of the artist; books on caves, books by Albert Speer, from the time of the wealthy German importer who taught her the word *spelunker*; books on revolution which date from the West Indian.

She takes up a man and his story wholeheartedly. She learns his language, figuratively or literally. At first she may try to disguise her condition, pretending to be prudent or ironic. 'Last week I met a peculiar character—' or, 'I had a funny conversation with a man at a party, did I tell you?' Soon a tremor, a sly flutter, an apologetic but stubborn smile, 'Actually I'm afraid I've fallen for him, isn't that terrible?' Next time you see her she'll be in deep, going to fortune tellers, slipping his name into every other sentence; with this mention of the name there will be a mushy sound to her voice, a casting down of the eyes, an air of cherished helplessness, appalling to behold. Then comes the onset of gloom, the doubts and anguish, the struggle either to free herself or to keep him from freeing himself; the messages left with answering services. Once she disguised herself as an old woman, with a grey wig and a tattered fur coat; she walked up and down, in the cold, outside the house of the woman she thought to be her supplanter. She will talk coldly, sensibly, wittily, about her mistake, and tell discreditable things she has gleaned about her lover, then make desperate phone calls. She will get drunk, and sign up for rolfing, swim therapy and gymnastics.

In none of this is she so exceptional. She does what women do. Perhaps she does it more often, more openly, just a bit more ill-advisedly, and more fervently. Her powers of recovery, her faith, are never exhausted. I joke about her, everybody does, but I defend her too, saying that she is not condemned to living with reservations and withdrawals, long-drawn-out dissatisfactions, inarticulate wavering miseries. Her trust is total, her miseries are sharp, and she survives without visible damage. She doesn't allow for drift or stagnation and the spectacle of her life is not discouraging to me.

She is getting over someone now; the husband, the estranged husband, of another woman at the farm. His name is Roy; he too is an anthropologist.

'It's really a low ebb falling in love with somebody who's lived at the farm,' she says. 'Really low. Somebody you know all about.'

I tell her I'm getting over somebody I met in Australia, and that I plan to be over him just about when I get the book done, and then I'll go and look for another job, a place to live.

'No rush, take it easy,' she says.

I think about the words 'getting over.' They have an encouraging, crisp, everyday sound. They are in tune with Kay's present mood. When love is fresh and on the rise she grows mystical, tentative; in the time of love's decline, and past the worst of it, she is brisk and entertaining, straightforward, analytical.

'It's nothing but the desire to see yourself reflected,' she says. 'Love always comes back to self-love. The idiocy. You don't want them, you want what you can get from them. Obsession and self-delusion. Did you ever read those journals of Victor Hugo's daughter, I think that's who it was?'

187

'No.'

'I never did either, but I read about them. The part I remember, the part I remember reading about, that struck me so, was where she goes out into the street after years and years of loving this man, obsessively loving him, and she meets him. She passes him in the street and she either doesn't recognize him or she does but she can't connect the real man any more with the person she loves, in her head. She can't connect them at all.'

5

When I knew X in Vancouver he was a different person. A serious graduate student, still a Lutheran, stocky and resolute, rather a prig in some people's opinion. His wife was more scatterbrained; a physiotherapist named Mary, who liked sports and dancing. Of the two, you would have said she might be the one to run off. She had blonde hair, big teeth; her gums showed. I watched her play baseball at a picnic. I had to go off and sit in the bushes, to nurse my baby. I was twenty-one, a simple-looking girl, a nursing mother. Fat and pink on the outside; dark judgements and strenuous ambitions within. Sex had not begun for me, at all.

X came around the bushes and gave me a bottle of beer.

'What are you doing back here?'

'I'm feeding the baby.'

'Why do you have to do it here? Nobody would care.'

'My husband would have a fit.'

'Oh. Well, drink up. Beer's supposed to be good for your milk, isn't it?'

That was the only time I talked to him, so far as I can remember. There was something about the direct approach, the slightly clumsy but determined courtesy, my own unexpected, lightened feeling of gratitude, that did connect with his attentions to women later, and his effect on them. I am sure he was always patient, unalarming; successful, appreciative, sincere.

6

I met Dennis in the Toronto Reference Library and he asked me out to dinner.

Dennis is a friend of X's, who came to visit us in Australia. He is a tall, slight, stiff, and brightly smiling young man—not so young either, he must be thirty-five—who has an elaborately courteous and didactic style.

I go to meet him thinking he may have a message for me. Isn't it odd, otherwise, that he would want to have dinner with an older woman he has met only once before? I think he may tell me whether X is back in Canada. X told me that they would probably come back in July. Then he was going to spend a year writing his book. They might live in Nova Scotia during that year. They might live in Ontario.

When Dennis came to see us in Australia, I made a curry. I was pleased with the idea of having a guest and glad that he arrived in time to see the brief evening light on the gully. Our house like the others was built out on posts, and from the window where we ate we looked out over a gully like an oval bowl, ringed with small houses and filled with jacaranda, poinciana, frangipani, cypress, and palm trees. Leaves like fans, whips, feathers, plates; every bright, light, dark, dusty, glossy shade of green. Guinea fowl lived down there, and flocks of rackety kookaburras took to the sky at dusk. We had to scramble down a steep dirt bank under the house to get to the wash-hut and peg the clothes on a revolving clothesline. There we encountered spider webs draped like tent-tops, matched like lids and basins with one above and one below. We had to watch out for the one little spider that weaves a conical web and has a poison for which there is no antidote.

We showed Dennis the gully and told him this was a typical old Queensland house with the high tongue-and-groove walls and the ventilation panels over the doors filled with graceful carved vines. He did not look at anything with much interest, but talked about China, where he had just been. X said afterwards that Dennis always talked about the last place he'd been and the last people he'd seen, and never seemed to notice anything, but that he would probably be talking about us, and describing this place, to the next people he had dinner with, in the next city. He said that Dennis spent most of his life travelling, and talking about it, and that he knew a lot of people just well enough that when he showed up somewhere he had to be asked to dinner.

Dennis told us that he had seen the recently excavated Army Camp at Sian, in China. He described the rows of life-size soldiers, each of them so realistic and unique, some still bearing traces of the paint which had once covered them and individualized them still further. Away at their backs, he said, was a wall of earth. The terracotta soldiers looked as if they were marching out of the earth.

He said it reminded him of X's women. Row on Row and always a new one appearing at the end of the line.

'The Army marches on,' he said.

'Dennis, for God's sake,' said X.

'But do they really come out of the earth like that?' I said to Dennis. 'Are they intact?'

'Are which intact?' said Dennis with his harsh smile. 'The soldiers or the women? The women aren't intact. Or not for long.'

'Could we get off the subject?' said X.

'Certainly. Now to answer your question,' said Dennis,

turning to me, 'They are very seldom found as whole figures. Or so I understand. Their legs and torsos and heads have to be matched up usually. They have to be put together and stood on their feet.'

'It's a lot of work, I can tell you,' said X, with a large sigh.

'But it's not that way with the women,' I said to Dennis. I spoke with a special, social charm, almost flirtatiously, as I often do when I detect malice. 'I think the comparison's a bit off. Nobody has to dig the women out and stand them on their feet. Nobody put them there. They came along and joined up of their own free will and some day they'll leave. They're not a standing army. Most of them are probably on their way to someplace else anyway.'

'Bravo,' said X.

When we were washing the dishes, late at night, he said, 'You didn't mind Dennis saying that, did you? You didn't mind if I went along with him a little bit? He has to have his legends.'

I laid my head against his back, between the shoulder blades.

'Does he? No. I thought it was funny.'

'I bet you didn't know that soap was first described by Pliny and was used by the Gauls. I bet you didn't know they boiled goat's tallow with the lye from the wood ashes.'

'No. I didn't know that.'

7

Dennis hasn't said a word about X, or about Australia. I wouldn't have thought his asking me to dinner strange, if I had remembered him better. He asked me so he would have somebody to talk to. Since Australia, he has been to Iceland, and the Faeroe Islands. I ask him questions. I am interested, and surprised, even shocked, when necessary. I took trouble with my make-up and washed my hair. I hope that if he does see X, he will say that I was charming.

Besides his travels Dennis has his theories. He develops theories about art and literature, history, life.

'I have a new theory about the life of women. I used to feel it was so unfair the way things happened to them.'

'What things?'

'The way they have to live, compared to men. Specifically with aging. Look at you. Think of the way your life would be, if you were a man. The choices you would have. I mean sexual choices. You could start all over. Men do. It's in all the novels and it's in life too. Men fall in love with younger women. Men want younger women. Men can get younger women. The new marriage, new babies, new families.'

I wonder if he is going to tell me something about X's wife; perhaps that she is going to have a baby.

'It's such a coup for them, isn't it?' he says in his malicious, sympathetic way. 'The fresh young wife, the new baby when other men their age are starting on grandchildren. All those men envying them and trying to figure out how to do the same. It's the style, isn't it? It must be hard to resist starting over and having that nice young mirror to look in, if you get the opportunity.'

'I think I might resist it,' I say cheerfully, not insistently. 'I don't really think I'd want to have a baby, now.'

'That's it, that's just it, though, you don't get the opportunity! You're a woman and life only goes in one direction for a woman. All this business about younger lovers, that's just froth, isn't it? Do you want a younger lover?'

'I guess not,' I say, and pick my dessert from a tray. I pick a rich creamy pudding with pureed chestnuts at the bottom of it and fresh raspberries on top. I purposely ate a light dinner, leaving plenty of room for dessert. I did that so I could have something to look forward to, while listening to Dennis.

'A woman your age can't compete,' says Dennis urgently. 'You can't compete with younger women. I used to think that was so rottenly unfair.'

'It's probably biologically correct for men to go after younger women. There's no use whining about it.'

'So the men have this way of renewing themselves, they get this refill of vitality, while the women are you might say removed from life. I used to think that was terrible. But now my thinking has undergone a complete reversal. Do you know what I think now? I think women are the lucky ones! Do you know why?'

'Why?'

'Because they are forced to live in the world of loss and death! Oh, I know, there's face-lifting, but how does that really help? The uterus dries up. The vagina dries up.'

I feel him watching me. I continue eating my pudding.

'I've seen so many parts of the world and so many strange things and so much suffering. It's my conclusion now that you won't get any happiness by playing tricks on life. It's only by natural renunciation and by accepting deprivation, that we prepare for death and therefore that we get any happiness. Maybe my ideas seem strange to you?'

I can't think of anything to say.

8

Often I have a few lines of a poem going through my head, and I won't know what started it. It can be a poem or rhyme that I didn't even know I knew, and it needn't be anything that conforms to what I think is my taste. Sometimes I don't pay any attention to it, but if I do, I can usually see that the poem, or the bit of it I've got hold of, has some relation to what is going on in my life. And that may not be what seems to be going on.

For instance last spring, last autumn in Australia, when I was happy, the line that would go through my head, at a merry clip, was this:

'Even such is time, that takes in trust—'

I could not go on, though I knew trust rhymed with dust, and that there was something further along about 'and the dark and silent grave, shuts up the story of our days.' I knew the poem was written by Sir Walter Raleigh on the eve of his execution. My mood did not accord with such a poem and I said it, in my head, as if it was something pretty and lighthearted. I did not stop to wonder what it was doing in my head in the first place.

And now that I'm trying to look at things soberly I should remember what we said when our bags were packed and we were waiting for the taxi. Inside the bags our clothes that had shared drawers and closet space, tumbled together in the wash, and been pegged together on the clothesline where the kookaburras sat, were all sorted and separated and would not rub together any more.

'In a way I'm glad it's over and nothing spoiled it. Things are so often spoiled.'

'I know.'

'As it is, it's been perfect.'

I said that. And that was a lie. I had cried once, thought I was ugly, thought he was bored.

But he said, 'Perfect.'

On the plane the words of the poem were going through my head again, and I was still happy. I went to sleep thinking the bulk of X was still beside me and when I woke I filled the space quickly with memories of his voice, looks, warmth, our scenes together.

I was swimming in memories, at first. Those detailed, repetitive scenes were what buoyed me up. I didn't try to escape them, didn't wish to. Later I did wish to. They had become a plague. All they did was stir up desire, and longing, and hopelessness, a trio of miserable caged wildcats that had been installed in me without my permission, or at least without my understanding how long they would live and how vicious they would be. The images, the language, of pornography and romance are alike; monotonous and mechanically seductive, quickly leading to despair. That was what my mind dealt in; that is what it still can deal in. I have tried vigilance and reading serious books but I can still slide deep into some scene before I know where I am.

On the bed a woman lies in a yellow nightgown which has not been torn but has been pulled off her shoulders and twisted up around her waist so that it covers no more than a crumpled scarf would. A man bends over her, naked, offering a drink of water. The woman, who has almost lost consciousness, whose legs are open, arms flung out, head twisted to the side as if she has been struck down in the course of some natural disaster—this woman rouses herself and tries to hold the glass in her shaky hands. She slops water over her breast, drinks, shudders, falls back. The man's hands are trembling, too. He drinks out of the same glass, looks at her, and laughs. His laugh is rueful, apologetic, and kind, but it is also amazed, and his amazement is not far from horror. How are we capable of all this? his laugh says, what is the meaning of it?

He says, 'We almost finished each other off.'

The room seems still full of echoes of the recent commotion, the cries, pleas, brutal promises, the climactic sharp announcements and the long subsiding patterns.

The room is brimming with gratitude and pleasure, a rich

195

broth of love, a golden twilight of love. Yes, yes, you can drink the air.

You see the sort of thing I mean, that is my torment.

9

This is the time of year when women are tired of sundresses, prints, sandals. It is already fall in the stores. Thick sweaters and skirts are pinned up against black or plum-coloured velvet. The young salesgirls are made up like courtesans. I've become feverishly preoccupied with clothes. All the conversations in the stores make sense to me.

'The neckline doesn't work. It's too stark. I need a flutter. Do you know what I mean?'

'Yes. I know what you mean.'

'I want something very classy and very provocative. Do you know what I mean?'

'Yes. I know exactly what you mean.'

For years I've been wearing bleached-out colours which I suddenly can't bear. I buy a deep-red satin blouse, a purple shawl, a dark-blue skirt. I get my hair cut and pluck my eyebrows and try a lilac lipstick, a brownish rouge. I'm appalled to think of the way I went around in Australia, in a faded wraparound cotton skirt and T-shirt, my legs bare because of the heat, my face bare too and sweating under a cotton hat. My legs with the lumps of veins showing. I'm half convinced that a more artful getup would have made a more powerful impression, more dramatic clothes might have made me less discardable. I have fancies of meeting X unexpectedly at a party or on a Toronto street, and giving him a shock, devastating him with my altered looks and late-blooming splendour. But I do think you have to watch out, even in these garish times; you have to watch out for the point at which the

splendour collapses into absurdity. Maybe they are all watching
out, all the old women I see on Queen Street: the fat woman with
pink hair; the eighty-year-old with painted-on black eyebrows;
they may all be thinking they haven't gone too far yet, not quite
yet. Even the buttercup woman I saw a few days ago on the
streetcar, the little, stout, sixtyish woman in a frilly yellow dress
well above the knees, a straw hat with yellow ribbons, yellow
pumps dyed-to-match on her little fat feet—even she doesn't aim
for comedy. She sees a flower in the mirror: the generous petals,
the lovely buttery light.

I go looking for earrings. All day looking for earrings which I
can see so clearly in my mind. I want little filigree balls of silver,
of diminishing size, dangling. I want old and slightly tarnished
silver. It's a style I well remember; you'd think the secondhand
stores would be sure to have them. But I can't find them, I can't
find anything resembling them, and they seem more and more
necessary. I go into a little shop on a side street near College and
Spadina. The shop is all done up in black paper with cheap,
spooky effects—for instance a bald, naked mannequin sitting on
a stepladder, dangling some beads. A dress such as I wore in the
fifties, a dance dress of pink net and sequins, terribly scratchy
under the arms, is displayed against the black paper in a way that
makes it look sinister, and desirable.

I look around for the tray of jewellery. The salesgirls are busy
dressing a customer hidden from me by a three-way mirror. One
salesgirl is fat and gypsyish with a face warmly coloured as an
apricot. The other is spiky and has a crest of white hair
surrounded by black hair, like a skunk. They are shrieking with
pleasure as they bring hats and beads for the customer to try.
Finally everybody is satisfied and a beautiful young lady, who is
not a young lady at all but a pretty boy dressed up as a lady,
emerges from the shelter of the mirror. He is wearing a black

197

velvet dress with long sleeves and a black lace yoke; black pumps and gloves; a little black hat with a dotted veil. He is daintily and discreetly made up; he has a fringe of brown curls; he is the prettiest and most ladylike person I have seen all day. His smiling face is tense and tremulous. I remember how when I was ten or eleven years old I used to dress up as a bride in old curtains, or as a lady in rouge and a feathered hat. After all the effort and contriving and my own enchantment with the finished product there was a considerable letdown. What are you supposed to do now? Parade up and down on the sidewalk? There is a great fear and daring and disappointment in this kind of display.

He has a boyish, cracking voice. He is brash and timid.

'How do I look, momma?'

'You look very nice.'

10

I am at a low point. I can recognize it. That must mean I will get past it.

I am at a low point, certainly. I cannot deal with all that assails me unless I get help and there is only one person I want help from and that is X. I can't continue to move my body along the streets unless I exist in his mind and in his eyes. People have this problem frequently, and we know it is their own fault and they have to change their way of thinking, that's all. It is not an honourable problem. Love is not serious though it may be fatal. I read that somewhere and I believe it. Thank God I don't know where he is. I can't telephone him, write letters to him, waylay him on the street.

A man I had broken with used to follow me. Finally he persuaded me to go into a café and have a cup of tea with him.

'I know what a spectacle I am,' he said. 'I know if you did have any love left for me this would destroy it.'

I said nothing.

He beat the spoon against the sugar bowl.

'What do you think of, when you're with me?'

I meant to say, 'I don't know,' but instead I said, 'I think of how much I want to get away.'

He reared up trembling and dropped the spoon on the floor.

'You're free of me,' he said in a choking voice.

This is the scene both comic and horrible, stagy and real. He was in desperate need, as I am now, and I didn't pity him, and I'm not sorry I didn't.

11

I have had a pleasant dream that seems far away from my waking state. X and I and some other people I didn't know or can't remember were wearing innocent athletic underwear outfits, which changed at some point into gauzy bright white clothes, and these turned out to be not just clothes but our substances, our flesh and bones and in a sense our souls. Embraces took place which started out with the usual urgency but were transformed, by the lightness and sweetness of our substance, into a rare state of content. I can't describe it very well, it sounds like a movie-dream of heaven, all banality and innocence. So I suppose it was. I can't apologize for the banality of my dreams.

12

I go along the street to Rooneem's Bakery and sit at one of their little tables with a cup of coffee. Rooneem's is an Estonian Bakery where you can usually find a Mediterranean housewife in a black dress, a child looking at the cakes, and a man talking to himself.

I sit where I can watch the street. I have a feeling X is somewhere in the vicinity. Within a thousand miles, say, within a hundred miles, within this city. He doesn't know my address but he knows I am in Toronto. It would not be so difficult to find me.

At the same time I'm thinking that I have to let go. What you have to decide, really, is whether to be crazy or not, and I haven't the stamina, the pure, seething will, for prolonged craziness.

There is a limit to the amount of misery and disarray you will put up with, for love, just as there is a limit to the amount of mess you can stand around a house. You can't know the limit beforehand, but you will know when you've reached it. I believe this.

When you start really letting go this is what it's like. A lick of pain, furtive, darting up where you don't expect it. Then a lightness. The lightness is something to think about. It isn't just relief. There's a queer kind of pleasure in it, not a self-wounding or malicious pleasure, nothing personal at all. It's an uncalled-for pleasure in seeing how the design wouldn't fit and the structure wouldn't stand, a pleasure in taking into account, all over again, everything that is contradictory and persistant and unaccommodating about life. I think so. I think there's something in us wanting to be reassured about all that, right alongside—and at war with—whatever there is that wants permanent vistas and a lot of fine talk.

I think about my white dream and how it seemed misplaced. It strikes me that misplacement is the clue, in love, the heart of the problem, but like somebody drunk or high I can't quite get a grasp on what I see.

What I need is a rest. A deliberate sort of rest, with new definitions of luck. Not the sort of luck Dennis was talking about. You're lucky to be sitting in Rooneem's drinking coffee, with people coming and going, eating and drinking, buying cakes, speaking Spanish, Portuguese, Chinese, and other languages that you can try to identify.

13

Kay is back from the country. She too has a new outfit, a dark-green schoolgirl's tunic worn without a blouse or brassiere. She has dark-green kneesocks and saddle oxfords.

'Does it look kinky?'

'Yes it does.'

'Does it make my arms look dusky? Remember in some old poem a woman has dusky arms?'

Her arms do look soft and brown.

'I meant to get down on Sunday but Roy came over with a friend and we all had a corn roast. It was lovely. You should come out there. You should.'

'Some day I will.'

'The kids ran around like beautiful demons and we drank up the mead. Roy knows how to make fertility dolls. Roy's friend is Alex Wather, the anthropologist. I felt I should have known about him but I didn't. He didn't mind. He's a nice man. Do you know what he did? After dark when we were sitting around the fire he came over to me and just sighed, and laid his head on my lap. I thought it was such a nice simple thing to do. Like a St. Bernard. I've never had anybody do that before.'

Two Heroes

BPNICHOL

1

IN THE BACK garden two men sit. They are talking with one another very slowly. Around them things are growing they are not conscious of. They are only conscious of each other in a dim way, enough to say that this is the person they are talking to. Much of it appears a monologue to us as we approach them over the wide lawn, thru the bower of trees, sit down between them on the damp grass & prepare to listen. There is nothing left to listen to. They have ceased speaking just as we appeared. They have finally reached an end to their conversation.

2

Once a long time ago they talked more easily. Once a long time ago the whole thing flowed. They were young men then. They had gone west at fifteen to fight in the metis uprising, urged on by accounts they read in the papers, & they would talk then as if they were conscious of future greatness, made copies of the letters they

mailed home, prepared a diary, talked, endlessly & fluently, talked
to whoever'd listen, of what they'd done, what they planned to do,
but i did not know them then, never heard them, never heard
them, can only write of what i learned second hand.

3

When the fight was over & Riel was dead & Dumont had fled
into the states, they went home again & became bored. They
would sit up nights talking about how grand it had been when
they were fighting the half breeds & reread their diaries &
dreamed of somehow being great again.

When the Boer War began they went to Africa to fight there &
oh it was great & yes they kept their journals up to date &
made more copies of letters that they mailed home, tying up
their journals & letters as they were done, tying them up in
blue ribbons they had brought along expressly for that
purpose, placing them inside waterproof tin boxes, locking
the locks & hiding the keys. They were very happy then. If you
had asked them they would not have said it was the killing but
rather the war for, as they were fond of saying, it was thru war
a man discovered himself, adventuring, doing heroic things as
everything they'd read had always taught them.

Their friends
stayed home of course, working in the stores, helping the cities
to grow larger, trying to make the country seem smaller & more
capable of taking in in one thought. And they thought of the
two of them, off then in Africa, & it was not much different to
them from when they'd been out west, Africa & the west being,

after all, simply that place they weren't.

4

Time passed. No one heard much from either of them. In GRIP one day appeared a story titled BILLY THE KID & THE CLOCKWORK MAN & it seemed there were things in the story reminded all their friends of both of them, even tho it wasn't signed, & they all read it & talked about it as if the two men had written it, chatting over cigars & brandy, over tea & cakes, as the late afternoon sun streamed thru the windows of their homes on the hill looked down towards the harbour, over the heart of the city, the old village of Yorkville & the annex, the stands of trees still stood there, & wondered aloud if they'd ever see the two of them again, if they would ever receive again those letters, those marvellous tales that so delighted them, & after all it would be very sad if they were dead but then no one had seen them for so long that they were not very real to them.

5

There are some say Billy the Kid never died the story began. There are some say he was too tough to die or too mean, too frightened or too dumb, too smart to lay his life down for such useless dreams of vanity, of temporary fame & satisfaction, that he & Garret were friends after all & Mr. Garret would never do such cruel deeds to anyone as sweet as young William was. I don't know. I read what I read. Most of it's lies. And most of those liars say Billy the Kid died.

There are those who like sequels though. There are those who like the hero to return even if he is a pimply-faced moron who never learned, like most of us, we shoot our mouths off with ease, never care where the words fall, whose skull they split, we're too interested in saying it, in watching our tongues move & our lips flap & Billy & his gun were a lot like that.

When you read a sequel you might learn anything. Of how Pat Garret faked Billy's death, of how the kid went north to Canada or south to Mexico or sailed off to Europe as part of a wild west show, but there's no sequel you'll read again that'll tell you the strange tale of Billy the Kid & the clockwork man.

6

Billy was in love with machines. He loved the smooth click of the hammers when he thumbed his gun, when he oiled & polished it so it pulled just right. He loved to read the fancy catalogues, study the passing trains, & when he met the clockwork man well there was nothing strange about the fact they fell in love at first sight.

It was a strange time in Billy's life. He was thinking a lot about his death & other things. He had this feeling he should get away. And one day, when he was oiling the clockwork man's main spring, Billy made the clockwork man a proposition & the clockwork man said he'd definitely think about it & he did, you could hear his gears whirring all day, & that night he said to Billy sure kid i'll go to Africa with you & he did, even tho they both felt frightened, worried because they didn't know what'd happen.

When they got to Africa it was strange. It wasn't so much the elephants or lions, the great apes or pygmies, the ant hills that were twenty feet high, it was the way their minds changed, became deranged I suppose, even more than Billy's had always been, so that they began seeing things like their future, a glimpse of how they'd die, & they didn't like it.

7

It was a good story as stories go. Most of their friends when they'd read halfway thru it would pause & wonder which one of them was Billy & which one the clockwork man & each had their own opinion about which of the two men was the bigger punk & which the more mechanical. The women who had known them would smile & say well isn't that just like him or point a finger at some telling sentence & wink & say that's just the way he'd talk.

The mothers of the two men agreed they should never have given them those mechanical banks or shiny watches & would not read much further than this. But the fathers who'd bought them their first guns were proud of them & read it all the way thru to the end even tho they didn't understand it & hoped they'd never have to read it again.

8

The problem with Africa was it was kind of damp & there was no good place where you could buy replacement parts. The clockwork man began to rust. He & the Kid sat up all night talking, trying to figure some way to save the clockwork man's life. There was no way. They were too broke to go back home. Besides they'd already seen that this was how the clockwork man would die.

They got fatalistic. They got cynical & more strange. They took to killing people just to make the pain less that was there between them but people didn't understand. They tried to track them down, to kill them, & they fled, north thru the jungles, being shot at as they went, as they deserved to be, being killers they weren't worth redeeming.

One day they ran out of bullets & that was the end. They tried to strangle a man but it lacked conviction & they just kept heading north, feeling worse & worse, & the men & women pursuing them cursed a lot but gave up finally when the bodies stopped dropping in their path.

The Kid & the clockwork man made it thru to the Sahara with no one on their tracks & lay down on their backs in the sand dunes & gazed up at the stars & fell asleep.

9

When Billy the Kid awoke the clockwork man was very still. There were ants crawling in & out of the rivet holes in his body & a wistful smile on his face. This looks like the end Bill he said & I can't turn to embrace you. Billy wiped away a tear and sighed. The clockwork man was only the second friend he'd ever had.

The clockwork man's rusty tin face was expressionless as he asked you going to head someplace else Bill & Bill shrugged & said i don't really know as there's much place else to go to & the clockwork man sighed then & looked pained as only a clockwork man can as the blowing sand sifted thru the jagged holes in his sides, settling over the gears, stilling them forever.

Goodbye Bill he said. Bill said goodbye & got up & walked away a bit before he'd let himself cry. By the time he'd dried his eyes & looked back the clockwork man was covered in by sand & Billy never did find his body even tho he looked for it.

208

10

There are strange tales told of Billy the Kid, of what happened next. I heard once he met up with Rimbaud in a bar & started bedding down with him & the gang he'd fallen in with. I don't know. There are a lot of stories one could tell if gossip were the point of it all.

If he went back home he died a quiet old man. If he stayed in Africa he was never heard from again. He's not a fit man to tell a story about. Just a stupid little creep who one time in his life experienced some deep emotion & killed anyone who reminded him of his pain.

And the clockwork man was no better than him. All we can say of him is he was Billy the Kid's friend & tho it's true there's very few can make that claim well there's very few would want to.

11

One year the two men returned. They were both greyer & quiet. They didn't speak much to friends. They'd talk but only if they thot you weren't listening. They had their tin boxes full of diaries, of letters, but then they never showed them, never opened them, never talked about what it was had happened over there between them. They were still the best of friends. They bought a house in the annex & lived together. They opened a small stationer's shop & hired a lady to run it for them & lived off that income. They never wrote again. In their last years, when we came to visit them a lot, they'd stare at my cousins & me & say yes it was grand but & gaze away & not say anything else unless you eavesdropped on the two of them when they were sure you weren't listening. Even then it was only fragmentary sentences they said, random images that grew out of ever more random thots & I was never able, tho I listened often, to draw the whole thing together into any kind of story, any kind of plot, would make the sort of book I longed to write. They died still talking at each other, broken words & scattered images, none of us around, unable to see or hear us if we had been, because of their deafness & their failing sight.

Art

LEON ROOKE

I TOLD THE WOMAN I wanted that bunch down near the pine grove by the rippling stream.

Where the cow is? she asked.

I told her yep, that was the spot.

She said I'd have to wait until the milking was done.

The cow mooed a time or two as we waited. It was all very peaceful.

How much if you throw in the maiden? I asked.

Without the cow? she asked, or *with*?

Both would be nice, I said.

But it turned out a Not For Sale sign had already gone up on the girl. Too bad. It was sweet enough with her out of the picture, but not quite the same.

I took my cut bunch of flowers and plodded on behind the cow over to the next field. I wanted a horse too, if I could get one cheap.

Any horses? I asked.

Not today, they said.

Strawberries?

Not the season, I was told.

At home, I threw out the old bunch and put the new crop in a vase by the picture window so the wife might marvel at them when she came in from her hard day's grind.

I staked the cow out front where the grass was still doing pretty well.

It was touch-and-go whether we'd be able to do the milking ourselves. It would be rough without a shed or stall.

———————

Oh, hand-painted! the wife said when she came in.

I propped her up in the easy chair and put up her feet. She looked a trifle wind-blown.

Hard day? I asked.

So-so, she said.

I mixed up a gin and tonic, nice as I knew how, and lugged that in.

A touch flat, she said, but the lemon wedge has a nice effect.

I pointed out the cow, which was tranquilly grazing.

Sweet, she said. Very sweet. What a lovely idea.

I put on the stereo for her.

That needle needs re-doing, she observed. The tip needs retouching, I mean.

It will have to wait until tomorrow, I told her.

She gave me a sorrowful look, though one without any dire reproach in it. She pecked me a benign one on the cheek. A little wet. I wiped it off before it could do any damage.

The flowers were a good thought, she said. I appreciate the flowers.

Well, you know how it is, I said. What I meant was that one did the best one could—though I didn't really have to tell her that. It was what she was always telling me.

She was snoozing away in the chair as I tip-toed off to bed. I was beginning to flake a little myself. Needed a good touch-up job from an expert.

We all do, I guess. The dampness, the mildew, the *rot*—it gets into the system somehow.

Not much to be done about it, however.

I thought about the cow. Wondered if I hadn't made a mistake on that. Without the maiden to milk her, there didn't seem to be much *point* in having a cow. Go back tomorrow, I thought. Offer a good price for the maiden, the stream, and the whole damned field.

Of course, I could go the other way: find a nice seascape somewhere. Hang that up.

Well, sleep on it, I thought.

——————————

The wife slipped into bed about two in the morning. That's approximate. The paint job on the hour hand wasn't holding up very well. The undercoating was beginning to show through on the entire clock face, and a big crack was developing down in the six o'clock area.

Shoddy goods, I thought. Shoddy artisanship.

Still, we'd been around a bit. Undated, unsigned, but somewhere in the nineteenth century was my guess. It was hard to remember. I just wished the painter had been more careful. I wished he'd given me more chest, and made the bed less rumpled.

Sorry, baby, she said. Sorry I waked you.

She whispered something else, which I couldn't hear, and settled down far away on her side of the bed. I waited for her to roll into me and embrace me. I waited for her warmth, but she remained where she was and I thought all this very strange.

What's wrong? I said.

She stayed very quiet and did not move. I could feel her holding herself in place, could hear her shallow, irregular breathing, and I caught the sweep of one arm as she brought it up to cover her face. She started shivering.

I am so sorry, she said. I am so sorry. She said that over and over.

Tell me what's wrong, I said.

No, she said, please don't touch me, please don't, please don't even think about touching me. She went on like this for some seconds, her voice rising, growing in alarm, and I thought to myself: Well, I have done something to upset her, I must have said or done something unforgivable, and I lay there with my eyes open wide, trying to think what it might be.

I am so sorry, she said. So very very sorry.

I reached for her hand, out of that hurting need we have for warmth and reassurance, and it was then that I found her hand had gone all wet and muddy and smeary.

Don't! she said, oh please don't, I don't want you to hurt yourself!

Her voice was wan and low and she had a catch in her voice and a note of forlorn panic. I lifted my hand away quickly from her wetness, though not quickly enough for I knew the damage already had been done. The tips of my fingers were moist and cold, and the pain, bad enough but not yet severe, was slowly seeping up my arm.

My drink spilled, she said. She snapped that out so I would know.

Christ, I thought. Oh Jesus Christ. God help us.

I shifted quickly away to the far side of the bed, my side, away from her, far as I could get, for I was frightened now and all I could think was that I must get away from her, I must not let her wetness touch me any more than it had.

Yes, she said shivering, do that, stay there, you must try and save yourself, oh darling I am so sorry.

We lay in the darkness, on our backs, separated by all that distance, yet I could still feel her warmth and her tremors and I knew there was nothing I could do to save her.

Her wonderful scent was already going and her weight on the bed was already decreasing.

I slithered up high on the sheets, keeping my body away from her, and ran my good hand through her hair and down around her warm neck and brought my face up against hers.

I know it hurts, I said. You're being so brave.

Do you hurt much? she said. I am so terribly, terribly sorry. I was dozing in the chair and opened my eyes and saw the dark shape of the cow out on the lawn and for an instant I didn't know what it was and it scared me. I hope I haven't hurt you. I've always loved you and the life we had in here. My own wounds aren't so bad now. I don't feel much of anything anymore. I know the water has gone all through me and how frightful I must look to you. Oh please forgive me, it hurts and I'm afraid I can't think straight.

I couldn't look at her. I looked down at my own hand and saw that the stain had spread. It had spread up to my elbow and in a small puddle where my arm lay, but it seemed to have stopped there. I couldn't look at her. I knew her agony must be very great and I marvelled a little that she was being so brave for I knew that in such circumstances I would be weak and angry and able to think only of myself.

Water damage, I thought, that's the hardest part to come to terms with. The fear that's over you like a curse. Every day you think you've reconciled yourself to it and come to terms with how susceptible you are, and unprotected you are, and then something else happens. But you never think you will do it to yourself.

Oil stands up best, I thought. Oh holy Christ why couldn't we have been done in oil.

You get confident, you get to thinking what a good life you have, so you go out and buy yourself flowers and a goddamn cow.

I wish I could kiss you, she moaned. I wish I could.

My good hand was already behind her neck and I wanted to bring my head down on her breasts and put my hand there too. I wanted to close my eyes and stroke her all over and lose myself in the last sweetness I'd ever know.

I will too, I thought. I'll do it.

Although I tried, I couldn't, not all over, so I stroked my hand through her hair and rolled my head over till my lips gently touched hers.

She sobbed and broke away.

It's too much, she said. I'm going to cry. I am, I know I am.

Don't, I said. Don't. If you do, that will be the end of you.

The tears burst and I spun above her, wrenching inside, gripping the sheet and wiping it furiously about her eyes.

I can't stop it! she said. It's no use. It burns so much but I can't stop it, it's so sad but I've go to cry!

She kept on crying.

Soon there was just a smear of muddled colour on the pillow where her face had been, and then the pillow was washing away.

The moisture spread, reaching out and touching me, filling the bed until at last it and I collapsed on the floor.

Yet the stain continued widening.

I had the curious feeling that people were already coming in, that someone already was disassembling our frame, pressing us flat, saying, Well here's one we can throw out. You can see how the house, the cow, etc., have all bled together. You can't recognize the woman anymore, or see that this once was a bed and ... well it's all a big puddle except those flowers. Flowers are a dime a dozen, but these are pretty good, we could snip out the flowers, I guess, give them their own small frame. Might fetch a dollar or two, what do you say?

Tall Cowboys and True

GAIL SCOTT

THEY LEFT ANNABELLE, the last frontier town, tucked under an outcrop in the Rockies. She locked her sleeping children carefully in the house trailer. She took his hand. They walked along the Main Street. Horses and oil tankers, hitched to the same posts, fitfully pawed the sand, eyeing each other nervously.

They passed a poor cowboy sitting in front of a blind house. His faded knees jerked over the edge of the verandah. It was hot. He waited for the explosion of bullets that would never come. He feared taking refuge in the house. It was damp and dark. The cowboy preferred the risks of riding the rail.

They came to the edge of town. The man squeezed her close. 'Baby, you're beautiful,' he said. 'We'll go places.' The woman's hand hardened. He told her to stop worrying. 'Your sister will take care of your kids.' Back in the trailer camp the women played cards while they waited in silence from the children's screams for the men to come in their loud boots, the beer gushing out of their bottles. She looked at his red sneakers and nodded.

They stuck out their thumbs in the dust by the side of the road. The cars went by oiled black. The metal waves reflected the sun painfully into her eyes. Behind her a crowd of ragged vultures cowered over an old Indian. A woman in sky-blue moccasins waded unevenly through the long grass towards him. After her ran a small girl with grasshopper legs. The young woman licked her dry lips and smiled at the child. The man saw nothing. He lit a cigarette, his thoughts galloping confidently towards the sunset.

Her children were alone in the trailer. They slept soundly. It was hot. She wanted to sit. The pavement was sticky. She raised her head towards the horizon. It was blocked by the carefully ticking crotches of grain elevators. She looked wildly around. Behind her, out of a deep ditch, rose a powerful white charger. A cowboy stepped forth in rich embroidered boots and a cowlick. He motioned them into a bower of plush purple flowers. She took her place in the back between rows of blossoming shirts, her man in the front, and the great white beast retook to the ditch leaping forward between the cool clay walls well below the burning gilt fields.

At last. She leaned back, breathing in the blotting paper perfume. Her man opened a soft volume of Lenin, his sneakers tucked noiselessly beneath him. The clay walls sped by outside. The children's cries receded. Through the rear-view mirror the cowboy watched her. She ignored him and sighed. 'Twas a good ride. His eye fastened on her moist lips slowly smiling at how her father hated hitchhikers. Oh the children. The children alone. She quickly looked up. The eye was fixed on the button on her left breast. DES AILES AUX GRENOUILLES it said over a small blue frog with butterfly wings. 'You French?' asked a well-honed voice tightening like a lasso.

From behind the cool white columns of my verandah I watch Véronique Paquette walk by terriblement décolletée. The priest gives her shit every Sunday but she still does it just the same. Across the street Claude Bédard flirts on the front lawn with his girlfriend Bijou. 'Frogs,' says my father one of three bank managers all brothers. Drunkenly, they flex their flabby lip muscles at Véronique from their rocking chairs on the hot prairie. Then my father looks up at me and screams: 'Stick your nose back in that Bible. It's Sunday.'

'You French?' repeated the well-honed voice honed even higher.

'Non. No. Mais. Ispeakit.' A nervous tickle titillated the pit of her stomach. The cowboy's eye flinted like steel in the mirror. He shifted into pass and the charger rose above the deep ditch into dry fields flaring with the fluorescent yellow of rape. There could be a fire you know. What if the fields caught on fire? The children alone in the trailer. The eye stared steadily. Her man was unaware. He turned the pages of State and Revolution, his sneakers tucked snugly beneath him. She began talking to the eye quite fast. 'It's beautiful here. Blue sky up above. All you need is love ...' She stopped, guilty, ridiculous.

'Yeah.' The eye watched. The voice grew golden again. 'Big money on the gasline. Bad years back home I come up here to work.' The eye unlatched from her lips and pointed prayerfully towards the horizon still cluttered with wooden crotches. 'Seas of oil,' he said. The car hood shone in the midnight sun. 'You from near here?' she asked in a small voice. He took a picture from his breast pocket and passed it back. 'My mother and I farm in Mackenzie.' The woman had a fair wide forehead like her son. Her lips were drawn back tight in a bun. On the back it was written: 'He who putteth his hand on the plough and looks back is in danger of internal damnation.'

Interlude: A True Cowboy In Love

'Look Ma no hands.' The police car careens sideways across the road
and hovers breathlessly over the high precipice. I put my hand on
my stomach, staring at the perpendicular cliffs hanging below.
'Don't look back,' says the new hitchhiker (with red sneakers) to me
and my children beside me. He winks in a friendly way. A clitoris
pounds in a closet. My uncle has sold me a trailer to spare the
family the shame. I am heading down the valley to hide my
fatherless children. I will push it through the pass to Annabelle. The
car tears away from the temptation and shoots into a curve. 'The
thing about police cars,' says the fat young driver whose pants stink,
'is you can drive no hands to hold onto guns.' Close behind him on
the front seat Ma smiles from under her greasy grey hair. 'I always
buy police cars,' he says to us over his shoulder. 'The way we take off
from stopsigns in curstairs. Boy do the cops get peed off.'

Ma puts her hand close to his unsavoury crotch. He grins at her
recklessly. We are descending rapidly as a white balloon towards the
town where the trailer is. The cliffs become sandy like a setting from
a cowboy movie sparsely henspecked with sage. But the cherry
blossoms waft up from the valley below where the Ogo Pogo has just
surfaced between the feet of a petrified water-skier. 'Maybe we'll see
the Ogo Pogo,' says Ma. Her hand creeps closer to the crotch. He
steps on the gas. We race through the town. There are cowboy boots
on the hotel steps and frightened moustaches on coffee cups in the
windows. On top of the false front façade it reads: CONFESS AND YE
SHALL SAVE.

The charger cowboy's crotch was impeccable. His Adam's apple
had tightened into a thoughful knot. 'You know you French and
folks in the east don't give prairie farmers their due profits for
wheat flour.' At last her man looked up from Lenin. 'Capitalism,'

he said. 'Centralized markets. You're too far from Toronto.'

The eye in the mirror turned momentarily towards him, but was intercepted en route by a six-inch fuchsia statue on the dashboard. It returned immediately to fix again on her face.

'Do you know the Lord?'

She looked out the window. The rape fields were still on fire under the horizontal rays of the midnight sun. It was hot in the trailer. The baby whimpered weakly while the three-year-old pushed the stool against the refrigerator door. He always did that to reach the handle and then of course he couldn't open the door because the stool was in the way. But suddenly the charger dipped again, not into a ditch but into a long narrow valley whose walls were cool blue green. The eye filled with a great grey light.

'This is called the Valley of the Peace,' said the voice. 'It was filled with fornicating good-for-nothings (excuse me miss he tipped his Stetson) with whom the settlers had to fight and teach how to farm.' They were approaching a long silver river. Aging deep-tanned faces rocked in rocking chairs in front of dilapidated wooden dwellings crushed by the ranch houses superimposed on their roofs.

'I don't feel so good,' she said to her companion. 'It's only a cat,' he said absently. His eyes were on the works of Lenin whose picture was strong and stern on the front cover. The fuchsia Christ smiled from the dashboard. The baby whimpered. She wished she could put a clothespin on his tongue. Peace. Now I'll have peace. Her father's hand is rummaging through the clothespin box. She feels the pain as he pries open her mouth.

The cowboy handed her a pamphlet. 'I am the way, the truth, and the life,' it said. She smiled sweetly, bravely, lips closed to hide her bleeding tongue. The tickle in her stomach turned into a giggle and rose to gag her. 'I've seen it before,' she said. Back in the trailer camp the boy was pushing a spoon between the baby's dried compressed lips.

'You mean you know Jesus?' asked the cowboy. His well-honed voice took on the timbre of a stained-glass window. 'It's always nice to meet someone else spreading the word of the Lord so that the peoples of the world can learn the errors of their ways.'

'That's racist,' she thought, spreading wide her legs in silent protest.

'That's racist,' said the Leninist, looking up from his book. 'Really,' she said, handing back the pamphlet. The hyenic laughter swelled within her. She squeezed her lips to keep it from hissing out. 'I've seen it ...'

The cowboy stopped the car. He turned around to look at her. She snapped her knees together. 'You mean you know the Lord and you looked back. He who putteth his hand on the plough and looks back is in danger of internal damnation.'

The charger minced forward, uncertainly. 'I don't feel so good,' she said to her companion, putting her hand on her stomach. 'The children ...' He didn't seem to hear. He said nothing.

The brilliant quicksilver river approached. 'In his relationship with you,' said the voice, hued higher again, 'did Jesus uh hold up his end of the stick?'

'What d'ya mean?' she said. Like giant feces the laughter moved in to her mouth. The eye saw the fishtails glittering at the corners of her lips.

'Help,' she said to her companion. He didn't hear for he was furiously writing notes on the flyleaf of his book.

'The stick,' said the cowboy more insistently, beginning to squirm in his seat. 'The stick. In his bargain with you did Jesus hold up his end of the stick?' Underneath like an error ran the quicksilver river.

The cowboy squirmed harder on his seat. 'The stick. Whose end of the stick?' he said louder. 'It was you who didn't hold up your end of the stick. It was, wasn't it? Wasn't it, huh? I know it was.'

Interlude: A True Cowboy In Love

The police car is racing down into the valley, past the sagebrush into the beautiful cherry blossoms. 'It smells like cherry Chiclets,' says the son. 'I bet anything we see the Ogo Pogo,' says Ma. The hitchhikers have left. She fondles his pee-stained pants.

'I know Jesus,' cried the cowboy, rocking back and forth. He grabbed the statuette, waving it over his head like a lariat. 'Jesus never lets down his end of the stick. The stick …'

The car hit the valley wall with a thud. The red sneakers floated out the window, the laces trailing behind like spurs. The cowboy bled over the steering wheel, pierced by the statuette.

Her strawberry hair rose up the side of the valley. At last it was dark on the prairie. She sped through the cool night in her white shirt and white jeans. The baby was almost dead. She would get there before the headlines. In the first light of dawn she sped past the ticking-crotch silhouettes into Annabelle. The cops were coming towards her trailer with can openers. She sped through the dust past the poor cowboy's house. He slept on the rail, his spurs stuck in the wood. Gently (so as not to waken him) she untangled his legs and shoved his young strong body into the damp dangers of the forbidden house. She reached her trailer two strides before the police. Then she was fleeing, a child in each arm, their skin soft and warm against hers. New sensations were rising along her spine.

Home

CAROL SHIELDS

IT WAS SUMMER, the middle of July, the middle of this century, and in the city of Toronto one hundred people were boarding an airplane.

'Right this way,' the lipsticked stewardess cried. 'Can I get you a pillow? A blanket?'

It was a fine evening, and they climbed aboard with a lightsome step, even those who were no longer young. The plane was on its way to London, England, and since this was before the era of jet aircraft, a transatlantic flight meant twelve hours in the air. Ed Dover, a man in his mid-fifties who worked for the Post Office, had cashed in his war bonds so that he and his wife, Barbara, could go back to England for a twenty-one day visit. It was for Barbara's sake they were going; the doctor had advised it. For two years she had suffered from depression, forever talking about England and the village near Braintree where she had grown up and where her parents still lived. At home in Toronto she sat all day in dark corners of the house, helplessly weeping; there was dust everywhere, and the little back garden where rhubarb and raspberries had thrived was overtaken by weeds.

227

Ed had tried to cheer her first with optimism, then with presents—a television set, a Singer sewing machine, boxes of candy. But she talked only about the long, pale Essex twilight, or a remembered bakeshop in the High Street, or sardines on toast around the fire, or the spiky multicoloured lupins that blossomed by the back door. If only she could get lupins to grow in Toronto, things might be better.

Ed and Barbara now sat side by side over a wing, watching the propellers warm up. She looked out the window and dozed. It seemed to her that the sky they travelled through was sliding around the earth with them, given thrust by the fading of the sun's colour. She thought of the doorway of her parents' house, the green painted gate and the stone gateposts that her father polished on Saturday mornings.

Then, at the same moment, and for no reason, the thought of this English house fused perfectly with the image of her own house, hers and Ed's, off Keele Street in Toronto, how snug it was in winter with the new fitted carpet and the work Ed had done in the kitchen, and she wondered suddenly why she'd been so unhappy there. She felt something like a vein reopening in her body, a flood of balance restored, and when the stewardess came around with the supper tray, Barbara smiled up at her and said, 'Why, that looks fit for a king.'

Ed plunged into his dinner with a good appetite. There was duckling with orange sauce and, though he wasn't one for fancy food, he always was willing to try something new. He took one bite and then another. It had a sweet, burned taste, not unpleasant, which for some reason reminded him of the sharpness and strangeness of sexual desire, the way it came uninvited at queer moments—when he was standing in the bathroom shaving his cheeks, or when he hurried across Eglinton Avenue in the morning to catch his bus. It rose bewilderingly like a spray of fireworks, a fountain that was always brighter than he remembered, going on from minute to minute, throwing sparks into the air and out onto the coolness of grass. He remembered, too, something almost forgotten: the smell of Barbara's skin when she stepped out of the bath and, remembering, felt the last two years collapse softly into a clock tick, their long anguish becoming something he soon would be looking back upon. His limbs seemed light as a boy's. The war bonds, their value badly nibbled away by inflation, had been well exchanged for this moment of bodily lightness. Let it come, let it come, he said to himself, meaning the rest of his life.

Across from Ed and Barbara, a retired farmer from Rivers, Manitoba sat chewing his braised duckling. He poked his wife in the knees and said, 'For God's sake, for God's sake,' referring, in his withered tenor voice, to the exotic meal and also to the surpassing pleasure of floating in the sky at nine o'clock on a fine summer evening with first Quebec, then the wide ocean skimming beneath him.

His wife was not a woman who appreciated being poked in the knees, but she was too busy thinking about God and Jesus and loving mercy and the colour of the northern sky, which was salmon shading into violet, to take offence. She sent the old man, her husband for forty years, a girlish, new-minded smile, then brought her knuckles together and marvelled at the sliding terraces of grained skin covering the backs of her hands. Sweet Jesus our Saviour—the words went off inside her ferny head like popcorn.

Not far from her sat a journalist, a mole-faced man with a rounded back, who specialized in writing profiles of the famous. He went around the world phoning them, writing to them, setting up appointments with them, meeting them in hotels or in their private quarters to spy out their inadequacies, their

tragedies, their blurted fears, so that he could then treat them—
and himself—to lavish bouts of pity. It was hard work, for the
personalities of the famous vanish into their works, but always,
after one of his interviews, he was able to persuade himself that it
was better, when all was said and done, to be a nobody. In
Canada he had interviewed the premier of a large eastern
province, a man who had a grey front tooth, a nervous tremor
high on one cheek and a son-in-law who was about to go to jail
for a narcotics offence. Now the journalist was going home to his
flat in Notting Hill Gate; in twenty-four hours he would be
fingering his collection of tiny glass animals and thinking that,
despite his relative anonymity, his relative loneliness, his
relatively small income and the relatively scanty degree of
recognition that had come his way—despite this, his prized core
of neutrality was safe from invaders. And what did that mean?—
he asked himself this with the same winning interrogation he had
practised on the famous. It meant happiness, or something akin
to happiness.

Next to him sat a high-school English teacher, a woman of
forty-odd years, padded with soft fat and dressed in a stiff
shantung travel suit. Once in England, she intended to take a
train to the Lake District and make her way to Dove Cottage
where she would sign her name in the visitors' book as countless
other high-school teachers had done. When she returned to
Toronto, a city in which she had never felt at home, though she'd
been born there, and when she went back to her class in
September to face unmannerly adolescents who would never
understand what *The Prelude* was about, it would be a comfort to
her to think of her name inscribed in a large book on a heavy oak
table—as she imagined it—in the house where William
Wordsworth had actually lived. The world, she suddenly saw, was
accessible; oceans and continents and centuries could be spryly

overleapt. From infancy she'd been drawn towards those things that were transparent—glass, air, rain, even the swimmy underwaterness of poetry. The atmosphere on the plane, its clear chiming ozone, seemed her true element, rarified, tender, discovered. Thinking this, she put back her head and heard the pleasurable crinkle of her new perm, a crinkle that promised her safe passage—or anything else she desired or could imagine.

They all were happy, Ed and Barbara Dover, the lip-smacking farmer and his prayerful wife, the English journalist, and the Toronto teacher—but they were far from being the only ones. By some extraordinary coincidence (or cosmic dispensation or whatever), each person on the London-bound flight that night was, for a moment, filled with the steam of perfect happiness. Whether it was the oxygen-enriched air of the fusiform cabin, or the duckling with orange sauce, or the soufflé-soft buttocks of the stewardess sashaying to and fro with her coffeepot, or the unchartable currents of air bouncing against the sides of the vessel, or some random thought dredged out of the darkness of the aircraft and fueled by the proximity of strangers—whatever it was, each of the one hundred passengers—one after another, from rows one to twenty-five, like little lights going on—experienced an intense, simultaneous sensation of joy. They were for that moment swimmers riding a single wave, tossed upwards by infection or clairvoyance or a slant of perception uniquely heightened by an accident of altitude.

Even the pilot, a Captain Walter Woodlock, a man plagued by the most painful and chronic variety of stomach ulcers, closed his eyes for the briefest of moments over Greenland and drifted straight into a fragment of dream. It couldn't have lasted more than thirty seconds, but in that short time he felt himself falling into a shrug of relaxation he'd almost forgotten. Afloat in his airy dimension, he became a large wet rose nodding in a garden, a gleaming fish smiling on a platter, a thick slice of Arctic moon reaching down and tenderly touching the small uplifted salty waves. He felt he could go on drifting forever in this false loop of time, so big and so blue was the world at that moment.

It must have been that the intensity and heat of this gathered happiness produced a sort of gas or ether or alchemic reaction—it's difficult to be precise—but for a moment, perhaps two, the walls of the aircraft, the entire fuselage and wings and tail section became translucent. The layers of steel, the rivets and bracing and ribwork turned first purple, then a pearly pink, and finally metamorphosed to the incandescence of pure light.

This luminous transformation, needless to say, went unnoticed by those in the aircraft, so busy was each of them with his or her private vision of transcendence.

But there was, it turned out, one witness: a twelve-year-old boy who happened to be standing on a stony Greenland beach that midsummer night. His name was Piers and he was the son of a Danish Lutheran clergyman who had come to the tiny Greenland village for a two-year stint. The boy's mother had remained behind in Copenhagen, having fallen in love with a manufacturer of pharmaceuticals, and none of this had been adequately explained to the boy—which may have been why he was standing, lonely and desperately confused, on the barren beach so late at night.

It was not very dark, of course. In Greenland, in the middle of the summer, the sky keeps some of its colour until eleven o'clock, and even after that there are traces of brightness, much like the light that adheres to small impurities suspended in wine. The boy heard the noise of the motors first, looked up frowningly and saw the plane, shiningly present with its chambered belly and elegant glassy wings and the propellers spinning their milky webs. He was too dazzled to wave, which was what he normally did when a plane passed overhead. What could it be? he asked himself. He knew almost nothing of science fiction, a genre scorned by his father, and the church in which he had been reared strictly eschewed angelic hosts or other forms of bodily revelation. A trick of the atmosphere?—he had already seen the aurora borealis and knew this was different. The word *phenomenon* had not yet entered his vocabulary, but when it did, a few years later, dropping like a ripe piece of fruit into his consciousness, he found that it could usefully contain something of the spectacle of that night.

Such moments of intoxication, of course, quickly become guilty secrets—this is especially true of children—so it is not surprising that he never told anyone about what he had seen.

Like his father, he grew up to become a man of God, though like others of his generation he wore the label with irony. He went first to Leiden to study, and there lost his belief in the Trinity. After that he received a fellowship to the Union Theological Seminary in New York where his disbelief grew, as did his reputation for being a promising young theologian. Before long he was invited to join the faculty; he became, in a few short years, the author of a textbook and a sought-after lecturer, and in his late thirties he fell in love with a nervous, intelligent woman who was a scholar of mediaeval history.

One night, when wrapped in each other's arms, she told him how women in the Middle Ages had pulled their silk gowns through a golden ring to test the fineness of the cloth. It seemed to him that this was the way in which he tested his belief in God, except that instead of determining the fineness of faith, he charted its reluctance, its lumpiness, its ultimate absurdity. Nevertheless, against all odds, there were days when he was able to pull what little he possessed through the ring; it came out with a ripply whoosh of surprise, making him feel faint and bringing instantly to mind the image of the transparent airplane suspended in the sky of his childhood. All his life seemed to him to have been a centrifugal voyage around that remembered vision—the only sign of mystery he had ever received.

One day, his limbs around his beloved and his brain burning with pleasure, he told her what he had once been privileged to see. She pulled away from him then—she was a woman with cool eyes and a listening mouth—and suggested he see a psychiatrist.

Thereafter, he saw less and less of her, and finally, a year later, a friend told him she had married someone else. The same friend suggested he should take a holiday.

It was summertime, the city was sweltering, and it had been some time since he had been able to pull anything at all through his gold ring. He considered returning to Greenland for a visit, but the flight schedule was unbelievably complicated and the cost prohibitive; only wealthy birdwatchers working on their life lists could afford to go there now. He found himself one afternoon in a travel agent's office next to a pretty girl who was booking a flight to Acapulco.

'Fabulous place,' she said. Glorious sun. Great Beaches. And grass by the bushel.

Always before, when the frivolous, leisured world beckoned, he had solemnly refused. But now he bought himself a ticket, and by the next morning he was on his way.

At the airport in Acapulco, a raw duplicity hangs in the blossom-sweet air—or so thinks Josephe, a young woman who works as a baggage checker behind the customs desk. All day long fresh streams of tourists arrive. From her station she can see them stepping off their aircraft and pressing forward through the wide glass doors, carrying with them the conspiratorial heft of vacationers-on-the-move. Their soft-sided luggage, their tennis rackets, their New York pallor and anxious brows expose in Josephe a buried vein of sadness, and one day she notices something frightening; 109 passengers step off the New York plane, and each of them—without exception—is wearing blue jeans.

She's used to the sight of blue jeans, but such statistical unanimity is unnerving, as though a comic army has grotesquely intruded. Even the last passenger to disembark and step onto the tarmac, a man who walks with the hesitant gait of someone in love with his own thoughts, is wearing the ubiquitous blue jeans.

She wishes there had been a single exception—a woman in a bright flowered dress or a man archaic enough to believe that resort apparel meant white duck trousers. She feels oddly assaulted by such totality, but the feeling quickly gives way to a head-shaking thrill of disbelief, then amusement, then satisfaction and, finally, awe.

She tries hard to get a good look at the last passenger's face, the one who sealed the effect of unreality, but the other passengers crowd around her desk, momentarily threatened by her small discoveries and queries, her transitory power.

In no time it's over; the tourists, duly processed, hurry out into the sun. They feel lighter than air, they claim, freer than birds, drifting off into their various inventions of paradise as though oblivious to the million invisible filaments of connection, trivial or profound, which bind them one to the other and to the small green planet they call home.

The Man Doll

SUSAN SWAN

I MADE THE DOLL for Elizabeth. I wanted to build a
surrogate toy that would satisfy my friend so completely I
would never have to listen to her litany of grievances against the
male sex again.

I constructed the doll by hand. I am a bio-medical engineer,
but at that time I was still an intern. I couldn't afford to buy
Elizabeth one of the million-dollar symbiotes called Pleasure
Boys which the wealthy women and gay men purchase in our
exclusive department stores.

I didn't like these display models anyhow. Their platinum hair
and powder-blue eyes (identical to the colouring of Pleasure
Girls) looked artificial and their electronic brains had over-
developed intellects. I wanted something different from the run-
of-the-mill life form for Elizabeth. I wanted a deluxe model that
would combine the virility component of a human male with the
intuitive powers of the female. In short, I wanted a Pleasure Boy
whose programming emphasized the ability to give emotional
support.

I made my doll in secret, requisitioning extra parts whenever some limbs or organs were needed at the Cosmetic Clinic in human repairs where I worked. So it was easy for me to get the pick of anatomical bargains. I particularly liked the selection of machine extensions offered by the Space Force Bank. After careful consideration, I chose long, sinewy hands, arms and legs, and made sure they were the type that could be willed into action in a twinkling. The Space Force Bank agreed to simulate the doll's computer brain from mine for $1,500. The exterior of the doll was made out of plastic and silicone that was lifelike to the touch. I placed a nuclear reactor the size of a baseball in the chest cavity, just where the heart is in the human body. The reactor warmed the doll by transmitting heat to a labyrinth of coils. The reactor uses a caesium source that yields an 80 per cent efficiency rate with a life expectancy of just over thirty years. The doll was activated by a handheld switch.

I smuggled the materials home from the Clinic and each night in my flat I worked on the doll. I wanted it to be a perfect human likeness, so exact in detail that Elizabeth wouldn't guess it was a symbiote. I applied synthetic hair in transplants (matched with my own hair colour) and shaped its face with the help of liquid silicone. My money had almost run out by the time I got to the sex organs, but luckily I was able to find a cheap set from a secondhand supplier. For $250 I bought an antique organ that belonged to a 180-year-old Pleasure Boy. I hoped it would work under pressure.

Our laws forbid symbiotes to waste human food. But I gave the doll a silicone esophagus and a crude bladder because I wanted it to have something to do on social occasions. Its body was able to ingest and pass out a water and sugar solution. Of course, the doll didn't defecate. Its nuclear waste products were internally controlled and required changing once every ten years.

At the last moment I realized I had forgotten to add dye to the pupils, so its eyes were almost colourless. But in all other aspects, my doll looked normal.

When I installed its reactor, the doll came to life, lolling contentedly in my apartment, ignoring the discomfort of its mummy case and its helmet of elastic bandages and gauze. The doll called me 'Maker' and, despite its post-operative daze, began to display a talent for understanding and devotion.

It could sense when I was in a blue mood and sighed sympathetically behind its bandages. When I came home, exhausted from catering to the scientists at the Clinic, the doll would be waiting for me at the door of my apartment, ready to serve me dinner. Soon, I was unable to keep my hands off it. I decided it wouldn't spoil my present to Elizabeth if I tried it out ahead of time. Playfully I stroked and kissed the symbiote, and showed it how to peel back its groin bandage so we could have sex. To my delight, the doll operated above normal capacity, thanks to its desire to give pleasure.

Like any commercial symbiote, my doll was capable of orgasm but not ejaculation. It is illegal for a doll to create life. The sole function of a symbiote must be recreational.

At the end of five months I removed its protective case and found myself staring at a symbiote who gazed back with a remarkable calm, loving air. It had red hair and freckles, just like me, and a pair of cute pear-shaped ears.

My desire to give the doll to Elizabeth vanished.

I fell in love with my creation.

I called the doll Manny.

The next year with Manny was happy. I felt confident; I worked at the Clinic with zeal and diligence, knowing that at the end of the day I would be going home to Manny; his cooking and his kisses! (Something about the way I had juxtaposed his two oricularis oris muscles made the touch of his lips sensational.)

Secretly, I worried Manny might harbour resentment about a life built around ministering to my needs. Pleasure Boys have no rights, but Manny was still an organism with a degree of self-interest. If I neglected his programmed needs, he might deteriorate. When I confessed my fear, the doll laughed and hugged me.

'I want to be the slave,' he said. 'I need to be in service.'

Over the next six months I began to see less of my doll. I had graduated to the rank of engineer in facial repairs and was neglecting our home life.

I decided it was time to give Manny some social experiences, so I asked Elizabeth to the flat for a meal.

I felt a thrill of pride when Elizabeth walked in and didn't give Manny a suspicious look. Manny wore an ascot and a tweed sports suit. He beamed at the two of us as he placed a spinach quiche on the table.

'You look familiar,' Elizabeth mused.

'Everybody says I look like Tina,' the doll said breezily.

'You do,' Elizabeth said. 'Where did you meet Tina anyhow?'

'I'd rather hear about you,' the doll replied. 'Are you happy?'

Elizabeth started and looked at me for an explanation. I grinned.

'Go on. Tell him about your troubles with men.'

'Tina, my problems would bore Manny,' Elizabeth said nervously.

'No they wouldn't,' Manny said. 'I like to help people with their troubles.'

Elizabeth laughed and threw up her hands.

'I can't find a man who is decent, Manny. Every affair starts off well and then I find the guy has feet of clay.'

I saw Manny glance down at his plastic feet. He was smiling happily.

'I must be too much of a perfectionist,' Elizabeth sighed, 'but there are days when I'd settle for a good machine.'

I nodded and noticed Manny's colourless eyes watching Elizabeth as if he were profoundly moved. I thought he could be a little less sympathetic. If he knew Elizabeth like I did, Manny would realize Elizabeth enjoyed feeling dissatisfied.

Suddenly, Manny reached over and patted Elizabeth's hand. Elizabeth burst into tears and Manny continued to hold her hand, interlocking his fingers with hers in a deeply understanding way. In profile, the doll looked serene. Elizabeth was staring at him through her tears with an expression of disbelief. I knew Elizabeth was waiting for the doll to frown and suggest that she pull herself together.

Of course, the doll's programming prohibited uncaring reactions. Manny was unique, not only among male symbiotes, but among men. What man loved as unselfishly as my doll?

During dinner, Elizabeth quizzed Manny about his background and the doll gracefully handled her questions.

'I'm Tina's invention,' he quipped. 'I call her "Maker." It's our private joke.'

Elizabeth giggled and so did Manny. I winced. Why did my doll sound so happy? The understanding look on Manny's face, as Elizabeth whined about her love life, was a bit sickening! I noticed the doll lightly brush against Elizabeth's shoulder when he replenished the wine, and in disgust, I stood up and cleared away the dishes. When I came out of the kitchen, Manny was standing by the door holding hands with Elizabeth.

'Elizabeth needs me now, Tina,' the doll said. He paused to help my friend on with her coat. Then he gave her shoulder a loving squeeze. 'Elizabeth, I feel as if I were made just for you.'

My doll leaned over and offered her his sensational oricularis oris muscles, and suddenly I felt angry.

'You can't leave me, Manny,' I said. 'I own you.'

'Tina. You don't mean what you say,' Manny replied sweetly. 'You know dolls have rights too.'

'Who says?' I cried. 'You can't procreate. You can't eat. And your retinas are colourless.'

'Manny eats,' Elizabeth said. 'I saw him.'

'He just drinks,' I said, starting to shout. 'Elizabeth, Manny is my doll. Don't you dare walk out of my apartment with my possession.'

'Manny is not a doll,' Elizabeth said. 'You're making it up because you're jealous.'

'Manny, I'm warning you. If you leave me, I'll deactivate your program.'

'My Maker is not the sort of human to be petty,' Manny replied. Hand-in-hand, my doll and Elizabeth walked out of the apartment. 'Goodbye, Tina dear,' Manny called in an extremely sincere tone. I threw myself at the closed door, beating my fists against it, screaming my doll's name. Then I sank to my knees. I had made the doll for Elizabeth, but decided to keep him for myself. For the first time, I realized it didn't matter. My programming ensured that Manny would be drawn to whoever had most need of him.

For the next month, I was too depressed to see Elizabeth and Manny. I felt angry with my friend for taking my doll, although I scolded myself for being irrational. Now that Manny was gone, I regretted the way I had neglected him. I daydreamed nostalgically about the activities we might have done together. Why hadn't we gone shopping, or out to the movies? It made me sad to think we had never strolled arm-in-arm in the park like a normal couple.

True to his programming, Manny called me every day to see how I was doing. My pride stopped me from listening to his concerned inquiries and I slammed the phone down. Then one evening my symbiote phoned late and caught me offguard. I'd had an argument with my Clinic supervisor. This time, I was glad to hear my doll's friendly baritone.

'Tina, I'm worried about you,' Manny chided. 'The grapevine says you're working too hard.'

'Hard enough,' I agreed, relieved that someone cared.

'Dinner here this Tuesday. I won't take no for an answer.'

That Tuesday, I changed out of my lab coat and headed for Elizabeth's apartment. At the entrance to the building, three dolls were talking to the doorman. One of the dolls, a Pleasure Girl with shoulder-length platinum hair, asked the doorman to let them in so they could see a friend. The doorman shook his head.

'No dolls allowed in before six,' the doorman said. 'ASTARTE TOWERS is a respectable space block.' He made a slashing motion in the air with his gloved hand. Then he pushed the female doll on its chest. The doll groaned as if it were hurt and tottered backwards. For a second, it looked like it was going to fall. Then it slumped onto the curb and began to weep pitifully. The two male dolls rushed over to comfort it. Except for the unactivated models in store windows, I had never observed dolls in a group before. The sight of the symbiotes acting like humans made me uneasy. I hurried past the sobbing doll and her companions, and ran into the lobby.

In the apartment, I found Elizabeth reading a newspaper. Manny was setting the table. Elizabeth looked relaxed. But Manny! Why, the doll looked beatific! His synthetic curls shone with a copper glow and a suntan had brought out more large brown freckles. Then I remembered hearing that Elizabeth had gone on a Caribbean cruise.

'How wonderful to see you, Tina,' Manny said. 'Are you still mad at your old symbiote?'

I shook my head.

Joyfully, he embraced me. He told me about his holiday and asked about my new job. I immediately began to describe the way I had engineered a dish-face deformity. When I finished, I realized that Elizabeth had been listening intently too; apparently, she had no interest in going into her usual litany of grievances against the male sex.

Suddenly, Elizabeth said, 'Did you see any dolls at the door?'

'One or two,' I admitted. 'What are they doing here?'

'A few come, every day. They sometimes bring a human. If they can get by the doorman, Manny lets them come in and talks to them.' Elizabeth sighed and shrugged. 'I suppose there's nothing wrong with it. Except I worry that they tire Manny.'

'Elizabeth, I am tireless,' Manny laughed, bending over and kissing my friend on the nape of her neck. I remembered just how tireless Manny could be.

Elizabeth grabbed his silicone hand and kissed it hungrily. 'Selfless, you mean.' She looked dreamy. 'Tina, where did you find this paragon?'

'I already told you. I made him for you.' I smiled.

'Do you think I'm going to believe that line of yours?' Elizabeth laughed. 'It's time you forgave me for being with Manny.'

'What are you talking about?' I asked.

'Elizabeth thinks I'm human,' Manny smiled. 'I've tried to show her I'm a doll, but she goes out of the room and refuses to listen.' He paused, bewildered. 'The dolls think I'm human, too.'

'No doll could make *me* happy,' Elizabeth giggled.

'Serving your needs fulfils my function,' Manny replied.

'Isn't Manny funny?' Elizabeth said. 'He says the cutest things!'

Before I could answer, the door opened and the symbiotes who had been arguing with the doorman rushed in uttering cries of glee.

'Pleasure Girl #024 found a way in through the back entrance,' one of the male dolls said triumphantly.

The female doll kissed Manny fiercely on both his cheeks.

'Pleasure Boy #025 is the one who suggested we try another door,' she said. 'Aren't we clever for sex toys?' Then she noticed Elizabeth and me, and she blushed guiltily. 'Excuse me. I forgot humans were listening.'

'Don't apologize,' said the other male doll. 'We have the right to breathe like anybody else.'

The dolls murmured agreement and then turned back to Manny, who was holding up a jug of liquid. I guessed it contained a sugar and water solution. Manny poured the liquid into glasses. The dolls lifted the glasses in a toast and pretended to drink Manny's solution.

I stared at the dolls without speaking to them. Once again, I felt uneasy. The symbiotes were claiming human privileges. Not only were they acting as if they had the right to consume precious food resources, but the dolls were also appropriating human metaphors. I wasn't certain about the design type of the other symbiotes, but no air passed through Manny's system. His lungs were a tiny non-functional sac next to the caesium reactor. I had stuck in the sac to designate lung space in case I decided later to give Manny a requirement for oxygen.

Now the dolls began to complain loudly about their lot as pleasure toys. My doll listened solemnly, stroking each of their hands in turn while Elizabeth and I looked on blankly. Then one of the male dolls threw himself at Manny's feet.

'Why are we discriminated against, Manny?' the doll wailed. 'Why can't we procreate like humans do?'

Tears slowly dripped from Manny's clear eyes. He held out his arms and embraced the dolls, who in turn cried and embraced each other. In the midst of the hubbub I slipped out and left Elizabeth with the emotional dolls. Then I hurried back to the Clinic and calmed myself by working until dawn repairing a pair of cauliflower ears.

Three months went by. This time Elizabeth rang up and asked me to meet her at the Earth Minister's television studio. Elizabeth said that Manny had left her to become a spokesman for a political lobby of humans and symbiotes.

Manny's group could be heard in the background of the Earth Minister's daily broadcasts shouting their demands. Elizabeth wanted me to persuade Manny to give up politics. She wanted Manny back so they could start a family. She said that she would do 'something unthinkable' that evening unless she could convince Manny to return.

Gently, I tried to point out that Manny was only a doll, but the more I pleaded with her to forget about my symbiote, the more desperate she sounded. I agreed to meet her at the studio. Just before I left my apartment, I stuck my handheld switch into my pocket. I decided the time had come to deactivate Manny. It was illogical for the symbiotes to think dolls had rights. I felt sympathy for them as organisms, but their aspirations were making pests out of what were once perfectly good recreational objects.

The studio was ten minutes by air, but it took me over half an hour to force my way through the crowd at the studio door. I noticed with a start that there were hundreds of human heads among the masses of synthetic ones.

Finally, I found a seat at the back of the auditorium. At that moment the lights dimmed and then flared brightly as the Earth Minister walked out onto a dais at the front of the room, followed by a television crew pushing cameras. The crowd immediately began to chant, 'Manny for Earth Minister' and 'Symbiotes are humans too.'

I heard a noise at the front of the room and Manny was lifted onto the platform. Then Manny shook hands with the Earth Minister, a stocky human with an anxious smile. Now the crowd cheered more wildly than before, and Manny turned and lifted up his arms as if he wanted to embrace them all. He looked striking in his deep-magenta safari suit.

Just then, Elizabeth appeared by my side, weeping.

'Isn't it awful?' she whispered. 'This swarm of dolls? Oh, Tina, I was just too busy with other things, so Manny went into politics. But I can't live without him.'

'Sure you can,' I sighed and looked over the crowd at Manny's synthetic head. 'You already are.'

Manny spotted me and waved. I hesitated, then smiled and waved back.

'Tina, you're not paying attention,' Elizabeth sniffed. 'I want Manny back. I want to have children with him.'

'Look, Elizabeth,' I said. I felt in my pocket for the switch. 'Manny is a doll—a do-it-yourself model. His brains cost over a thousand dollars and his sex organs were two-fifty.'

Elizabeth blushed. 'Manny has talked about the help you gave him, but no symbiote could do what he does.'

'He's a Pleasure Boy,' I argued. 'I should know. I made him. Haven't you noticed he doesn't eat or defecate? And that's not all. He can't procreate either.'

'Nothing you say will make me believe Manny is a doll,' Elizabeth shouted, and then she slapped my face!

Angrily, I grabbed her and dragged her towards the dais.

'I'll show you his extensions, his hair strips, his silicone mouth ...!'

'Tina! Please! Don't hurt Manny!' Elizabeth cried, ducking her head as if she expected me to hit her. Even though I am bigger than Elizabeth, I was surprised at how easily cowed she was.

I tightened my grip on my friend's arm. 'I'm going to take you up there,' I yelled, 'and deactivate him in front of everyone. Manny the doll has come to an end.'

'No, Tina! I'll do what you want! I'll forget him!' Elizabeth said and plucked at my arm. 'I know Manny's a doll, but I love him. I've never loved anybody before.'

She bowed her head, and for a second I relaxed my grip. At that moment, a great gust of sighs filled the studio and the oscillating physical mass knocked us apart as it pushed towards the dais where Manny sat. The Earth Minister toppled from his seat and the crowd hoisted Manny into the air.

Suddenly, the doll looked my way. His placid, colourless eyes met mine. I pulled the switch out of my pocket and threw it away. In the next moment, the mass of dolls and humans carried Manny off on a sea of hands. I wasn't surprised—as I strained for a last glimpse—to see a blissful look on my doll's face.

The Man with Clam Eyes

AUDREY THOMAS

I CAME TO THE sea because my heart was broken. I rented a cabin from an old professor who stammered when he talked. He wanted to go far away and look at something. In the cabin there is a table, a chair, a bed, a woodstove, an aladdin lamp. Outside there is a well, a privy, rocks, trees and the sea.

(The lapping of waves, the scream of gulls.)

I came to this house because my heart was broken. I brought wine in green bottles and meaty soup bones. I set an iron pot on the back of the stove to simmer. I lit the lamp. It was no longer summer and the wind grieved around the door. Spiders and mice disapproved of my arrival. I could hear them clucking their tongues in corners.

(The sound of the waves and the wind.)

This house is spotless, shipshape. Except for the spiders. Except for the mice in corners, behind the walls. There are no clues. I have brought with me wine in green bottles, an eiderdown quilt, my brand-new *Bartlett's Familiar Quotations*. On the inside of the front jacket it says, 'Who said: 1. In wildness is the preservation of the world. 2. All hell broke loose. 3. You are the sunshine of my life.'

I want to add another. I want to add two more. Who said, 'There is no nice way of saying this'? Who said, 'Let's not go over it again'?   The wind grieves around the door. I stuff the cracks with rags torn from the bottom of my skirt. I am sad. Shall I leave here then? Shall I go and lie outside his door calling whoo—whoo—whoo like the wind?

(The sound of the waves and the wind.)

I drink all of the wine in one green bottle. I am like a glove. Not so much shapeless as empty, waiting to be filled up. I set my lamp in the window, I sleep to the sound of the wind's grieving.

(Quiet breathing, the wind still there, but
soft, then gradually fading out. The passage
of time, then seagulls, and then waves.)

How can I have slept when my heart is broken? I dreamt of a banquet table under green trees. I was a child and ate ripe figs with my fingers. Now I open the door—

(West-coast birds, the towhee with
its strange cry, and the waves.)

The sea below is rumpled and wrinkled and the sun is shining. I can see islands and then more islands, as though my island had spawned islands in the night. The sun is shining.

I have never felt so lonely in my life. I go back in. I want to write a message and throw it out to sea. I rinse my wine bottle from last night and set it above the stove to dry. I sit at the small table thinking. My message must be clear and yet compelling, like a lamp lit in a window on a dark night. There is a blue bowl on the table and a rough spoon carved from some sweet-smelling wood. I eat porridge with raisins while I think. The soup simmers on the back of the stove. The seagulls outside are riding the wind and crying ME ME ME. If this were a fairy tale, there would be someone here to help me, give me a ring, a cloak, a magic word. I bang on the table in my frustration. A small drawer pops open.

(Sound of the wind the waves lapping.)

Portents and signs mean something, point to something, otherwise—too cruel. The only thing in the drawer is part of a manuscript, perhaps some secret hobby of the far-off professor. It is a story about a man on a train from Genoa to Rome. He has a gun in his pocket and is going to Rome to kill his wife. After the conductor comes through, he goes along to the lavatory, locks the door, takes out the gun, then stares at himself in the mirror. He is pleased to note that his eyes are clear and clam.   *Clam?* Pleased to note that his eyes are clear and clam?   I am not quick this morning. It takes me a while before I see what has happened. And then I laugh. How can I laugh when my heart is cracked like a dropped plate? But I laugh at the man on the train to Rome, staring at himself in the mirror—the man with clam eyes. I push aside the porridge and open my *Bartlett's Familiar Quotations.* I imagine Matthew Arnold—'The sea is clam tonight …' or Wordsworth—'It is a beauteous evening, clam and free …'

I know what to say in my message.   The bottle is dry. I take the piece of paper and push it in. Then the cork, which I seal with wax from a yellow candle. I will wait until just before dark.

(The waves, the lapping sea. The gulls, loud
and then gradually fading out. Time passes.)

Men came by in a boat with a pirate flag. They were diving for sea urchins and when they saw me sitting on the rocks they gave me one. They tell me to crack it open and eat the inside, here, they will show me how. I cry No and No, I want to watch it for a while. They shrug and swim away.   All afternoon I watched it in pleasant idleness. I had corrected the typo of course—I am that sort of person—but the image of the man with clam eyes wouldn't leave me and I went down on the rocks to think. That's when I saw the divers with their pirate flag; that's when I was given the gift of the beautiful maroon sea urchin. The rocks were as grey and wrinkled as elephants, but warm, with enormous pores and pools licked out by the wind and the sea. The sea urchin is a dark maroon, like the lips of certain black men I have known. It moves constantly back/forth, back/forth with all its spines turning. I take it up to the cabin. I let it skate slowly back and forth across the table. I keep it wet with water from my bucket. The soup smells good. This morning I add carrots, onions, potatoes, bay leaves and thyme. How can I be hungry when my heart is broken? I cut bread with a long, sharp knife, holding the loaf against my breast. Before supper I put the sea urchin back into the sea.

(Sound of the wind and the waves.)

My bottle is ready and there is a moon. I have eaten soup and drunk wine and nibbled at my bread. I have read a lot of unfamiliar quotations. I have trimmed the wick and lit the lamp and set it in the window. The sea is still tonight and the moon has left a long trail of silver stretching almost to the rocks.

(Night sounds. A screech owl.
No wind, but the waves lapping.)

I go down to the sea as far as I can go. I hold the corked bottle in my right hand and fling it towards the stars. For a moment I think that a hand has reached up and caught it as it fell back towards the sea. I stand there. The moon and the stars light up my loneliness. How will I fall asleep when my heart is broken?

(Waves, then fading out. The sound
of the wild birds calling.)

I awoke with the first bird. I lay under my eiderdown and watched my breath in the cold room. I wondered if the birds could understand one another, if a chickadee could talk with a junco, for example. I wondered whether, given the change in seasons and birds, there was always the same first bird. I got up and lit the fire and put a kettle on for washing.

(The iron stove is opened and the wood lit.
It catches, snaps and crackles.
Water is poured into a large kettle.)

When I went outside to fling away the water, he was there, down on the rocks below me, half-man, half-fish. His green scales glittered like sequins in the winter sunlight. He raised his arm and beckoned to me.

(Sound of the distant gulls.)

We have been swimming. The water is cold, cold, cold. Now I sit on the rocks, combing out my hair. He tells me stories. My heart darts here and there like a frightened fish. The tracks of his fingers run silver along my leg. He told me that he is a drowned sailor, that he went overboard in a storm at sea. He speaks with a strong Spanish accent.

He has been with the traders who bought for a pittance the sea-otters' pelts which trimmed the robes of Chinese mandarins. A dozen glass beads would be bartered with the Indians for six of the finest skins.

With Cook he observed the transit of Venus in the cloudless skies of Tahiti.

With Drake he had sailed on 'The Golden Hind' for the Pacific Coast. They landed in a bay off California. His fingers leave silver tracks on my bare legs. I like to hear him say it—Cal-ee fórn-ya. The Indians there were friendly. The men were naked but the women wore petticoats of bulrushes.

Oh how I like it when he does that.

He was blown around the Cape of Good Hope with Diaz. Only they called it the Cape of Storms. The King did not like the name and altered it.   Oh.   His cool tongue laps me. My breasts bloom in the moonlight. We dive—and rise out of the sea, gleaming. He decorates my hair with clamshells and stars, my body with sea-lettuce. I do not feel the cold. I laugh. He gives me a rope of giant kelp and I skip for him in the moonlight. He breaks open the shells of mussels and pulls out their sweet flesh with his long fingers. We tip the liquid into our throats; it tastes like tears.   He touches me with his explorer's hands.

(Waves, the sea—loud—louder. Fading out.)

I ask him to come with me, up to the professor's cabin. 'It is impóss-ee-ble,' he says. He asks me to go with him. 'It is impóss-ee-ble,' I say. 'Not at all.'

I cannot breathe in the water. I will drown. I have no helpful sisters. I do not know a witch.

(Sea, waves, grow louder, fade,
fading but not gone.)

He lifts me like a wave and carries me towards the water. I can feel the roll of the world. My legs dissolve at his touch and flow together. He shines like a green fish in the moonlight. 'Is easy,' he says, as my mouth fills up with tears. 'Is nothing.' The last portions of myself begin to sift and change.

I dive beneath the waves! He clasps me to him. We are going to swim to the edges of the world, he says, and I believe him.

I take one glance backwards and wave to the woman in the window. She has lit the lamp. She is eating soup and drinking wine. Her heart is broken. She is thinking about a man on a train who is going to kill his wife. The lamp lights up her loneliness. I wish her well.

Le Baiser
de Juan-Les-Pins

LOLA LEMIRE TOSTEVIN

I T IS RAINING. From the tall narrow windows the different greys of the roofs and sky are the usual greys that one reads about in books on Paris. The cobblestone streets a perfect setting for a Renoir film where almost every shot begins with someone exiting or entering a frame, leaving several frames in between empty. It has rained almost every day since I arrived a month ago, the studio dank with the breath of old velvet furniture and drapes. Too much time spent gazing out windows or reading about France in France and not enough time writing what should be written. I have become inaccessible to myself.

I haven't seen Christine since she left Canada so I look forward to a visit at her studio this morning on rue Villiers de l'Isle-Adam, a name I came across last night in *Flaubert's Parrot*. Only the French would designate such a short street after some obscure writer. My studio is on rue Edouard Vaillant near Levallois. Who were these men?

Christine is working on an installation for an upcoming show, six tall diptychs the size of French windows. Half of them are black and white photographs three feet wide and eight feet high, some of a classic Roman Venus taken from different angles, others shots of streets lined with tombs. She has paired each photograph with either a framed sheet of stainless steel or a sheet of lead in the same dimensions as the photographs and hung them on walls painted midnight blue. The various greys of the photographs, the stainless steel and lead, stand out like tall narrow windows against the midnight wall. The lead panels, she explains, are inert surfaces that reflect nothing but when I walk past the stainless steel a shadow stirs against its surface.

Her studio is just around the corner from Père Lachaise and after lunch we stroll through the hush of the cemetery where she took several of the photographs. As we track down Colette, Bernhardt, Proust, Apollinaire, she explains how her diptychs play out the relation between image and object. Her photographs of the tombs, which idealize, encapsulate the history of the body's decay, are records of the mortal remains, she says. The presence of the dead evoked by monuments marked by their name. We look for Beauvoir and Sartre but can't find them. Who decides who will be buried at Lachaise, the living or the dead?

Christine wants to spend the rest of the afternoon working on the installation so we make plans to meet for the evening performance of Roman Polanski's interpretation of Gregor Samsa. As I wend my way towards Place Des Vosges past Victor Hugo's house I'm reminded of the extravagant musical about to open in Toronto. Les Miz. The irony of having his words adapted to tunes, accordions and kettledrums in spite of his steadfast hatred of music. I stop at the Bibliothèque Historique for an hour in the reading room with its magnificent ceiling, scrutinize original manuscripts because they remain the most reliable witnesses to the literary past. Walk towards Hôtel Salé which has been converted into the Musée Picasso. The viewing starts on the first floor with Picasso's famous 'Self-Portrait' from the Blue

Period. Muffled in a black coat against a blue background, he gazes out with a look that is both disillusioned and passionate. The allegorical starting point.

The layout of the museum is such that twenty rooms represent different periods—Blue, Rose, Cubist, Classic, Avignon, Guernica ... Biographical information and photographs relating to each period grace the entrance of each room as if to better tally the movement of time. Like a family album. Picasso at seven with his sister Lola. A note in his handwriting that her dress is black with a blue sash and white collar and his suit white with a navy-blue overcoat and a blue beret, round out the details that faded sepia can't convey. Snapshots of special events—Picasso as a Matador at a ball, meetings with friends, wives, lovers, children—take on mythical proportions as most viewers spend more time inspecting the photographs and the biographical details than the paintings. More interest in what can be translated into certainty.

By the time I reach Mougins, the last years, the drizzle outside has flourished into a downpour. Two hours still before meeting Christine, so I retrace my steps from the erotic drawings of his old age. Are these the evidence of an old man's obsession or the aesthetic affirmation of a vibrant life? I search early paintings of women for an answer, especially those that follow the first bloom of infatuation, but in their fashionable abstract configurations the women no longer speak for themselves. As if each one had been discharged from who she was and condemned to the puerility of the artist's dreams.

———

Polanski is brilliant. As Samsa awakens to his nightmare world, the transformation from man to insect is not as discernible on stage as on the shadow projected on the backdrop. It would have been too contrived to alter his appearance with make-up or costumes and what the audience sees as the subtle changes of his body lying on the bed or crawling on the floor is projected as slowly evolving deformations by Samsa's shadow. That other realm through which we imagine our other selves. There are at least a dozen curtain calls and Polanski receives a standing ovation. This is what I come to Paris for.

After the performance, Christine suggests a late dinner at a favourite Moroccan restaurant in Le Marais but when we get there the owner is just closing up. Within a few seconds, however, a show of amplified disappointment extracts an invitation to join him, his family and a few friends, as long as we don't mind couscous. He's always liked Canadians he concedes and the evening promises to be an animated and generous occasion in spite of one friend, a young Frenchman dressed in what is best described as a walking piece of art. In a tone drenched with hauteur he declares, as he retreats towards the exit, that he intensely dislikes Canadians, '*Ils sont comme les boches.*' The owner hollering after him, '*Quel caractère de cochon!*' Like Giraudoux, their favourite playwright, many French still equate foreigners to fleas on a dog, a menace to their spirit of perfection. 'I guess it's not camp to be Canadian,' Christine whispers and laughs. The couscous is the best I've ever tasted, the large mutton bones filled with marrow that we scoop and spread on chunks of crusty bread. Our hosts are delighted to learn that Christine and I are artist and writer. 'If you were stranded on an island and had the choice of one book, which would you choose?' someone asks. 'My own,' I counter and the evening progresses through loud debates and louder songs until well past two.

Because it's too late for the métro and the restaurant owner won't 'accept Canadian money,' Christine and I decide to splurge on separate taxis. Fortified by too much wine and earnest resolutions to set to work first thing in the morning we walk towards a taxi stand near La Bastille. The procedure requires that you hire the car at the head of the line so I ask the peculiar man leaning against the first car if he will take me to Levallois. He is very short, the top of his head barely reaching my shoulders. Not exactly a midget but his proportions are all wrong and his head, too large for his body, is haloed by a mane of long white hair that juts out like a hooded capuchin monkey.

No sooner have I settled into the seclusion of the back seat than the driver turns around to inspect me and I am struck with the error of my choice. It is almost three A.M. and I am driving through deserted streets of Paris with a monkey who keeps turning to gawk. Part of me cautions that I should get out at the next red light but another part convinces me that I am paranoid. 'How long have you driven a cab?' Twenty years confirms my paranoia. He turns again and stares. I feel compelled to strike some semblance of a conversation if only as a precautionary measure. 'You have an accent, are you Spanish?'

'Portuguese, but I've lived here many years. And you, you're not French.' Canadian, I reply.

'Ah! I wouldn't have guessed that. Swedish, Swiss perhaps, but not Canadian.' He turns to confirm his first impression. His face is dissonant, none of his features co-operate, my apprehension due more to his appearance than to the fact that he keeps taking his eyes off the road.

'Are you married?' Yes. 'Is your husband here with you?' Yes, I lie and to justify the folly of a woman on her own so late at night I add, 'I wasn't alone, I was with friends.' This odious little man bores me. Why should I explain myself to a taxi driver. I will definitely make a quick exit at the next red light.

'It's impossible to get taxis around here at this time of night.'

The monkey reads minds. When he twists his body to look back, I realize it's because he's too short for his rear-view mirror. Those very people you would prefer to be invisible are always those who think they have the right to connect with you eye to eye. When my husband and I lived here it took months to learn how to glaze my focus and walk past beggars and ogling men. As if they didn't exist.

'I said it's impossible to get taxis at this time.' Indifference makes the monkey belligerent.

'There are over fifteen thousand taxis crawling the sewers of this city day or night.' The reference to sewers should generate the appropriate association. He looks like a rat and sooner or later you have to play the game according to the rules of this predatory city. And the rules require that you begin with those who are clearly at a disadvantage.

After a few moments' silence, he leans towards the passenger seat and retrieves two pillows on which he perches to receive a better view through the mirror. I dismiss him with a sneer and turn my head towards the darkness on my right. The sky is the same inert grey as Christine's lead panels. With his eyes fastened to me I feel the distance I need beginning to dissolve. I am confined to the space of a mirror which frames his bushy eyebrows, his dark eyes and the bridge of his misshapen nose. I am visited by a wretched face that holds me hostage to its wretchedness.

'It amuses madame perhaps that I'm so short?'

'Yes.' Some shortcomings are such that you can only react to them with callousness.

'And that I'm ugly, madame finds that amusing or offensive?'

'At the moment I find it neither amusing nor offensive. If anything I find it rather tedious. Your fate has nothing to do with me.'

'On the contrary madame, your fate may have a lot to do with me.'

There are moments, fleeting seconds during the course of an event when the outcome of your next word or action balances by such a thin thread, your heart stops for the duration of several beats. One altered breath would upset that balance. My eyes lift to the mirror and meet his. The light behind their disillusionment is not unfamiliar.

'But madame may leave if she wishes,' and he stops the car.

'I'm very tired. Just take me home. Please.' The last word a precautionary whisper.

To get to Pont Levallois from La Bastille, it is necessary to cross the entire city from the southeast to the northwest and I am astounded to discover that in spite of fifteen minutes in the cab, we haven't crossed the city at all. We are travelling along Jean Jaures on the northeastern side of Paris. My friend Guansé has a studio on this street, so I know it well.

'Why are we still going north instead of west?' I ask.

'It is much quicker at this time to cross the city along the Boulevard, madame.'

'I have a friend who lives on this street, perhaps I should stop here.'

'As you wish madame,' and again he stops the car.

We are at least fifteen blocks from Guansé's studio and I don't even know if he's home. 'No. No, there's no point in waking him up. Go on.'

The mirror stares. 'What does he do, this friend who lives on this street?'

'He's an artist. Catalan.' Another safeguard. After all, in France, Spain isn't so different from Portugal and he wouldn't hurt someone who has a friend who is a foreigner and Catalan.

'Ah yes, the French love artists especially if they're Catalan.

Unfortunately, they don't feel the same about foreign taxi drivers.'

'They don't feel the same about most foreigners,' I reply and the mirror smiles.

'What about madame, how does she feel about them?'

'Who? Artists, foreigners or taxi drivers?'

'All of them, madame.'

'I like some artists, I seldom think of people as foreigners and I don't know any taxi drivers.'

'But madame knows many artists. I would bet that madame knows many live ones as well as dead ones. She comes to Paris to visit museums.'

I am relieved that we are finally on the Boulevard Périphérique, travelling west towards Levallois. The conversation threatens to veer towards the privileged artist versus the underprivileged cab driver and I'm in no mood for social criticism. He is setting me up for a large tip which I will gladly pay if I make it home.

'You know why I drive a cab at night?' he continues, 'it's because I've had it driving tourists to and from museums. People are nicer at night when they've been eating and drinking. Did madame go to a museum today?'

'Yes. Musée Picasso.'

'Ah Picasso! And did madame enjoy it? Does madame find Picasso's paintings beautiful?' The mirror will not give up.

'Art isn't necessarily beautiful. Picasso's shapes are compositions, metaphors for larger ranges of experience.' Why am I speaking to this monkey about art.

'Larger than what, madame?'

'Larger than what we usually experience, I suppose.' Under the yellow lights of the Boulevard, against space as blank as a monitor, traces of red tail-lights sweep by.

'Most of my passengers tell me his paintings are abstract. That way they don't have to tell me what they mean,' he continues, the perfect model of persistence.

'Because you have this conversation with most of your passengers,' I retaliate with a sarcastic upper hand. It is my turn to glare at the mirror. His eyes are no longer staring, no longer steady or merely curious. They shift from side to side in search of an image that exceeds the mirror's surface. 'Do you think his bodies are abstract?' he asks.

'It depends on the period. Some are abstract.'

'Can madame define for me the value of an abstract body?' His tone a challenge that can't be dismissed.

'I suppose it resides in its form and is independent of the subject of the painting. It has nothing to do with meaning or with the body painted as much as with lines, colours and surfaces. The subject can't be compared to other subjects but exists in itself through its own form.'

The mirror is broad with a distorted smile. 'Bravo madame. You are the first passenger to give me such an eloquent answer. Is madame an artist?' His voice is filled with scorn.

'A writer,' my reaction urgent to dissociate itself from his branding.

We have taken the exit at Porte Champerret, a few minutes from Edouard Vaillant and I am relieved that this conversation can finally come to an end. He is not a violent man but my disinterest has been eroded. There are circuitous ways of breaking into a person's isolation and the monkey has proven to be a master. The meter registers 120 francs, not a surprising sum considering his route, but there's no point complaining at this stage. When he stops a few doors from my building, I hand him 200 francs and ask for 60 francs change.

My arm holding the money is extended over the front seat

while he looks through his wallet. He is stalling and I expect him to say he doesn't have the proper change when suddenly he seizes my forearm and yanks it with such force I assume he wants to drag me to the front. Within a few seconds however, he has pulled himself over the front seat using my arm as a lever and is half sitting, half lying across me in the back. I hold onto my briefcase with my left arm while trying to open the door on my right but his grip prevents me from reaching the door. His hand is enormous, disproportionate to the length of his arm, the fingers short, stubby like a paw's. 'You can let go of your purse, I don't want your damn money.'

'What do you want then?'

'I want you to sit here for a few more minutes and talk to me. You needn't be afraid, I won't hurt you.'

'You are hurting me now. Let go of my arm.'

He loosens his grip and orders me to face him. 'Tell me, if I were a Picasso invention would you find me interesting? Would you spend hours figuring out why my nose is flat, my nostrils so dilated? How would you interpret a chin that juts too much to one side and legs that are so short and bandy?'

His face is only a few inches away, his teeth are in a state of advanced decay, his breath oppressive. Our eyes have locked, his waiting for an answer, mine hoping he will find it without my having to speak it. But my silence makes him impatient. *'Tu réponds, non!'*

'You already know the answer,' I mutter in a whisper.

'You find me disgusting.'

'If you stalk all your clients to ask them if they find you disgusting you must have your answer by now.'

'I want *your* answer.' He clenches my arm. 'Do you find me disgusting?' Yes. 'But you don't find Picasso's bodies disgusting, merely abstract.' As he speaks, his left arm enlaces my neck while

266

his right hand slowly slips from my arm to my shoulder. The flat of his palm glides down my chest, stops at my breast. The cotton of my blouse and the lace of my brassiere grate gently back and forth against my nipple. I am wedged in his vise-like grip against the car's seat, my feet dangling halfway to the floor so that I am unable to regain a foothold. His smile exposes more rotting teeth and as he leans to kiss me, his target eye hovering over mine, my mouth fills with the taste of fermented decay. Repugnance and fear paralyze me.

After a long and astonishingly tender kiss, he begins to trace with his tongue, a slow path along my jawline, inside my ear, down the side of my neck to my collarbone, into the opening of my blouse. As his mouth searches, reaches a nipple, I am startled by the convulsive turbulence that invades me. A warm sensation shoots to the pit of my stomach, explodes inside my groin. I am horrified. This reaction is banned, taboo, transgresses everything I know to be right. Yet the sensation has assumed the force of an unknown, unnamed law that possesses me so completely it divests me from who I am. Who I thought I was.

'Please, let me go.'

'Very well madame,' and without the slightest hesitation he releases his grip, delves into his pocket, hands me 60 francs change. '*Bonsoir madame,*' his tone casual, with no hint of regret or apology.

As soon as I reach the studio I rush to the bathroom and stand at the mirror as if to corroborate what has just happened. Explain or at least tame my unexpected reaction. Except for a long line of spittle that runs from my jawbone to the opening of my blouse, the mirror remains mute. His saliva. I scrub my neck, rinse my mouth, brush my teeth, still the taste of decay lingers.

Four A.M. From my briefcase I retrieve the guide to the Picasso museum, flip through it and an image, dated 1925, lunges at me. In an explosion of garish colours, two intertwining bodies kiss, their limbs and organs so topsy-turvy it is impossible to tell which ones belong to the man or to the woman. Each detail, a mouth which could also be an eye or female genitals, a phallic nose, a corrugated cardboard foot, is part of a puzzle whose pieces have been scattered in order to bind the two figures in a passionate but violent embrace. The commentary beside the image states 'art is never chaste.'

I pick up my pen and on the first page of the French scribbler I bought almost a month ago, I begin to write. *Le Baiser de Juan-Les-Pins. It was raining.*

Lily and the Salamander

MILDRED TREMBLAY

L ILY SITTER BEGAN her spring cleaning two weeks before
Easter. She took out her rubber gloves and her Old Dutch.
She filled the red plastic pail to the brim with hot, steaming water
and hauled it over to the cupboard. Grunting a little, she hiked
her slightly plump body up onto the metal stool and began
taking down the assortment of junk that always finds its refuge
on top shelves of kitchen cupboards.

Twice a year now, for more than fifteen years, Lily had been
cleaning her shelves in this manner. Nobody had ever noticed it
or commented on this job of work. Not her husband nor, later,
her children.

Nobody knew these intimate details of Lily Sitter's workaday
life—how she washed behind the stove every Friday, or did the
refrigerator on Wednesday and the toilet bowl on Tuesdays.
Sometimes, she would try to communicate these activities, but
nobody had ever listened beyond the opening sentence. Why
should they? It was terribly dull.

She took down all the chipped china cups with unmatched
saucers, the stacks of old plates and bowls, two broken toasters,

a collection of empty Nabob coffee cans, and a clumsy old popcorn popper nobody ever used anymore. When they were all down and arrayed out on the counter, Lily got down off her stool and stood there looking at them.

Suddenly, she couldn't remember why they were all arranged on the counter like that. What was she doing with them? Slowly, she reached out a clumsy, rubber-covered finger and poked a coffee can.

— What? she said. What?

She picked up a cup with a gorgeous blood-red rose painted on it and turned it over in her hands again and again.

— What?

And at three o'clock that afternoon when Marvin came home from his bowling game, that's where he found her. She had in her hands a plastic Xmas bowl, painted with wreaths and berries.

— What? she was saying. What?

Marvin took the bowl from her hands and steered her over to the kitchen table and sat her down.

— Have you seen it? she asked.

— Seen what? Marvin stared at her dumbfounded.

— My book, she said.

— What book?

— The one I was reading. She put her head down and stared at her hands, frowning. I can't remember what page I was on? Eh? About the middle?

Lily sat in the doctor's office awaiting a verdict.

The examination had been made difficult by the fact that Lily had been unable to tell the doctor how she was feeling. When he had said—Well, Mrs. Sitter, how are you? she had been obliged to answer—I don't know.

She didn't seem to be feeling much of anything except perhaps shrouded in woolly grey dust balls on the outside and more of the same within. It embarrassed her not to have anything to report to the doctor, who had impaled her with a sterilized eye, and it crossed her mind to make up something, but she didn't have the courage.

Surreptitiously, she pushed her fingers hard into her stomach looking for a pain, an ache, anything, and at the same time she sent her mind scurrying the hidden paths within her body, but all she could feel were the heavy grey dust balls.

They were swathed about her heart and lungs; they had crowded into her womb. There was a very large and woolly one caught in her brain just behind her eyes. It was difficult to think through it.

The doctor sat regarding her, considering possibilities. A twitchy, beige-coloured moustache like a small scrub brush sat under his nose, and he picked at it reflectively as he stared at her. She saw that he considered her hapless, and she didn't dare ask him about her book, although she wanted to, quite badly.

She tried to look hapless. She tucked her feet under the chair. Her mind went to her clothes. What did she have on? The possibility that, under her coat, she was stark naked, occurred to her. With a quick, terrified glance, she looked down at her lap; but no, there was a skirt showing where her coat fell open, her good brown suit skirt.

The doctor rose and called Marvin into a small antechamber.

— Female disorder, he pronounced. Probably premature menopause. Should get her started thinking about her hysterectomy. He took out his pen and began a rapid scribble. Estrogen, he said. Mind she takes it twice a day. We'll take out the IUD and try her on the pill. And anti-depressants, just in case. He paused for a moment to shake the ink up. Valium on arising. And iron pills, by god, almost forgot the iron pills! The pen was out of ink, and he began opening and shutting drawers looking for another one.

In the next room, a nurse appeared with a needle and shot Lily's behind full of a colourless substance.

— What was in that? Lily asked, but the nurse just smiled and didn't answer. I can't remember, Lily thought, hiking up her pantyhose, but I guess I'm the kind of person who always asks dumb questions.

When they got back home, Lily sat down at the kitchen table and took all the pills out of her purse and lined them up in front of her. She didn't know what they were or when to take them.

— I feel very strange, Marvin, she said. Will you sit down and talk to me for a minute?

— I might, said Marvin, if you hurry up about it.

— Well, Lily said, and her eyes looked wide and dark as burnt chocolate in her pale face, well, for instance, I know you're my husband, I know that! But I can't remember how I'm supposed to feel about you?

She looked down at her hands, twisting the gold wedding band around and around on her finger.

— For instance, do I love you?

— Well of course you love me! I'm your husband. Marvin snorted and shook his head in disgust. You've always admired me! He spoke loudly as if she had suddenly become hard of hearing. You've always looked up to me!

Lily considered this information gravely for a moment.

— But, she replied, lifting her head and frowning, I know lots of wives who don't love their husbands. My mother, for instance ...

— That's different! Marvin sat down at the table and leaned over towards his wife to make her understand better. Your father—well, shit! you know ... he isn't quite the sort of man I am, now is he? When it comes to being smart, I mean that family certainly isn't known for its brains!

This thought almost made Marvin laugh, and he couldn't resist the temptation to elaborate a little.

— Just look at your Aunt Nettie for God's sake! And your old man, another thing now, d'you think women ever found him sexy? A little skinny jerk like that? How could you compare him to me. What kinda dummy are you anyway?

Marvin looked at her appealingly, inviting her agreement.

Lily didn't answer at once. She was staring at him now in an open and childlike way, almost as if seeing him for the first time. He creaked back uneasily in his chair and attempted a shrug.

— Not to sound conceited, he said, just all in the family, like.

— But Marvin, she said, frowning, you aren't very attractive. You are quite overweight, aren't you? And your hair is too thin and stringy. Didn't you used to have thick, blonde curls? And you have sort of a peevish look around your mouth—sulky! That's it!

She smiled, glad to have pinned it down so neatly.

— It's not nice at all, is it? she said.

She stopped suddenly. Marvin was standing over her. His usually pallid face was mottled and dark with anger.

— Oh, I'm sorry! she said. It's just so strange how I feel. Of course if you say you're attractive and I love you, of course I must! I'll try to remember it.

But she was thinking in a confused way—Marvin doesn't know who he is either.

When Marvin had left the room, Lily reached out and picked up one of the pill bottles. She began to think about the doctor. I wonder if he knows who he is? she thought. She sat for another minute, and then she got up and took all the pills and shoved them back in a corner on the top shelf behind the coffee cans.

The back door opened, and one of Lily's daughters came into the kitchen. She came in noisily; throwing her books onto the cupboard and without speaking to her mother, she went directly to the fridge and pulled the door open.

For a split second, the kitchen background faded away and the body and presence of the girl stood out very clearly to Lily: Vivien. It's Vivien. How chunky and strong her arms look. Vicious. She almost pulled that door off its hinges. She's ugly. Mean mouth. I don't like her. My Vivien. Deep inside of Lily's body, a tremor began; she felt she was going to faint.

— Nothing to eat in here! the girl began to complain, whining, but malicious too. Never nothing to eat in this house!

She slammed the fridge door shut and turned to confront her mother.

Confusedly, Lily thought of her other children. Who were they? What did they really look like? Surely they weren't all like this girl? Overwhelmed, she put her head down into her hands.

— Why are you sitting there like that, Vivien said. Why isn't supper started!

Lily peeked out through her fingers at this stranger, her first-born child.

— What do I usually make for supper? she said.

That night Marvin made out an activity list for Lily for the next day so that she could remember what she was supposed to do. Get car washed, he wrote. Phone TV man. Get supper. He sat for a moment chewing his pencil, trying to think. What did women do all day anyway? he asked Lily, but Lily couldn't remember. Suddenly he thought of something. What had she been mucking around in out there in the kitchen when he'd found her? Oh, the shelves. Finish spring cleaning, he wrote down. Well, that would have to do for a start.

Lily followed Marvin's lists as well as she could, although peculiar things began to happen around the house; for instance although meals were abundant and the TV always in good repair, dirt and dust piled up undisturbed in the most unlikely places. However, Marvin got better at the lists, so they managed for a while.

The younger children were sent to Aunt Nettie's, dumb as she was. Marvin announced that it didn't take any brains to look after kids anyway; just give them a good clout on the head now and then to let them know who's boss. Lily cried when they left. She had discovered that they were normally lovable children, not cold and strange like Vivien, but she couldn't always remember what to do with them, and it became too risky leaving them alone with her.

And so they went along in this way for a while, but gradually Lily began to forget about the lists too. After Vivien and Marvin had left in the mornings, Lily would go seriously to work to look for her book. Clothes flew from drawers and closets; sheets were stripped from beds. Sometimes she would go out into the yard and look under the big rocks in the rock garden or lift the heavy damp arms of the big cedar tree and shake them about. Once she went next door to old Mrs. Lafleur's to ask if she had seen it. She stood patiently knocking and waiting on the porch for a long time, but the old lady would not come to the door, though Lily knew she was at home.

When she was not looking for her book, she took to sitting, unmoving, for long hours at a time in Marvin's big chair in the living room.

The room was of a medium size and it was furnished with an imitation Spanish chesterfield suite, with coffee tables to match. The coffee tables were decorated with elaborate, glued-on plastic carvings. They had purchased this furniture, not too many years ago, at a Simpson Sears sale, and it had been an occasion of considerable excitement in their lives. But it had quickly lost its charm, and now as she looked at it, there seemed something almost evil about it—it sat there, day after day, looking back at her with a sort of mindless brutishness. There was a rug also—a green circular affair—she saw now that patches of its shaggy hair were falling out in clumps near the chesterfield, exposing a dirty grey scalp.

She wondered, as she sat there, who had been this woman, Lily Sitter, who had gone with this man, Marvin, this fat, blonde, baby-faced man, and purchased all of these things which now surrounded her?

Across from where she sat, placed on one of the ugly little tables, was a framed picture of herself—her wedding portrait. There she was, all veiled and satined and gartered, ready to be handed over to Marvin, supposedly intact. From out of the lace and lacquered curls, the round young face beamed idiotically into the future; into a living room of imitation Spanish furniture and moulting shag rugs. Sometimes she would pick the picture up and stare at it for a while, but she could find no sense to it. One day, walking past, she took it and put it away in a drawer.

In the long silences, she became aware of the presence of the house. It would start its communications shortly after Marvin left in the mornings; it was like a vast uneasy stomach, creaking and rumbling and farting faintly off in its depths. Sometimes though, it would suddenly become very quiet as if it had become aware of her sitting there and was watching her.

It occurred to her that the house had a voice, and that one day it might draw a great heaving sigh and begin to speak to her. It would speak her name—Lily, Lily!—and she waited in a sort of curious dread for this to happen.

Mostly though, it just rumbled about, carrying on with its life. One morning the fridge went on with such a loud belch that she went into the kitchen to look at it. It was getting old; it was losing its shine.

— How do I feel about you, fridge? she said.

She knew she felt something. Was it pity? Or hate? She couldn't decide. She stood looking at it for a moment, and then she reached her hand around behind it, groping, and pulled out the plug.

— I think I'll call that a mercy killing, she said, and laughed.

After that, she went around and pulled out every plug she could find. Her laughter rose up in torrents from deep within her belly and leapt, naked and wild, out into the room, out the door and down into the street.

All the plump, little, aproned women, in all the plump, tidy, little houses, stopped in their rounds and listened intently when they heard it.

Of course, when Marvin came home from work and found the fridge defrosted and water all over the floor, he didn't laugh; he was furious.

And who could blame him, really?

He took Lily by the shoulders and shook her violently, his fingers digging like knives into the soft flesh of her arms. She begged him to stop, he was hurting her, but this only seemed to enrage him further and reaching out, he took her by the neck and lifting her off the floor, began to throttle her. His weak blonde hair was falling every which way and his face, pushed up close to hers, had turned the colour of raw beefsteak.

— Crazy woman! he yelled, spit flying from his mouth onto Lily's cheeks. Crazy woman!

Lily felt he might kill her, and with fingers fluttering like dying butterflies, she picked weakly at his hands, trying to release their grip. She would have begged for her life if she'd been able to speak. From the other room, she heard excited footsteps, and Vivien came bursting in. Lily reached a hand blindly out towards her, but Vivien made no move, only stood there, watching, her eyes wide and alert. Lily's ears began to ring; at the back of her skull a crimson cloud ballooned up, ready to explode, and Marvin's face, distorted, unreal, loomed and blocked out the whole world. But at the last moment, she was thrown across the room, skidding through the water and crashing up against the wall like a half-dead, discarded cat. As if from a long distance, she could hear Vivien talking forcefully to her father.

— We've got to do something about her, she was saying, she's a ree-tard. The kids at school all call her a ree-tard.

Lily was afraid to get beaten again so she resolved to do better.

For two whole days, she didn't allow herself to look for her book, except for one quick peek in Marvin's bowling bag.

And she decided to take up jogging, it was said to work miracles, she'd read an article in one of Marvin's magazines. It had said also that sometimes, while jogging, you could have orgasms (she looked the word up in the dictionary to make sure she hadn't misunderstood, for it seemed a strange thing). Lily was interested in orgasms for the same reason a poor man is interested in money—she never had any. Well, god knows maybe that's what's wrong with me, she reflected, and even though she couldn't understand how such a thing could be managed while running in public, she was willing to give it a try.

And so the next morning, all the plump little women with all their flat-faced, large-headed, peanut-butter-stuffed little children, were treated to the sight of Lily Sitter, wearing a turtleneck sweater to hide her black and blue throat, bursting out of her front door and galloping madly off down the street. Lily ran all the way down the street, turned right on the Avenue, ran one block down past the graveyard, jumped over the wall to look under a pile of wreaths on a new grave, jumped out again, and ran all the way down to the beach. By the time she got there, she was huffing and puffing a lot, but not from orgasm; she was just very short on wind.

She had conceived the idea that when she got to the beach, she would look for some suitable logs and stumps to use as furniture in her living room, for she had decided to get rid of the Spanish, which had been silently moving in closer to her, inch by inch, every day. However, the beach was covered with such a variety of large, interesting-looking stones that she spent the rest of the day looking for her book.

Unfortunately, the jogging, in Lily's case, did not produce any miracles, and as she seemed unable to think of any other solution, she was soon back sitting in her living room contemplating the green rug.

Sitting there, with her eyes wide open, she began to have dreams. She dreamed of books—books with 1,000 pages, with 10,000 pages, and books with 12,375 pages, that is, one for every day of her life. She dreamed she found her book; it sat on a table, a strong light falling across it; it was black bound, and hurriedly she ran to open it. But the pages were covered with undecipherable markings, thrown about on the white paper like wet, black tea leaves, and tears of disappointment streamed like rivers down her exhausted cheeks.

She decided to try out various roles, to see if by chance she might stumble on to something that would help her remember. After some long and careful thought, she decided it was possible that she was a young girl about six or seven years old.

The more she thought about this idea the better she liked it, and one day, sitting there, a strange and painful shiver rushed through all of her bones, and it came to her immediately afterwards that her name was Lily Marie Josephine Hoskins, and she was six-and-a-half years old. It astounded her that she could have forgotten such an important thing, and her whole being flooded with such a tremendous relief and happiness that she jumped to her feet, laughing and clapping her hands.

Down the street to play with Billy! and out the door she ran, calling back at the empty house—Be back for supper, Mamma! But running down the street her feet felt too clumsy, and looking down, she saw that her feet were not those of a child. Frightened, she went quickly back home.

Other times, she thought she remembered that she was an old lady, and she went hobbling and wheezing about, with her nose thrust forward sniffing out odours.

— Smells like stale bread in here! she would say in her high cracked old lady's voice, or, smells like mice, or old apples, or whatever happened to catch her fancy. Smells like death, she said one day and spent the whole day jumping around quickly to catch her own death who stood behind her, but she could never turn about fast enough.

One day, she was sure she was a young mother in love with her newborn baby. She went up the steps to Vivien's room and took from its box under the bed a salamander Vivien had imprisoned there.

She made some tiny blankets from scraps and wrapped it tenderly and carried it about all the day long. She bathed its bumpy little body, and at lunch time, she pushed mashed bananas into its stubborn little crocodile mouth. One lidless, reptilian eye gleamed out at her adoringly from a corner of the blanket when she rocked it and sang 'Lullabye and Goodnight.'

When Vivien arrived home and saw what she was doing, she took the salamander away, and flailing her short, chunky arms, she hit her mother about the head and shoulders with hard, mean punches, not stopping until her mother had fallen to the floor.

Easter came and went, and the days moved on towards early

summer. One day Lily, sitting in her living room, woke from a dream of a book with only one sentence in it. The sentence was 'Nov schmoz ka pop,' and it was repeated, page after page. She noticed that the sun, in its summer orbit, was streaming into the room with more strength. Pale lemon oblongs of light lay across the dark chesterfield and revealed new bare patches on the shag rug.

She sat for a while watching the sun patterns, when gradually she became aware of a new sound in the house, as of short, clean notes picked on a tight string. She listened carefully for a moment and then nodded her head in satisfaction—she knew what it was. The little salamander had escaped from Vivien's room and was coming down the stairs.

Its tiny feet picked their way down, touching against the varnished wood with fastidious little clacks. By now, the sun had reached Lily's chair, and it fell in heavy warmth across her face. She closed her eyes, listening intently. The clacking grew louder, very close to her face now and strangely familiar.

Suddenly, she realized that somehow the salamander had curled its cold body in behind her ear, seeking fire from her brain. She reached up her hand to remove it, but could not; it had become terribly tangled in her hair. She pulled and tugged at it frantically until it opened its long, crooked mouth and began to scream. The screams were thin and far away, but yet intimately known to her.

Without warning, Lily's whole body convulsed into a taut, excruciating arch, as if it would explode, and then it was thrown violently back into the chair.

Memory flooded in in great roaring streams.

The last page; she had been on the last page.

The Death of Robert Browning

JANE URQUHART

I N DECEMBER OF 1889, as he was returning by gondola from the general vicinity of the Palazzo Manzoni, it occurred to Robert Browning that he was more than likely going to die soon. This revelation had nothing to do with either his advanced years or the state of his health. He was seventy-seven, a reasonably advanced age, but his physical condition was described by most of his acquaintances as vigorous and robust. He took a cold bath each morning and every afternoon insisted on a three-mile walk during which he performed small errands from a list his sister had made earlier in the day. He drank moderately and ate well. His mind was as quick and alert as ever.

Nevertheless, he knew he was going to die. He also had to admit that the idea had been with him for some time—two or three months at least. He was not a man to ignore symbols, especially when they carried personal messages. Now he had to acknowledge that the symbols were in the air as surely as winter. Perhaps, he speculated, a man carried the seeds of his death with him always, somewhere buried in his brain, like the face of a woman he is going to love. He leaned to one side, looked into the deep waters of the canal, and saw his own face reflected there. As broad and distinguished and cheerful as ever, health shining vigorously, robustly from his eyes—even in such a dark mirror.

Empty Gothic and Renaissance palaces floated on either side of him like soiled pink dreams. Like sunsets with dirty faces, he mused, and then, pleased with the phrase, he reached into his jacket for his notebook, ink pot and pen. He had trouble recording the words, however, as the chill in the air had numbed his hands. Even the ink seemed affected by the cold, not flowing as smoothly as usual. He wrote slowly and deliberately, making sure to add the exact time and location. Then he closed the book and returned it with the pen and pot to his pocket, where he curled and uncurled his right hand for some minutes until he felt the circulation return to normal. The celebrated Venetian dampness was much worse in winter, and Browning began to look forward to the fire at his son's palazzo where they would be beginning to serve afternoon tea, perhaps, for his benefit, laced with rum.

A sudden wind scalloped the surface of the canal. Browning instinctively looked upwards. Some blue patches edged by ragged white clouds, behind them wisps of grey and then the solid dark strip of a storm front moving slowly up on the horizon. Such a disordered sky in this season. No solid, predictable blocks of weather with definite beginnings, definite endings. Every change in the atmosphere seemed an emotional response to something that had gone before. The light, too, harsh and metallic, not at all like the golden Venice of summer. There was something broken about all of it, torn. The sky, for instance, was like a damaged canvas. Pleased again by his own metaphorical thoughts, Browning considered reaching for the notebook. But the cold forced him to reject the idea before it had fully formed in his mind.

Instead, his thoughts moved lazily back to the place they had been when the notion of death so rudely interrupted them; back to the building he had just visited. Palazzo Manzoni. *Bello, bello* Palazzo Manzoni! The colourful marble medallions rolled across Browning's inner eye, detached from their home on the Renaissance façade, and he began, at once, to reconstruct for the thousandth time the imaginary windows and balconies he had planned for the building's restoration. In his daydreams the old poet had walked over the palace's swollen marble floors and slept beneath its frescoed ceilings, lit fires underneath its sculptured mantels and entertained guests by the light of the chandeliers. Surrounded by a small crowd of admirers he had read poetry aloud in the evenings, his voice echoing through the halls. *No R.B. tonight,* he had said to them winking, *Let's have some real poetry.* Then, moving modestly into the palace's impressive library, he had selected a volume of Dante or Donne.

But they had all discouraged him and it had never come to pass. Some of them said that the façade was seriously cracked and the foundations were far from sound. Others told him that the absentee owner would never part with it for anything resembling a fair price. Eventually, friends and family wore him down with their disapproval and, on their advice, he abandoned his daydream though he still made an effort to visit it, despite the fact that it was now damaged and empty and the glass in its windows was broken.

It was the same kind of frustration and melancholy that he associated with his night dreams of Asolo, the little hill town he had first seen (and then only at a distance), when he was twenty-six years old. Since that time, and for no rational reason, it had appeared over and over in the poet's dreams as a destination on the horizon, one that, due to a variety of circumstances, he was never able to reach. Either his companions in the dream would persuade him to take an alternate route, or the road would be impassable, or he would awaken just as the town gate came into view, frustrated and out of sorts. 'I've had my old Asolo dream again,' he would tell his sister at breakfast, 'and it has no doubt ruined my work for the whole day.'

Then, just last summer, he had spent several months there at the home of a friend. The house was charming and the view of the valley delighted him. But, although he never once broke the well-established order that ruled the days of his life, a sense of unreality clouded his perceptions. He was visiting the memory of a dream with a major and important difference. He had reached the previously elusive hill town with practically no effort. Everything had proceeded according to plan. Thinking about this, under the December sky in Venice, Browning realized that he had known since then that it was only going to be a matter of time.

The gondola bumped against the steps of his son's palazzo.

Robert Browning climbed onto the terrace, paid the gondolier, and walked briskly inside.

———————

Lying on the magnificent carved bed in his room, trying unsuccessfully to surrender himself to his regular pre-dinner nap, Robert Browning examined his knowledge like a stolen jewel he had coveted for years; turning it first this way, then that, imagining the reactions of his friends, what his future biographers would have to say about it all. He was pleased that he had prudently written his death poem at Asolo in direct response to having received a copy of Tennyson's 'Crossing the Bar' in the mail. How he detested that poem! What *could* Alfred have been thinking of when he wrote it? He had to admit, none the less, that to suggest that mourners restrain their sorrow, as Tennyson had, guarantees the floodgates of female tears will eventually burst open. His poem had, therefore, included similar sentiments, but without, he hoped, such obvious sentimentality. It was the final poem of his last manuscript which was now, mercifully, at the printers.

Something for the biographers and for the weeping maidens; those who had wept so copiously for his dear departed, though soon to be re-instated wife. Surely it was not too much to ask that they might shed a few tears for him as well, even if it was a more ordinary death, following, he winced to have to add, a fairly conventional life.

How had it all happened? He had placed himself in the centre of some of the world's most exotic scenery and had then lived his life there with the regularity of a copy clerk. A time for everything, everything in its time. Even when hunting for lizards in Asolo, an occupation he considered slightly exotic, he found he could predict the moment of their appearance; as if they knew he was searching for them and assembled their modest population at the sound of his footsteps. Even so, he was able to flush out only six or seven from a hedge of considerable length and these were, more often than not, of the same type. Once he thought he had seen a particularly strange lizard, large and lumpy, but it had turned out to be merely two of the ordinary sort, copulating.

Copulation. What sad dirge-like associations the word dredged up from the poet's unconscious. All those Italians; those minstrels, dukes, princes, artists, and questionable monks whose voices had droned through Browning's pen over the years. Why had they all been so endlessly obsessed with the subject? He could never understand or control it. And even now, one of them had appeared in full period costume in his imagination. A duke, no doubt, by the look of the yards of velvet which covered his person. He was reading a letter that was causing him a great deal of pain. Was it a letter from his mistress? A draught of poison waited on an intricately tooled small table to his left. Perhaps a pistol or a dagger as well, but in this light Browning could not quite tell. The man paced, paused, looked wistfully out the window as if waiting for someone he knew would never, ever appear. Very, very soon now he would begin to speak, to tell his story. His right hand passed nervously across his eyes. He turned to look directly at Robert Browning who, as always, was beginning to feel somewhat embarrassed. Then the duke began:

> At last to leave these darkening moments
> These rooms, these halls where once
> We stirred love's poisoned potions
> The deepest of all slumbers,
> After this astounds the mummers
> I cannot express the smile that circled
> Round and round the week
> This room and all our days when morning
> Entered, soft, across her cheek.
> She was my medallion, my caged dove,
> A trinket, a coin I carried warm,
> Against the skin inside my glove
> My favourite artwork was a kind of jail
> Our portrait permanent, imprinted by the moon
> Upon the ancient face of the canal.

The man began to fade. Browning, who had not invited him into the room in the first place, was already bored. He therefore dismissed the crimson costume, the table, the potion housed in its delicate goblet of fine Venetian glass and began, quite inexplicably, to think about Percy Bysshe Shelley; about his life, and under the circumstances, more importantly, about his death.

Dinner over, sister, son and daughter-in-law and friend all chatted with and later read to, Browning returned to his room with Shelley's death hovering around him like an annoying directionless wind. He doubted, as he put on his nightgown, that Shelley had ever worn one, particularly in those dramatic days preceding his early demise. In his nightcap he felt as ridiculous as a humorous political drawing for *Punch* magazine. And, as he lumbered into bed alone, he remembered that Shelley would have had Mary beside him and possibly Clare as well, their minds buzzing with nameless Gothic terrors. For a desperate moment or two Browning tried to conjure a Gothic terror but discovered, to his great disappointment, that the vague shape taking form in his mind was only his dreary Italian duke coming, predictably, once again into focus.

Outside the ever calm waters of the canal licked the edge of the terrace in a rhythmic, sleep-inducing manner; a restful sound guaranteeing peace of mind. Browning knew, however, that during Shelley's last days at Lerici, giant waves had crashed into the ground floor of Casa Magni, prefiguring the young poet's violent death and causing his sleep to be riddled with wonderful nightmares. Therefore, the very lack of activity on the part of the water below irritated the old man. He began to pad around the room in his bare feet, oblivious of the cold marble floor and the dying embers in the fireplace. He peered through the windows into the night, hoping that he, like Shelley, might at least see his double there, or possibly Elizabeth's ghost beckoning to him from the centre of the canal. He cursed softly as the night gazed back at him, serene and cold and entirely lacking in events—mysterious or otherwise.

He returned to the bed and knelt by its edge in order to say his evening prayers. But he was completely unable to concentrate. Shelley's last days were trapped in his brain like fish in a tank. He saw him surrounded by the sublime scenery of the Ligurian coast, searching the horizon for the boat that was to be his coffin. Then he saw him clinging desperately to the mast of that boat while lightning tore the sky in half and the ocean spilled across the hull. Finally, he saw Shelley's horrifying corpse rolling on the shoreline, practically unidentifiable except for the copy of Keats' poems housed in his breast pocket. *Next to his heart,* Byron had commented, just before he got to work on the funeral pyre.

Browning abandoned God for the moment and climbed beneath the blankets.

'I might at least have a nightmare,' he said petulantly to himself. Then he fell into a deep and dreamless sleep.

———————

Browning awakened the next morning with an itchy feeling in his throat and lines from Shelley's *Prometheus Unbound* dancing in his head.

'Oh, God,' he groaned inwardly, 'now this. And I don't even *like* Shelley's poetry any more. Now I suppose I'm going to be plagued with it, day in, day out, until the instant of my imminent death.'

How he wished he had never, ever, been fond of Shelley's poems. Then, in his youth, he might have had the common sense *not* to read them compulsively to the point of total recall. But how could he have known in those early days that even though he would later come to reject Shelley's life and work as being too impossibly self-absorbed and emotional, some far corner of his brain would still retain every syllable the young man had committed to paper. He had memorized his life's work. Shortly after Browning's memory recited: *The crawling glaciers pierce me with spears / Of their moon freezing crystals, the bright chains / Eat with their burning cold into my bones,* he began to cough, a spasm that lasted until his sister knocked discreetly on the door to announce that, since he had not appeared downstairs, his breakfast was waiting on a tray in the hall.

While he was drinking his tea, the poem 'Ozymandias' repeated itself four times in his mind except that, to his great annoyance, he found that he could not remember the last three lines and kept ending with *Look on my works, ye Mighty, and despair.* He knew for certain that there were three more lines, but he was damned if he could recall even one of them. He thought of asking his sister but soon realized, that, since she was familiar with his views on Shelley, he would be forced to answer a series of embarrassing questions about why he was thinking about the poem at all. Finally, he decided that *Look on my works, ye Mighty, and despair* was a much more fitting ending to the poem and attributed his lack of recall to the supposition that the three last lines were either unsuitable or completely unimportant. That settled, he wolfed down his roll, donned his hat and coat, and departed for the streets in hopes that something, anything, might happen.

Even years later, Browning's sister and son could still be counted upon to spend a full evening discussing what he might have done that day. The possibilities were endless. He might have gone off hunting for a suitable setting for a new poem, or for the physical characteristics of a duke by examining handsome northern Italian workmen. He might have gone, again, to visit his beloved Palazzo Manzoni, to gaze wistfully at its marble medallions. He might have gone to visit a Venetian builder, to discuss plans for the beautiful tower he had talked about building at Asolo, or out to Murano to watch men mould their delicate bubbles of glass. His sister was convinced that he had gone to the Church of S.S. Giovanni e Paolo to gaze at his favourite equestrian statue. His pious son, on the other hand, liked to believe that his father had spent the day in one of the few English churches in Venice, praying for the redemption of his soul. But all of their speculations assumed a sense of purpose on the poet's part, that he had left the house with a definite destination in mind, because as long as they could remember, he had never acted without a predetermined plan.

Without a plan, Robert Browning faced the Grand Canal with very little knowledge of what, in fact, he was going to do. He looked to the left, and then to the right, and then, waving aside an expectant gondolier, he turned abruptly and entered the thick of the city behind him. There he wandered aimlessly through a labryrinth of narrow streets, noting details; *putti* wafting stone garlands over windows, door knockers in the shape of gargoyles' heads, painted windows that fooled the eye, items that two weeks earlier would have delighted him but now seemed used and lifeless. Statues appeared to leak and ooze damp soot, window-glass was fogged with moisture, steps that led him over canals were slippery, covered with an unhealthy slime. He became peculiarly aware of smells he had previously ignored in favour of the more pleasant sensations the city had to offer. But now even the small roof gardens seemed to grow as if in stagnant water, winter chrysanthemums emitting a putrid odour, which spoke less of blossom than decay. With a kind of slow horror, Browning realized that he was seeing his beloved city through Shelley's eyes and immediately his inner voice began again: *Sepulchres where human forms / Like pollution nourished worms / To the corpse of greatness cling / Murdered and now mouldering.*

He quickened his steps, hoping that if he concentrated on physical activity his mind would not subject him to the complete

version of Shelley's 'Lines Written Among the Euganean Hills.'
But he was not to be spared. The poem had been one of his
favourites in his youth and, as a result, his mind was now capable
of reciting it to him, word by word, with appropriate emotional
inflections, followed by a particularly moving rendition of 'Julian
and Maddalo' accompanied by mental pictures of Shelley and
Byron galloping along the beach at the Lido.

When at last the recitation ceased, Browning had walked as
far as possible and now found himself at the edge of the
Fondamente Nuove with only the wide flat expanse of the
Laguna Morta in front of him.

He surveyed his surroundings and began, almost
unconciously, and certainly against his will, to search for the
islanded madhouse that Shelley had described in 'Julian and
Maddalo': *A building on an island; such a one / As age to age might
add, for uses vile / A windowless, deformed and dreary pile.* Then
he remembered, again against his will, that it was on the other
side, near the Lido. Instead, his eyes came to rest on the cemetery
island of San Michele whose neat white mausoleums and tidy
cypresses looked fresher, less sepulchral than any portion of the
city he had passed through. Although he had never been there,
he could tell, even from this distance, that its paths would be
raked and its marble scrubbed in a way that the rest of Venice
never was. Like a disease that cannot cross the water, the rot and
mould of the city had never reached the cemetery's shore.

It pleased Browning, now, to think of the island's clean-boned
inhabitants sleeping in their whitewashed houses. Then, his
mood abruptly changing, he thought with disgust of Shelley, of
his bloated corpse upon the sands, how his flesh had been
saturated by water, then burned away by fire, and how his heart
had refused to burn, as if it had not been made of flesh at all.

Browning felt the congestion in his chest take hold, making

his breathing shallow and laboured, and he turned back into the city, attempting to determine the direction of his son's palazzo. Pausing now and then to catch his breath, he made his way slowly through the streets that make up the Fondamente Nuove, an area with which he was completely unfamiliar. This was Venice at its most squalid. What little elegance had originally existed in this section had now faded so dramatically that it had all but disappeared. Scrawny children screamed and giggled on every narrow walkway and tattered washing hung from most windows. In doorways, sullen elderly widows stared insolently and with increasing hostility at this obvious foreigner who had invaded their territory. A dull panic began to overcome him as he realized he was lost. The disease meanwhile had weakened his legs, and he stumbled awkwardly under the communal gaze of these women who were like black angels marking his path. Eager to be rid of their judgemental stares, he turned into an alley, smaller than the last, and found to his relief that it was deserted and graced with a small fountain and a stone bench.

The alley, of course, was blind, went nowhere, but it was peaceful and Browning was in need of rest. He leaned back against the stone wall and closed his eyes. The fountain murmured *Bysshe, Bysshe, Bysshe* until the sound finally became soothing to Browning and he dozed, on and off, while fragments of Shelley's poetry moved in and out of his consciousness.

Then, waking suddenly from one of these moments of semi-slumber, he began to feel again that he was being watched. He searched the upper windows and the doorways around him for old women and found none. Instinctively, he looked at an archway with was just a fraction to the left of his line of vision. There, staring directly into his own, was the face of Percy Bysshe Shelley, as young and sad and powerful as Browning had ever known it would be. The visage gained flesh and expression for a glorious thirty seconds before returning to the marble that it really was. With a sickening and familiar sense of loss, Browning recognized the carving of Dionysus, or Pan, or Adonis, that often graced the tops of Venetian doorways. The sick old man walked towards it and, reaching up, placed his fingers on the soiled cheek. 'Suntreader,' he mumbled, then he moved out of the alley, past the black, disapproving women, into the streets towards a sizeable canal. There, bent over his walking stick, coughing spasmodically, he was able to hail a gondola.

All the way back across the city he murmured, 'Where have you been, where have you been, where did you go?'

———————

Robert Browning lay dying in his son's Venetian palazzo. Half of his face was shaded by a large velvet curtain which was gathered by his shoulder, the other half lay exposed to the weak winter light. His sister, son, and daughter-in-law stood at the foot of the bed nervously awaiting words or signs from the old man. They spoke to each other silently by means of glances or gestures, hoping they would not miss any kind of signal from his body, mountain-like under the white bedclothes. But for hours now nothing had happened. Browning's large chest moved up and down in a slow and rhythmic fashion, not unlike an artificially manipulated bellows. He appeared to be unconscious.

But Browning was not unconscious. Rather, he had used the last remnants of his free will to make a final decision. There were to be no last words. How inadequate his words seemed now compared to Shelley's experience, how silly this monotonous bedridden death. He did not intend to further add to the absurdity by pontificating. He now knew that he had said too much. At this very moment, in London, a volume of superfluous words was coming off the press. All this chatter filling up the space of Shelley's more important silence. He now knew that when Shelley had spoken it was by choice and not by habit, that the young man's words had been a response and not a fabrication.

He opened his eyes a crack and found himself staring at the ceiling. The fresco there moved and changed and finally evolved into Shelley's iconography—an eagle struggling with a serpent. *Suntreader.* The clouds, the white foam of the clouds, like water, the feathers of the great wings becoming lost in this. *Half angel, half bird.* And the blue of the sky, opening now, erasing the ceiling, limitless so that the bird's wing seemed to vaporize. *A moulted feather, an eagle feather.* Such untravelled distance in which light arrived and disappeared leaving behind something that was not darkness. *His radiant form becoming less radiant.* Leaving its own natural absence with the strength and the suck of a vacuum. No alternate atmosphere to fill the place abandoned. *Suntreader.*

And now Browning understood. It was Shelley's absence he had carried with him all these years until it had passed beyond his understanding. *Soft star.* Shelley's emotions so absent from the old poet's life, his work, leaving him unanswered, speaking through the mouths of others, until he had to turn away from Shelley altogether in anger and disgust. The drowned spirit had outdistanced him wherever he sought it. *Lone and sunny idleness of heaven.* The anger, the disgust, the evaporation. *Suntreader, soft star.* The formless form he never possessed and was never possessed by.

Too weak for anger now, Robert Browning closed his eyes and relaxed his fists, allowing Shelley's corpse to enter the place in his imagination where once there had been only absence. It floated through the sea of Browning's mind, its muscles soft under the constant pressure of the ocean. Limp and drifting, the drowned man looked as supple as a mermaid, arms swaying in the current, hair and clothing tossed as if in a slow, slow wind. His body was losing colour, turning from pastel to opaque, the open eyes staring, pale, as if frozen by an image of the moon. Joints unlocked by moisture, limbs swung easy on their threads of tendon, the spine undulating and relaxed. The absolute grace of his death, that life caught there moving in the arms of the sea. Responding, always responding to the elements.

Now the drowned poet began to move into a kind of Atlantis consisting of Browning's dream architecture; the unobtainable and the unconstructed. In complete silence the young man swam through the rooms of the Palazzo Manzoni, slipping up and down the staircase, gliding down halls, in and out of fireplaces. He appeared briefly in mirrors. He drifted past balconies to the tower Browning had thought of building at Asolo. He wavered for a few minutes near its crenellated peak before moving in a slow spiral down along its edges to its base.

Browning had just enough time to wish for the drama and the luxury of a death by water. Then his fading attention was caught by the rhythmic bump of a moored gondola against the terrace below. The boat was waiting, he knew, to take his body to the cemetery at San Michele when the afternoon had passed. Shelley had said somewhere that a gondola was a butterfly of which the coffin was a chrysalis.

Suntreader. Still beyond his grasp. The eagle on the ceiling lost in unfocused fog. *A moulted feather, an eagle feather, well I forget the rest.* The drowned man's body separated into parts and moved slowly out of Browning's mind. The old poet contented himself with the thought of one last journey by water. The coffin boat, the chrysalis. Across the Laguna Morta to San Michele. All that cool white marble in exchange for the shifting sands of Lerici.

And the Four Animals

SHEILA WATSON

THE FOOTHILLS SLEPT. Over their yellow limbs the blue sky crouched. Only a fugitive green suggested life which claimed kinship with both and acknowledged kinship with neither.

Around the curve of the hill, or out of the hill itself, came three black dogs. The watching eye could not record with precision anything but the fact of their presence. Against the faded contour of the earth the things were. The watcher could not have said whether they had come or whether the eye had focused them into being. In the place of the hills before and after have no more meaning than the land gives. Now there were the dogs where before were only the hills and the transparent stir of the dragonfly.

Had the dogs worn the colour of the hills, had they swung tail round leg, ears oblique and muzzles quivering to scent carrion, or mischief, or the astringency of grouse mingled with the acrid smell of low-clinging sage, the eye might have recognized a congruence between them and the land. Here Coyote, the primitive one, the god-baiter and troublemaker, the thirster after power, the vainglorious, might have walked since the dawn of creation—for Coyote had walked early on the first day.

The dogs, however, were elegant and lithe. They paced with rhythmic dignity. In the downshafts of light their coats shone ebony. The eye observed the fineness of bone, the accuracy of adjustment. As the dogs advanced they gained altitude, circling, until they stood as if freed from the land against the flat blue of the sky.

The eye closed and the dogs sank back into their proper darkness. The eye opened and the dogs stood black against the blue of the iris for the sky was in the eye yet severed from it.

In the light of the eye the dogs could be observed clearly—three Labrador retrievers, gentle, courteous, and playful with the sedate bearing of dogs well-schooled to know their worth, to know their place, and to bend willingly to their master's will. One stretched out, face flattened. Its eyes, darker than the grass on which it lay, looked over the rolling hills to the distant saw-tooth pattern of volcanic stone. Behind it the other two sat, tongues dripping red over the saw-tooth pattern of volcanic lip.

The dogs were against the eye and in the eye. They were in the land but not of it. They were of Coyote's house, but become aristocrats in time which had now yielded them up to the timeless hills. They, too, were gods, but civil gods made tractable by use and useless by custom. Here in the hills they would starve or loose themselves in wandering. They were aliens in this spot or exiles returned as if they had never been.

The eye closed. It opened and closed again. Each time the eye opened the dogs circled the hill to the top and trained their gaze on the distant rock. Each time they reached the height of land with more difficulty. At last all three lay pressing thin bellies and jaws against the unyielding earth.

Now when the eye opened there were four dogs and a man and the eye belonged to the man and stared from the hill of his head along the slope of his arm on which the four dogs lay. And the fourth which he had whistled up from his own depths was glossy and fat as the others had been. But this, too, he knew in the end would climb lacklustre as the rest.

So he opened the volcanic ridge of his jaws and bit the tail from each dog and stood with the four tails in his hand and the dogs fawned graciously before him begging decorously for food. And he fed the tail of the first dog to the fourth and the tail of the fourth to the first. In the same way he disposed of the tails of the second and the third. And the dogs sat with their eyes on his mouth.

Then he bit the off-hind leg from each and offered it to the other; then the near-hind leg, and the dogs grew plump and shone in the downlight of his glance. Then the jaw opened and closed on the two forelegs and on the left haunch and the right and each dog bowed and slavered and ate what was offered.

Soon four fanged jaws lay on the hill and before them the man stood rolling the amber eyes in his hands and these he tossed impartially to the waiting jaws. Then he fed the bone of the first jaw to the fourth and that of the second to the third. And taking the two jaws that lay before him he fed tooth to tooth until one tooth remained and this he hid in his own belly.

Sampling Today's Fiction: The Black Fish

GEORGE BOWERING

L INDA HUTCHEON KNOWS very well that there is no such thing as the last word and I say amen to that.

Gail Geltner's contradictory and intertextual Odalisque is framed and framed again, and such is the nature of parody, something is left wide open, and whatever it is, you are in it. Put it another way—it is hard to gaze at her without in some way becoming her. Because of all the ironic frames it is difficult not to feel one's own nakedness. Gaze all you want to at the conventional reclining skin, your eyes will come to see most of this picture looking back at you, overdressed men, television set, Gail Geltner. What a cover for a book of 'stories'!

So Ingres did not have the last word on beauty, commodified or etherealized, and Geltner makes art to show that she does not either, and neither do you. People who hanker for 'closed systems' are unsettled by that suggestion. Readers of likely stories enjoy it—they are the fictional descendants of Scheherazade, who told and told stories because she did not like the implications of the last word.

The largest and most logical closed system is the universe, or the notion of the universal. Universities were created on that premise. The National Library and the 'Canadian Tradition' and the Global Village are constructed on that model. Modernist writers and their collectors liked the idea. In one of the best Canadian literature textbooks, Oxford's *An Anthology of Canadian Literature in English*, edited by Russell Brown, Donna Bennett and Nathalie Cooke, a Canadian modernist is introduced this way: 'Certainly Callaghan's tendency to generalize is consistent with his interest in "timeless" issues. His novels are concerned with the universal problem of mankind's imperfect condition.' What an irony!

As Linda Hutcheon has pointed out, the postmodern writer tends to disregard or distrust any claims to the universal. That makes sense for a West-coast woman of a storytelling pre-Mackenzie people, who may be told often that the experience that ties Canadians together is boyhood skating after a hockey puck. In January people in Prince Rupert stand in the rain and look quizzically at billboards that show studded car tires crunching through a 'Canadian winter.'

George Woodcock tells of the time when he hospitably showed Northrop Frye the panorama of Vancouver harbour with its margin of high-timbered mountains, and Frye said that the scene filled him with dread.

During the heyday of thematic criticism, in the seventies especially, Frye's name was often invoked by critics and other commentators who promoted a totalizing system called the 'Canadian Tradition.' According to this, the Canadian psyche was formed by a fear of nature and winter, and expressed in habitation and the arts as variations on what Frye called the 'Garrison Mentality.' The untamed forest was full of wolves and tomahawks, and the dark places of the mind were a forest.

But I will never forget an image near the end of an Alice Munro story called 'Labor Day Dinner.' It has been a typically complex Munro story, working out the equations of love and power, and now two adults in the front of a half-ton truck, and two girls in the back, are heading to their rural home over a back road late at night. At right angles to the road and ahead of them there is a dark-green car with two drunks in it, with the lights off in the moonlight, going eighty and ninety miles an hour:

> There isn't time to say a word. Roberta doesn't scream. George doesn't touch the brake. The big car flashes before them, a huge, dark flash, without lights, seemingly without sound. It comes out of the dark corn and fills the air right in front of them the way a big flat fish will glide into view suddenly in an aquarium tank. It seems to be no more than a yard in front of their headlights. Then it's gone—it has disappeared into the corn on the other side of the road. They drive on.

Then while the family of four heads home, they do not feel the universal, or if they do we are not told that they do. We are told that they 'feel as strange, as flattened out and borne aloft, as unconnected with previous and future events as the ghost car was, the black fish.'

The white whale is an American version of otherly nature, according to the usual critics, and a synecdoche for the huge prize the obsessed American individual spends his life pitting himself against. The Canadian, we are told, is inside the whale, and the white is snow, and the Canadian writer is intent on metaphors such as that. The weather in Manitoba, for instance, makes it hard to be an individual. You could perish on the way back from the outhouse if the blizzard makes you lose your grip

305

on the rope strung between the outhouse and the back porch.

Such metaphorical and symbolic writing (and reading) can be fun if it is not all you do, but it can also lead you too quickly through the surface of the actual writing into the maw of the symbolic monster. We are all going to die, and certainly that is a simple and profound universal. But the interesting thing about life is living. If we are all headed towards the same end, why not pay attention to the words that happen before then, pay attention to all the differences in the places we are visiting now?

Eternal themes and the symbols that tell their stories are meant to persuade us that we dream the dreams of Ulysses, or that we are the dream characters in some cosmic dreamer's odyssey. All right. But too often the merchants of unity find it in their interest to eradicate or devalue difference. Ordinary people, asked to look at your strange new story will say, 'well, it's certainly *different*,' and hope this way to start getting back to their familiar lives.

Postmodern writers are interested in difference. Difference can be a matter of the way a writer gets her sentences put together. Claire Harris's first page lets any reader know that there are alternatives to the paragraph with a topic sentence. Difference can happen because the writer (or reader) does not resemble the main figures in the official narrative. 'Language all her life is a second language,' wrote the poet Sharon Thesen. So no matter how many 'typical' Canadian girls identify with Anne of Green Gables, they will have to learn to read differently when they come to J.B. Joe's 'Cement Woman.'

They might say 'that's different.' When you have standards, as for instance when you are in a packing house sorting peaches, you have seen the picture on the label, and you throw away the culls, you are impatient with too much difference. In J.B. Joe's story you will hear 'There is always time to fling away the everyday.' Now what do you do? You can consign such weird fictions to some margin, call them folklore or call them 'experimental.' Call them 'way out.' But J.B. Joe's narrator pronounces these 'last' words: 'I am at the centre of the universe. I place the rattle in a soft cloth bag.' To some European explorers or clergymen those two sentences would seem to be contradictory.

That might be a good word to describe the stories in this book.

The stories in this book are not as difficult to read as all that, though. Like its predecessor, *Fiction of Contemporary Canada* (Coach House Press, 1980), it is a collection of stories that depart from the form of the regular, but not all that much. It is a sampler, this book, but a sampler from a body of work the size of which might surprise you.

The stories are not all that easy to read as you might think, though. If you need to be reminded of that look closely at the title of Sheila Watson's story and explain it to me.

Fiction of Contemporary Canada is still a pretty good anthology, I think. *Likely Stories* is not so much a replacement for it as it is an updating of the news about difference in this country. This new anthology has a higher percentage of women writers— that is an obvious difference. An equally important one is the fact that there are in this book more writers who speak the kinds of difference that come before decisions about style and structure.

When the question of creating a new Coach House anthology of postmodern fiction came up, I remembered what I said in the introductory notes to the first one: '… an avant-garde literature fan might say that what we have here is a collection of *slightly* postmodern pieces, some fables, a few quirks in presentation, basically several ways of showing a loss of faith in the realist story. … A later volume might sport what happens next.'

When the question of creating a new anthology came up, I said let me get a co-editor, so that some difference in the editing process might operate. Let me ask Linda Hutcheon. What a good idea! I have customarily brought my attention to the aesthetics of making difference, to problems of composition, as if perhaps the 'universal' somehow gave rise to its own need for criticism, as if the social and political were somehow matters for the written text itself, as if postmodernism were an excrescence of modernist aesthetics. Linda Hutcheon has written lots of books about the postmodern, and she knows what has been happening. She said that postmodernism questions authority, and that speaking from a minority position is a likely condition out of which to tell that story. Wouldn't we love to hear Sweeney's take on T.S. Eliot, I thought! Linda Hutcheon said that there is getting to be less white bread in Canada.

So what we are presenting here is not a profile of the national consciousness, not a list of contents for the Northern Experience, and certainly not the timeless and universal drama of the human condition. These are stories told by writers who like language, for readers who are not in a hurry to get home. Guy Davenport, in his essay about *Erewhon*, wrote: 'The familiar owns our love, the strange claims our intelligence.' That is probably what Linda Hutcheon was telling me. This is just to say thank you for the first word.

Notes on Contributors

DAVID ARNASON was born in Gimli, Manitoba. He was founder and editor of the *Journal of Canadian Fiction* and of Turnstone Press. His short story collections are *Fifty Stories and a Piece of Advice, The Circus Performers' Bar* and *The Happiest Man in the World*.

MARGARET ATWOOD lives in Toronto. Her newest books are a collection of short stories, *Wilderness Tips,* and a collection of short fiction, *Good Bones*.

GEORGE BOWERING lives in Vancouver. He has published five novels and four books of short fiction. He has edited numerous books of short stories, and written essays about stories by Murray Bail, Nathaniel Hawthorne, Audrey Thomas, Rudy Wiebe, Douglas Woolf and others. He has recently finished writing a collection of stories titled *Diggers*.

DIONNE BRAND was born in the Caribbean and has lived in Toronto for the past twenty years. She has published several books of poetry including *'Fore day morning, Earth Magic* (for children), *Primitive Offensive* and *No Language Is Neutral*.

DAVID BROMIGE was born in London, England and emigrated to Canada in his teens. He has lived in California for the last twenty years and his writing is more often anthologized south of the 49th than north of it. In 1988 he won the Western States Book Award for his selected poems, *DESIRE*. His latest book of poetry, *Tiny Courts*, is from Brick Books.

MATT COHEN was born in Kingston, Ontario. His novels include *The Sweet Second Summer of Kitty Malone, Nadine* and *Emotional Arithmetic*. His short story books include *Café Le Dog* and *Living on Water*. In 1991 he was awarded the John Glassco Translation Prize.

BRIAN FAWCETT was born in 1944 and grew up in Prince George, B.C. He attended Simon Fraser University where he studied with R. Murray Schafer and Robin Blaser. Recent books are *The Secret Journal of Alexander Mackenzie, Capital Tales* and *My Career with the Leafs*, all from Talon Books.

TIMOTHY FINDLEY was born in Toronto in 1930. From 1950-1962 he worked as a professional actor in Canada, the U.S. and the U.K. His books include *The Wars, Famous Last Words, Not Wanted on the Voyage* and *Stones*.

DOUGLAS GLOVER was born and raised on a tobacco farm in southwestern Ontario. He has published three story collections and two novels. In 1990 he won a National Magazine Award for Fiction. His book *A Guide to Animal Behaviour* was nominated for the 1991 Governor General's Award.

CLAIRE HARRIS settled in Calgary after coming to Canada from Trinidad in 1966. She is the author of four collections of poetry and the recipient of several awards including a Commonwealth Prize for Poetry and the Writer's Guild of Alberta Poetry Award. Her work can be found in more than a dozen anthologies including the *Oxford Anthology of Poetry by Canadian Women,* and Penguin's *Book of Caribbean Verse.*

LINDA HUTCHEON has written numerous books on postmodernism, including: *A Poetics of Postmodernism: History, Theory, Fiction; The Canadian Postmodern; The Politics of Postmodernism;* and most recently, *A Postmodern Reader,* co-edited with Joseph Natoli. When not writing about postmodernism, she is teaching it in the Department of English and Centre for Comparative Literature at the University of Toronto.

J.B. JOE is the founder and president of the Face of Raven Theatre Workshop Society based in Chemainus, B.C. She holds a B.A. in Fine Arts from the University of Victoria and a Masters in Fine Arts from the University of British Columbia. She is a member of the Penelakut Indian Band, Kuper Island, B.C.

ERIC McCORMACK was born in Scotland and emigrated to Canada in 1966. He teaches at St. Jerome's College, Waterloo. His published works include a collection of short stories, *Inspecting the Vaults,* which won the 1988 Commonwealth Writers Prize, and two novels, *The Paradise Motel* and *The Mysterium.*

DAVID McFADDEN was born in Hamilton, Ontario. A former newspaper reporter, he taught at the David Robinson University Centre for a number of years, during which time he founded the magazine *Writing.* Three of his books—*On the Road Again, The Art of Darkness* and *Gypsy Guitar*—were nominated for Governor General's Awards.

ALICE MUNRO was born in Wingham, Ontario. Her books include *Lives of Girls and Women, The Moons of Jupiter,* and *The Progress of Love.*

BPNICHOL wrote eleven books of poetry, four novels, several children's books and one collection of short fiction. *The Martyrology,* his lifework, is recognized internationally as a major poetic achievement. He was a member of the sound poetry ensemble The Four Horsemen. He died in 1988.

LEON ROOKE is an author, playwright and editor. His books include *The Happiness of Others, A Good Baby, Shakespeare's Dog, A Bolt of White Cloth,* and *Who Do You Love?*

GAIL SCOTT is the author of *Spare Parts,* a collection of short stories, *Heroine,* a novel, and *Spaces Like Stairs,* a book of essays. A third book of fiction, *Main Brides, Against Ochre Pediment and Aztec Sky,* will be published by Coach House Press in 1993. She was co-founder of *Spirale,* a French-language critical review, and of *Tessera,* a bilingual journal of feminist writing and criticism.

CAROL SHIELDS was born in Oak Park, Illinois and now lives and teaches in Manitoba. Her books include *A Fairly Conventional Woman, Various Miracles* and *Swann.*

SUSAN SWAN is a novelist, performer, editor and teacher. She is the author of *The Biggest Modern Woman in the World* and *The Last of the Golden Girls,* and the co-editor, with Margaret Dragu and Sarah Sheard, of *Mothers Talk Back.*

AUDREY THOMAS was born in Binghamton, New York and emigrated to Canada in 1959. She is a novelist, short story writer and radio playwright. Her latest novel, *Graven Images*, will be published in 1993 by Penguin Canada.

LOLA LEMIRE TOSTEVIN has published four books of poetry, including *'sophie*, and she has just finished her first novel *Frog Moon*. She teaches creative writing at York University, Toronto.

MILDRED TREMBLAY lives in Nanaimo, B.C. Her stories have appeared in many literary magazines, including *Canadian Fiction Magazine*, and she has won several awards for her writing. *Dark Forms Gliding*, a collection of her short stories, was published by Oolichan Books.

JANE URQUHART was born in Geraldton, Ontario. She is the author of one collection of short stories, two novels—*The Whirlpool* and *Changing Heaven*—and three books of poetry.

SHEILA WATSON was born in New Westminster, B.C. She is the author of *The Double Hook*, a novel, and *Deep Hollow Creek*, a novel written at the end of the nineteen-thirties and published for the first time without any major revision by McClelland & Stewart in 1992.